to

Half Way

Halfway
to
Half Way

SUZANN
LEDBETTER

MIRA®

MIRA

ISBN-13: 978-0-7783-2450-8
ISBN-10:   0-7783-2450-8

HALFWAY TO HALF WAY

www.MIRABooks.com

Printed in U.S.A.

For Dave, my forever prince,
who proved happily ever after isn't just the stuff
of fairy tales and fiction.

ACKNOWLEDGMENTS

Yet another battalion of advisers and sources gave generously of their time and provided answers for a desperately in-need novelist's weird questions. Thank you SO much: Darren L. Moore, Greene County (Missouri) Prosecuting Attorney; Cheryl Smith and Pat Tripoli, Research Dept., Joplin (Missouri) Public Library; Tracey Gillenwater, LOM, Clayton Jones Agency/American Family Insurance, Nixa, Missouri; American Family Insurance consultants, John C. Christensen, Don P. Minter; John S. Korte, Manager, Life & Health Section, Missouri Department of Insurance; Mark A. Elliston, Elliston Law Offices, Webb City, Missouri, Jim Hamilton, Senior Staff Writer, Community Publishers, Inc., and Veda Boyd and Jimmie Jones.

And a special thanks to Mm. [Robin] Rue, stellar literary agent and fortune-teller's namesake, and to Lara Hyde, my new editor who jumped into this project at the (ahem) halfway mark, but with full-tilt enthusiasm from day one.

1

It was shortly after daybreak when Hannah Garvey snuck through Valhalla Springs' brick-and-wrought-iron gates. Actually, she drove through them. It only felt like sneaking. As the retirement community's resident operations manager, Hannah was supposed to be on site and available, 24/7. Although the employment manual didn't expressly forbid sleeping with the sheriff at his house a couple of nights a week, she assumed it was an unwritten rule.

Posted in no uncertain numerals was Valhalla Springs' inchmeal speed limit. Hannah rode the Blazer's brakes up the gentle slope, as if abiding by that rule washed out breaking the big one. Again. And again. And—well, over the past two months, the rough estimate of her serial sneak-outs and sneak-backs was in the low twenties.

Aware that her scruples were as thin as her brake shoes, Hannah steeled herself for the scourge that callous disregard would inevitably wreak on four hundred innocent senior citizens. A fire. A flood. Hordes of locusts, at the very least.

Except once again, the bearded, smite-happy Almighty she'd been terrified of as a child must have been looking elsewhere the past eleven hours or so. A lawnmower's echo was the lone disclaimer to "The closest thing to Paradise" part of Valhalla Springs' advertising slogan.

Dandelions didn't dare sprout in the manicured acreage tended by an army of groundskeepers. Birds twittered happy songs in the trees and squirrels ran double-helixes around their trunks. Mare's-tail clouds festooned a brilliant blue Ozarks sky, honeysuckle perfumed the air and...

Delbert Bisbee's turquoise '58 Edsel was parked in Hannah's circle driveway.

Compared to a fire, flood or insect swarm, a Delbert drop-in was at most a point-zero-seven on the Divine Retribution Meter. And a nine-point-nine on the God Has a Wicked Sense of Humor scale.

Hannah shut her eyes, counted to one, then opened them. Alas, the vintage Ford with a snazzy Continental kit was not a mirage.

It never had been before. Why would this otherwise splendid mid-July morning be any different?

The first time Delbert and his gang of elderly gumshoes commandeered Hannah's cottage for their headquarters, she'd had the locks changed. Ditto the second time. Before a third set was installed, "Sam Spade" Bisbee had purchased a lock-pick gun from Private Spy Supply.

Since then, neither rain, sleet nor dark of night deterred the retired post office supervisor and his henchpersons from trooping into Hannah's house at will. Even when she was home and definitely not alone. Or dressed to receive visitors, as they said in the good old days before lock-pick guns were invented.

Hannah toyed with the idea of making a U-turn and leaving central Missouri for somewhere remote, such as Nepal, except she wouldn't get far on a quarter tank of gas. Besides, Valhalla Springs' geriatric Mod Squad had several sort-of solved homicides, felonious assaults and a couple of kidnappings to its credit. Tracking down an AWOL resident operations manager before she crossed the Kinderhook County line would be a snap.

After she'd parked her truck, Hannah opened the passenger door and grabbed her purse from the floorboard. The leather overnight bag beside it, she'd carry in after Delbert left. Years of experience had shown that lying about where you'd been had a lot more credibility without luggage, than with it.

"Moomph," said Malcolm, her impatient passenger and eighty-five-pound other love of her life.

The instant she freed him, the giant Airedale-wildebeest went airborne and landed kersplat on the lawn like a belly-down B-52 with fur. From this perspective, it was clear his ancestry included Dalmatian, golden retriever, Irish setter, Russian wolfhound and a wanton fling with a Shetland pony.

While he watered his three favorite trees, Hannah entered the cottage and deposited her purse on the desk. A wooden railing separated the office nook from the spacious great room. Apart from an oak dining set used as a conference table, the cottage was furnished like a private residence. Which it was, when the gumshoes, prospective tenants, current ones, department supervisors, lost tourists and the odd paroled convict weren't cluttering it up.

"Delbert?" she called. "Where are you?"

A cranky, disembodied "Right here" shot her seventeen inches vertically, then into a neat, horizontal half twist. Hand clapped to her chest, she was momentarily blinded by Delbert's madras Bermudas, red-checked gingham shirt and yellow smiley face crew socks—a typical Bisbee ensemble that was probably visible from one of Pluto's moons.

"Damn you, Delbert," she wheezed. "You scared the living crap out of me."

The snowy-haired home invader was standing on a metal toolbox, poking a screwdriver into her thermostat's exposed innards. "Didn't you see my car out front?"

"Yes, but—"

"Then you knew I was here when you came in—"

"Yes, but—"

"—from wherever you'd gallivanted off to." He gave Hannah a withering paternal up-and-down. "And I guess I don't have to ask where *that* was."

Delbert in protective father-figure mode was annoying and endearing. Delbert with a screwdriver in his fist kindled memories of perfectly functional appliances being reduced to rubble.

First things first. "I guess not," she said. "You know I can't start on the payroll without picking up the time sheets from the department supervisors."

This was true. It had no bearing on his remark, but Hannah's twenty-five years in the advertising industry qualified as a Ph.D. in the ol' bait and switch.

"Oh. Well." He sawed a finger under his nose.

"Now that you mention it, ladybug, I reckon this is the second Tuesday of the month."

The pet name sufficed as an apology for implying she'd spent the night having mind-blowing sex with Sheriff David Hendrickson. Just because the human love of her life had left to respond to a meth lab explosion before they'd had a chance to get naked didn't make her feel any better about deceiving Delbert.

Guilt from being caught doing something you shouldn't paled in comparison to getting away with it and feeling like a two-faced slimeball. Hannah's confession was in the composition stage when she heard a distinct *zzzt*.

The screwdriver sailed past her left ear. A puff of smoke shot toward the ceiling. Sparks showered downward like tiny meteorites. Delbert yelled, "Battle stations! Mayday! Get the fire extinguisher! *Quick!*"

Minutes later, the wall beside the breakfast room doorway was a seething blotch of powdery yellow residue several shades brighter than Mr. Fix-It's socks. His complexion pretty much matched his shirt and the fire extinguisher's red-enameled barrel. He handed it back to her with a quiet, but sincere "Oops."

It's said you can choose your friends, but not your family. Delbert and the gumshoe gang had become both. As with her real family—long gone to that single-wide trailer park in the sky—the urge to strangle him, or the other four, on a fairly frequent basis went with the territory.

Hannah inquired, "Are you sure the fire's out?"

"Ya gotta have flames to have a fire." Delbert straightened to a full five foot three, which put the top of his head level with her chin. "Leave it to a woman to make Mount Rushmore out of a molehill."

Misogyny was his premier line of defense. Objecting to it was, in the immortal words of her great-uncle Mort, like teaching a pig to sing. Hannah set down the fire extinguisher and made a mental note to have it recharged. And buy a backup. Maybe two.

"Next question," she said. "Why were you ramming a screwdriver into my thermostat?"

"Because every window in the ding-danged house was open when I pulled up out front."

She cocked her head, gnawed her lower lip, then finally had to admit she had no clue what the hell he was talking about.

"It hit eighty-eight degrees yesterday afternoon," Delbert said, as though addressing a toddler, or a lunatic. "It's supposed to be over ninety today. Not bad for July, but when I saw your windows open, I figured the central air was on the fritz."

Hannah eyed the mustardy mess with a rectangular lump in the middle, formerly known as a climate-control device. "I'll bet it is now."

He nodded, then hung his head. "I was just trying to help, ladybug."

Valhalla Springs had a full-time maintenance department. Reminding Delbert of it was akin to telling Malcolm to recite the Analects of Confucius in Mandarin.

Hannah hugged Delbert's sparrow shoulders. "My windows were open because I like real air. And fans. Especially at night." She planted a smooch on his sweet Old-Spice-scented cheek. "We didn't have air-conditioning when I was a kid, then I spent two-thirds of my life in a hermetically sealed condo in Chicago. Listening to a fan and the crickets are like revisiting my childhood. The good parts."

Shrewd, milky-blue eyes rose to her brown ones, and the corners of Delbert's mouth quirked into a smile. In a tone both affectionate and crabby, he said, "Has anybody ever told you, you're nuttier than a fruitcake factory?"

"Uh-huh." Hannah laughed. "But you haven't for quite a while."

"I would have, if I'd known you were such a nature freak." He squatted to retrieve the screwdriver and chucked it in the toolbox. "Real air, my sweet aspidistra. Next you'll trade in that feminazi mobile for an ox team and a wagon."

He pondered the sunlight streaming through the French doors to the deck. "It's not as hot in here as you'd expect, though. Must be the shade—trees keep it cooler longer."

That and relative isolation. A stocked, spring-fed lake and the adjacent community center separated the manager's cottage from the residential area and Main Street's commercial district. Across Valhalla Springs Boulevard and a jog east was an eighteen-hole championship golf course. Any whisper of a breeze from any direction was Hannah's to enjoy.

With Mother Nature as her nearest neighbor, she should also have privacy out the wazoo. And mostly did, for about seventy-three hours after she moved in last April. Coming home to find the first gumshoe meeting in progress because *they* wanted privacy had significantly lessened her hope of having some.

Delbert pulled a chartreuse ball cap with Eat Well, Stay Fit, Die Anyway embroidered on it from his back pocket. "Since you've got bookkeeping to do, I'd best shove off. If you want, I'll mosey by Maintenance and report that bum thermostat."

"No rush, unless you're in one. I can't work a calculator without coffee."

A sly grin said her marginal math skills were gender-related, not caffeine-oriented. "One cup. Then I gotta get crack-a-lackin'."

Availing himself of a bar stool, Delbert shucked the rubber band from the county weekly newspaper he must have brought in with him. "I'm teeing off with Leo Schnur in a few minutes. Suki Allen's invited me over for lunch, then after my siesta, I've gotta decide whether to take Carol Flaherty or Pat Fortune to the square dance tonight."

His harem was a source of amusement and no speculation whatsoever. The childless, five-time divorcée was the George Clooney of Valhalla Springs—either in spite of, or because of, his pledge to never say "I do" again.

Hannah's mother never married, but her romantic learning curve was similarly steep. Caroline Garvey's lifelong quest for Mr. Right netted a parade of Mr. Couldn't Be More Wrongs, an illegitimate daughter, chronic alcoholism, incurable poverty and an early grave.

Avoiding that fate was simple. Never get involved with anyone other than a Mr. Wrong, whom Hannah wouldn't marry if she were comatose, or who had no desire to marry her. The bonus was the appearance of a committed relationship without the angst, complications and heartache. It also resolved a lot of trust issues. It's easy not to fear Mr. Wrong will leave, when you don't want him around forever, anyway.

As Hannah filled the coffee carafe with tap water, she thought David Hendrickson should have been the ultimate Mr. Wrong. A divorced, dedicated county sheriff seven years her junior? No threat whatsoever to her theory, much less to the vow of celibacy she took on her fortieth birthday.

They'd both put up a good fight. Well, *she* had. A whole seven, maybe eight days had elapsed from the time she fell in like to when she fell hopelessly in love with the tall, handsome, smart, smart-ass lawman.

Hannah flipped the coffeemaker's switch to Brew and took two mugs from the cabinet. She'd designed the Valhalla Springs logo and slogan embossed on the cups—a souvenir of her former life as a senior account executive at Chicago's Friedlich & Friedlich agency.

When exactly her dream career became drudgery was impossible to peg. The result was an "I quit" memo to the agency's fraternal CEOs. To this day, Hannah wasn't sure how a courtesy call to Jack

Clancy, her longtime client and dearest friend, turned into the resident manager's job at his upscale retirement community.

Now all she had to do to become Mrs. Sheriff was plan their wedding, find her own replacement, leave the second family she loved, the only real home she'd ever had, and move to the house David was building twenty-five miles away.

No problem, as long as she ignored minor qualms, such as not wanting to quit her job and a severe reluctance to move to "the corner of East Jesus and plowed ground." David's new house wasn't as far from Valhalla Springs as Nepal, but his closest neighbor was miles away and her love of nature was somewhat selective.

Fresh air and crickets, good. A surrounding forest, a meadow teeming with wildflowers, bunnies, birds, squirrels and deer, very good. Snakes, skunks, ticks, chiggers, poison ivy, probably bears, maybe wolves, not good. *Way* not good.

Newspaper pages rattled behind her. "This county rag gets skimpier every week," Delbert said. "If I subscribed, I'd cancel."

"You did," Hannah reminded him. "The day I started mine."

The aroma of bubbling Tip of the Andes followed

her to the utility room. She filled Malcolm's food vat, then let him in the side door. Reverse the order and he'd dive into the kibble can and eat his way out.

"Hey, ladybug. Get a load of this."

She detoured to the coffeemaker, filled the mugs and set Delbert's in front of him. He sucked down a healthy swig as he tapped a three-by-four photograph below the fold. "Looks like Chlorine Moody's got herself between a rosebush and a bulldozer."

Hannah realized the picture's blurriness was the fault of her forty-three-year-old eyes, not the photographer. She hiked a shoulder, preferring not to admit her presbyopia to a retired unhandyman who didn't need reading glasses.

Delbert went on. "The caption says Chlorine is fighting the city over a new natural gas line being laid in the alley behind her house."

Hannah's nose wrinkled, remembering her one, thankfully brief, encounter with the woman. "If anyone can beat city hall, it's her. Saying she's rude is almost a compliment."

Delbert harrumphed. "Near as I can tell, that pickle-puss of hers would stop traffic on I-44. This picture was taken last Friday. I'll bet that bulldozer driver still ain't sleeping through the night."

They both jumped at a *zing,* like lightning striking

a telephone line. "What the—" Delbert glanced around. "What was that?"

Hannah's eyes riveted on the breakfast room's damaged wall, expecting it to burst into flames. Then from the great room came a faint and rather cheesy rendition of "Me and Bobby McGee."

Her cell phone. The secret cell phone that allowed her to maintain the appearance of being on duty in Valhalla Springs while she was at David's. It was still in her purse on the desk where she'd left it.

"What was what?" she blurted, praying Delbert's ears weren't as sharp as his vision.

"That noise," he said, coinciding with the cell phone's second ring. "Now it sounds like an ice cream truck going by."

Delbert slid off the bar stool just as Malcolm the Wonder Dog streaked from the utility room. *Burf-burfing* like a maniac, the dog blew by, nearly knocking Delbert out of his sandals. "Glorioski zero, this *is* a goddamn fruitcake factory."

For once, Hannah was thankful that Malcolm was genetically predisposed to *burf* at the front door when the phone rang, and *burf* at the phone when the doorbell rang.

"Malcolm, hush up!" she yelled. *Louder, boy.*

A pause, then a fresh blast of *burfing* indicated the

mutt was slow on the telepathic uptake, or the stupid cell phone was singing again.

Muttering something about muzzles, Delbert stomped over to fetch his toolbox, then past Hannah and out the utility room door. Her relief that another guilty secret was safe didn't offset the shame of having so many.

Sneaking around behind Delbert's and everyone else's backs was over. He hadn't given her engagement to David a seal of approval, but that wasn't the problem. Even grouchy father figures don't believe any man on earth is good enough for their daughter figures. What he'd never forgive was finding Hannah gone, if an emergency arose.

Strange though it was that Valhalla Springs residents slept better knowing she was there, they did. As if the development were a horizontal apartment complex and Hannah was the doorman—an omniscient, easily ignored presence vital to their peace of mind.

Malcolm gallumped into the kitchen, a triumphant knight in shaggy armor who'd saved the fair maiden from… The nobody's home look in his eyes said he wasn't sure what, but bravery with or without a clue should be rewarded.

She peeled open a can of Vienna sausages and dumped them in his bowl, then popped an English muffin into the toaster for herself. She'd buttered it, topped off her coffee and sat down at the bar before she realized the old fart had taken the newspaper with him.

2

David Hendrickson rolled a stubby pencil back and forth across his knuckles. His other hand held the telephone receiver away from his ear. Truth be told, he could have laid it on the desk and not missed a word of Mrs. Bumgartner's weekly 911 call.

"That roofer charged me a hundred-and-sixteen dollars just to fix some loose shingles," she squawked. "Stole me blind, he did. Now, you get off your duff and arrest him. Right this very minute."

"Ma'am, I can't—"

"What do you mean, *can't?* You're the sheriff, aren't you? I'll have you know, my taxes pay your salary."

David's taxes paid his salary, too, but he doubted that she'd appreciate the irony. Nor did she want the roofer arrested, any more than the pharmacist who'd allegedly shorted her a pill last week, or the mechanic who'd worked on her car the week before that.

Sad, how often the world's lonely and alone alienate the few friends they have left, then manufacture excuses to call strangers just for somebody to talk to.

David looked out the door to his office. Chief Deputy Jimmy Wayne McBride was munching a slice of cold pizza and staring off into space. The understaffed, underfunded Kinderhook County cop shop wasn't blessed with slow days. David's second-in-command only appeared to be lollygagging. And he ought to know better than to do it in plain sight.

"Tell you what, Mrs. Bumgartner," David said into the phone. "I'll send a man over to take a complaint report. But don't you go to baking cookies or anything. He might be obliged for a glass of sweet tea, but he can't stay longer than ten, maybe fifteen minutes."

Judging by the hum on the line, that wasn't the response the Macedonia Free Will Full Gospel Church's organist had expected. David grinned. All's fair in love and law enforcement. Jimmy Wayne wasn't expecting to waste an hour writing a report destined for the shredder, either.

Mrs. Bumgartner sniffed, then sniped, "It's about time you did something about the scoundrels running amok from one end of this county to t'other. I'll have you know, Clara Haines told—"

"Beg pardon, ma'am, but the quicker I hang up, the quicker I can send that deputy."

"Of *all* the— Uh, well, all right, but you tell him to wipe his shoes on the mat. I won't abide him tracking in dirt on my fresh-mopped floors."

David was still chuckling when he shut his office door on Jimmy Wayne's verbal resignation. An estimated thirty seconds would elapse before he passed off Mrs. Bumgartner to the handiest rookie.

His oak banker's chair squeaked and groaned as David sat down again. It and the massive desk were relics of an era when Sanity, the county seat, was a one-horse town with the ugliest courthouse in Missouri. The century-old, three-story brick box disproved the notion that no-bid government contracts and construction kickbacks were modern inventions.

David's gaze lowered from a top-floor view of the square's west side to a farm truck nosed into the curb. A bumper sticker affixed to its rear window was a smaller version of the yard signs that leaned against the office gun safe.

On both, the message spelled out in bold red ink was Reelect David Hendrickson for Kinderhook County Sheriff on August 3. Brief and to the point, he granted, but a skosh shy of accurate.

Technically he wasn't an incumbent. The governor

promoted him from chief deputy when the duly elected sheriff, Larry Beauford, died in office. And August 3 marked the county's primary election, not the general one.

It might as well be, though, David admitted. He'd filed as a Republican because Beauford won three terms from that side of the ballot. David's nemesis, Jessup Knox, filed the same way, for the same reason. Whoever won at the polls in three weeks had nobody to beat in November, except a Democrat who once ran unopposed and lost to a write-in candidate.

All politics is local, they say. Whoever *they* were, David fervently believed that sheriffs should be hired, like chiefs of police. Being a "come-here," not a native Kinderhook Countian, he might not get the job, but in a place where everyone seemed to be everyone else's Cousin Bob, it was a neat trick to arrest scofflaws and win a popularity contest at the same time.

Fingers laced behind his head, he leaned back in his chair and stared at the paint flaking off the stamped tin ceiling. The three hours' sleep he'd managed last night after that meth lab blew to Kingdom Come had him feeling closer to sixty-seven, than thirty-seven. Legs outstretched, he'd settled in for a sweet little nap, when some fool with a death wish rapped on the door.

Lucas Sauers, his personal attorney and campaign manager, didn't wait for an invitation. "You busy?" he asked, closing the door behind him. "I told 'em to hold your calls for a few minutes."

David grunted an obscenity. "What this office needs is a maximum-security dead bolt. A big brass sucker that locks from the inside. With a *key.*"

Luke dragged a chair closer to the window air conditioner. The unit lacked for BTUs, but sounded like a Harley stuck in first gear. "Sorry I didn't make the Sunrise Optimists' meeting. How'd your speech go?"

"Nobody threw eggs at me. All but a couple of members came up afterward and said I had their votes."

"Oh, yeah? How many turned out for it?"

"Twelve, maybe fourteen all told." David's sigh expressed his love of politics in general and campaigning in particular. "Could be the makings of a landslide."

"Don't we wish." Luke removed a business-size envelope from an inner jacket pocket. "But this'll knock some planks off Jessup Knox's platform. The ones stamped 'Hendrickson is a fiscal liability.'"

A drum roll was almost audible as Luke ripped the envelope in half. "That, my friend, was a hearing notice for Lydia Quince's wrongful death lawsuit against you and the sheriff's department." The asundered envelope sailed over the nameplate on David's desk. The pieces landed on a stack of requisition forms awaiting his signature.

Luke gestured *ta-da,* his expression as smug as a terrier with a mole in its mouth. "Just as I predicted, the plaintiff fired her counsel and dropped the suit."

The million-dollar civil complaint had hung over David's head for three months. At the outset, Luke vowed to stall by every available legal means. The court system's molasses-in-January momentum seemed to lend credence to his opinion that Mrs. Quince preferred getting on with her life to putting it on hold for a jackpot that might not materialize.

Subtle encouragement from her cousin, Jimmy Wayne McBride, probably convinced her to give up. David ordered him to zip his lip, but suspected insubordination. Friendship and loyalty aside, his chief deputy didn't want to be the sheriff—officially, or de facto, which he would be, if Knox were elected.

Neither the anguish of shooting Quince's estranged husband, even in self-defense, nor the resulting lawsuit's recrimination would vanish like smoke in a wind. Not for David, anyway. He regarded the mangled envelope. "What's the catch?"

"No catch. No settlement. No strings. The slate's

clean." Luke chuckled. "Here's where you start wax-
ing poetic about what a genius you have for a lawyer."

Still skeptical, but relief quickening behind his
breastbone, David tipped forward and extended his
hand. "Mr. Sauers, for a lawyer, you're a bona fide,
nickel-plated genius."

They shook on it, Luke accepting David's thanks
with a joke about the forthcoming bill for services.
"Too bad I'm not a psychic genius." He motioned at
the unread *Sanity Examiner* atop David's in-basket.
"You'd owe me a bonus, if I'd picked up a vibe yesterday afternoon when the suit was actually dropped.

"I can't swear Chase Wingate would've stopped his
presses, but waiting till next week's edition to get the
word out puts us seven days closer to primary day."

The timing wasn't a surprise to David. The plaintiff's attorneys weren't his biggest fans. You'd think
they would be, considering the ratio of clients in need
of defending rose in proportion to the increase in arrest warrants since David took the oath of office.

Then again, the son of one of the firm's partners
was awaiting trial for arson and related charges. The
fifteen-year-old and two buddies celebrated the
Fourth of July by torching a fireworks stand. No one
was hurt, but David refused to write it off as a prank
in exchange for their fathers' paying restitution.

He said, "You'll have a press release about the suit ready for next week's paper."

"Absolutely. A full-blown feature, if I can swing it. It won't be as splashy as Wingate's headline story when Quince filed it against you, but I'll push for every inch I can."

Trusting your instincts was a law enforcement officer's stock in trade. David's weren't infallible, but he'd regretted ignoring them far more often than he'd regretted following them. "One of my dad's favorite sayings is 'Just because you can, doesn't mean you should.' Maybe that applies here."

"How?"

"What if all that story does is remind undecided voters that I was suspended from duty and a tick away from a grand jury indictment for second-degree homicide?"

To his credit, rather than responding with a knee-jerk argument, Luke mulled the possibility at length. "I'm afraid that's a risk we have to take. If we don't go public, what's to stop Jessup Knox from continuing to use it as a campaign issue?"

"Who says he won't, anyway?"

"If he does and constituents know it's been dropped, they'll know he's slandering you outright." Luke noted the look on David's face. "I hear ya.

That's his entire strategy. Let me think about it. We have almost a week before Wingate puts the next *Examiner* to bed."

He sat back in the chair. "Which reminds me, did you talk to Hannah about my idea?"

David rolled his eyes. "No."

"Why not? I promise you, a boxed come-one, come-all wedding invitation in the paper the week before the election would bring people out in droves."

"I am *not*—"

"Then front and center in the August 3 edition, there'll be photos of the sheriff and his lovely bride." Luke bracketed his fingers like a picture frame. "Even if we had it, money can't buy that kind of warm fuzzy publicity. I don't have to tell you, we *need* it."

Rather than grab his enthusiastic but occasionally insane campaign manager by the belt and throw him out the nearest window, David groaned and scrubbed his face with his hands.

"Unless you and Hannah elope, you'll have to invite half the county to the wedding, anyway," Luke said. "So what's the difference? Elvis can lie till he's blue, but he can't steal thunder from a romantic Sunday-afternoon wedding in the park."

The nickname for David's opponent derived from Knox's slicked-back pompadour and muttonchop sideburns. Elvis's wannabe twin also had less law-enforcement experience than his idol. The late King of Rock 'n' Roll never wore a badge but did serve two years' active duty in the military. Jessup Knox hadn't even rung a bell at Christmas for the Salvation Army.

"Sauers, I'm telling you for the last time. Hannah's stuck at Valhalla Springs until she hires her own replacement. But even if that happened tomorrow, there isn't going to be a wedding until I can count on more than three weeks' worth of job security."

Luke crossed his arms. "Worst case scenario, it'd be next January before Knox is sworn into office. That's more like six months' job security."

"Good plan," David shot back. "Then me and Hannah will both be unemployed."

His loan payments on the new house and the cost of hiring contractors to finish it, had already put the hurt on his checkbook. If he lost the election, alternative job prospects were nil. Bump down to deputy with Knox in the sheriff's seat? Elvis probably wouldn't hire him and David had serious qualms about working for an idiot. The Sanity Police Department would be a demotion of a different but equally undesirable stripe. Some were born to be highway patrol officers; David was not.

That left federal branches of service, most of them

known by acronyms, and none conducive to a Kinder-hook County address.

"Doing something is better than this stalemate you're in," Luke said. "You want to get married. She wants to get married. So get a license, rings, an event permit from the Parks Department and get married already. Everything after that's just details."

David visually measured the window casing. It was plenty wide and tall enough for him to push Luke through. But with his luck, Luke would land in the shrubbery, dust himself off and be yapping across the desk at him again before David sat back down in his chair.

As Genius Lawyer said when he'd originally suggested his dumb-ass nuptials-as-vote-getter idea, desperate times called for desperate measures.

"Tell you what, Sauers. If you can talk Hannah into it, I'll do all the above, find a preacher, get measured for a tux and reserve the limousine."

"Really? You mean it?" Luke's voice yodeled up the scale like a middle-schooler's. "Seriously?"

David's tongue pressed his teeth to keep a straight face. If Luke managed to survive that little chat with Hannah, his ears ought to stop ringing by about Friday noon.

Unless Hannah said yes…

Which, David thought, was about as likely as his having to scrape snow off his windshield tomorrow morning.

3

Wednesday morning, a throbbing sun graphic back-dropped the KJPP weatherperson's forecast of a scorcher. True to prediction, the midday heat index hovered near the century mark.

Hannah was huddled over the stove stirring her last can of chicken noodle soup when the doorbell rang. A vaporous mewl of joy burst from her lips. She turned off the burner and scuttled from the kitchen as fast as her fuzzy plush house shoes allowed.

The savior she'd expected to find on the porch was not tattooed on his respective biceps with an anchor and an arrow-pierced heart. Nor was he named Henry Don Tucker.

The Grounds and Greens Department supervisor was flanked by his assistant and son-in-law, Pinky Dobbs. A trio of younger, sweatier employees slouched behind them. All five exchanged owl-eyed glances. As a group, they faded back a step and stood as inert as a Martian expeditionary force encountering their first Earthling.

Henry Don slowly removed a straw cowboy hat, as though demonstrating how to comply with a no-false-moves order. His Adam's apple bounced, then his mouth moved.

"What? I can't—" Hannah peeled off her earmuffs. "Sorry about that. You were saying?"

Henry Don's basset-hound eyes traveled from the sweater under her chenille robe to her fleece-lined sweatpants and up again. "I—uh, well, seems like a silly question, but I asked if you was ailin'."

"I appreciate the concern." Hannah chuckled. "But I'm not sick, I'm—"

"There, there, hon." Henry Don held a work boot against the screen door. "Just relax and everything's gonna be fine."

A crunching noise heralded a blue-and-white county cruiser pulling into the driveway. Pinky Dobbs looked from it to Henry Don to Hannah. His natural flush intensified. "I get it," he murmured. "Here we go again."

"Uh-huh." Henry Don peered in the direction of the development's entrance. "No ambulance yet." A key ring keeper was unclipped from his belt and handed off to a crewman. "You boys better move the truck down the road a-piece to make room, though."

The designated driver and both coworkers sprinted for the green king-cab pickup with the Valhalla Springs logo on the door.

"Ambulance?" Hannah said. "What ambulance?"

David Hendrickson emerged from the patrol unit as gracefully as his six-foot-three-inch frame allowed. He was dressed in street clothes, but a curt "Hold it" had the desired effect on the fleeing groundskeepers. Adding, "Y'all stay put, now," he strode to the porch, his expression a mixture of cop-face and confusion.

"Afternoon, Mr. Tucker, Mr. Dobbs." David motioned Henry Don away from the door. To Hannah, he said, "Still living in a one-bedroom refrigerator, eh?"

A rhetorical question, she presumed, thrilled to have another pair of male eyes inventorying her bag-lady ensemble. "What's this about an ambulance?"

Henry Don whispered, "I hope it's here quick, Sheriff. She's gettin' agitated, same as Owen McCutcheon did, back before they come for him."

Pinky chimed in, "Even after that shot they give him, it was a booger wrasslin' him into that backward coat with all them buckles and such."

Hannah's mouth fell open. Disjointed syllables stuttered out, then she doubled over laughing.

Owen McCutcheon, the previous operations manager, was labeled eccentric, but a decent-enough guy, until he started covering the windows with aluminum foil to deflect particle beams. In truth, after Owen's breakdown and transport to a mental health facility, he was finally receiving the treatment his family had denied him for years.

Henry Don and Pinky weren't convinced that Hannah's grasp on reality wasn't slipping until they entered the cottage. Malcolm was curled up on the sofa under a Scooby-Doo beach towel. The muttsicle raised his head, whimpered and retucked his snoot between his paws.

Henry Don sucked in a deep breath and exhaled. "After melting out yonder on the porch, it feels plumb wonderful in here to me."

"Give it a minute or two," David said. A wink reminded Hannah that playing wilderness camp-out under a comforter with a big, hot sheriff was an excellent remedy for a broken central air-conditioning system.

Pinky shivered and thrust his hands in his pockets. "You've got a hundred pounds more insulation on you, Henry Don. It's colder'n a witch's—er, cold enough to freeze the— Uh, well, it's sure to goodness cold in here, all right."

Feeling vindicated, Hannah sat down at the desk and arranged the robe over her legs. "Now that we've established I'm reasonably sane, and before Pinky turns blue, care to tell me why you're here?"

The department superintendent deferred to the sheriff, sitting on the arm of the sofa. When David gestured *be my guest,* Henry Don pulled a sheaf of folded checks from his T-shirt pocket. "The bank told us and the boys that these weren't no good."

Hannah's heart skipped a beat. A CPA in town monitored the development's cash flow. She plied the computer keyboard for an online review of the account's current balance. Another zero or two, and she might commit grand larceny and flee to a country with no extradition treaty with the U.S. "There's no reason they shouldn't have cleared, Henry Don. My guess is, the teller transposed the account number when she punched it in."

"He didn't punch in nothin'," Pinky said. "Took one look at your John Hancock down at the bottom and all but accused us of forging it."

On closer inspection, it did appear as though she'd clenched a pen between her toes and countersigned her name below *Tripp Irving, CPA.* Wearing mittens to finish yesterday's last batch of checks had produced the same effect.

Henry Don was now bear-hugging himself. Pinky bounced on his heels like a child waiting his turn for the restroom. She said, "I'll bet you guys can't wait to get back outside now."

"Uh-uh," Henry Don chattered. "Don' know how you stan' it in here."

"Funny you should say that." Hannah raised her poor, trembling hands, which only seconds ago had nimbly manipulated the computer's keyboard. "I'd be happy to replace the checks, but my signature will probably look worse now than it did yesterday."

Wise to her—which wasn't always a good thing—David said, "It looks to me like the sooner the AC is fixed, the sooner you can pay these men their due."

Hannah nodded vigorously. "Maintenance was supposed to take care of it last night. Now it's one-thirty and—"

"Don't you worry, hon." Henry Don raced Pinky to the door. "There'll be somebody here in ten minutes, if we have to chain his ankle and drag him behind the truck."

David contained his laughter until they were out of earshot. "Darlin', you've got about twice more orneriness in you than any one woman ought to have."

Hannah sat down on his lap and curled an arm

around his neck. "Whatever works. I'm tired of shlumping around in this Nanook of the North outfit."

He waggled his eyebrows. "That could be arranged."

"Not in ten minutes, it can't." She nibbled his lower lip, her tongue flicking the outer edge. "Even you can't thaw me out that fast."

A lecherous groan reverberated in David's chest. "Flip off the circuit breaker." A warm, broad hand slithered under Hannah's sweater, then her bra. "The bedroom door's got a lock on it."

She arched her back as most of her muscles began to liquefy. Some, oh yes, a sweet, sensitive few, tightened and started to swell. Just before her mind completely melted, she gasped, "Circuit breaker?"

"Umm hmm," David mumbled, his mouth otherwise occupied, then added, "For the AC."

Hannah's eyes opened. She cocked her head, replaying the conversation. Particular attention was given a select verb and a couple of nouns.

She wriggled upright and tugged down her sweater. "Do you mean, I could have flipped off the breaker, instead of freezing my ass off for the past twenty-nine hours?"

Her tone and abrupt change of trajectory probably accounted for his slack-jawed expression. The majority of his blood supply having diverted well south of his brain triggered a "Yeah," rather than insisting she'd imagined any reference to electrical circuitry.

It also strengthened her opinion that mechanical lie detectors would never be as accurate as foreplay, which was how she'd confirmed a former lover was cheating on her with a flight attendant.

"But," David said, "before I left this morning, I asked if you wanted me to kick off the breaker."

"Did I happen to be awake at the time?"

"Your eyes were open. And you shook your head."

"Ha. Nice try, Hendrickson. You know as well as I do that conscious isn't the same as awake."

His mouth crooked into that irresistible grin. "Okay, I did neglect to ask how many fingers I was holding up." Four of them dove under the hem of her sweater and began the trek upward again. "Surely, I can think of some way to make it up to you."

Hannah nodded at the maintenance department van turning into the driveway. Henry Don Tucker's pickup hovered so close behind, it could be attached to a tow chain. "Not with the cavalry coming to my rescue."

The look David leveled at the two-vehicle caravan should have blistered their paint jobs. He stood and did the hip maneuvers common to hula hoop aficionados and the sexually deprived.

"Reminds me of the bad old days." He smoothed his shirtfront and adjusted his sport coat's lapels. "Back when someone or something interrupted every time I rounded second base and charged for third."

"There could be extra innings," she said, "if they can fix the AC as fast as Delbert broke it."

"I wish." Although fleeting, David's tongue-intensive kiss had its usual effect on Hannah's equilibrium and libido. Meaning the former whirled off its axis and the latter shifted into overdrive.

"It's your fault I started what I didn't have time to finish." He glanced at the men stamping up the sidewalk. "I'll have to boogie to make that ice cream social down in Passover as it is. One look at you and politics is the last thing on my mind."

Hannah surveyed her ensemble. "You're a strange man, Sheriff."

"Nope. Just crazy in love with a redhead and tired of—" He grimaced.

"Tired of what?"

"Being tired," he finished, a bit too quickly. "I don't suppose you've talked to Luke today."

"Luke Sauers?" The leap from unrequited horniness to his campaign manager bewildered her. "No. Why?"

"Just wondering." His smile seemed forced. "I'll call you as soon as I can, sugar."

Hannah stared after him as he passed the incoming crew on the porch. She was usually as adept at reading his mind as he was hers. How Luke factored in, she couldn't guess. What David was tired of was hardly a mystery, but if he thought she was using her job as a stalling tactic, he was...

Well, he wasn't right. Sure, he'd hired subcontractors to finish the house faster, instead of doing it himself. But just last month, who'd said they might as well postpone the wedding until after the election?

Mother Nature and Murphy's Law preordained that by four o'clock, all the cottage's circuit breakers were shut off until the repairman scored a replacement thermostat in town. And consequently, the humidity was outpacing the air temperature.

Oven had replaced *igloo* as the operative word for the great room. Hannah elected to conduct an employment interview on the back deck. The roofed front porch was arguably a degree or two cooler, but too visible to curious passersby—specifically, Ida-Clare Clancy.

The gumshoe gang's second-in-command would not kill to retake Hannah's job, but targeted maiming wasn't entirely out of the question. After the previous manager's restrained departure, Jack had taken leave of his senses long enough to let his bossy, my-way-or-the-highway mother take charge.

A geriatric civil war erupted almost immediately, although civility on both sides was in short supply. Hannah considered IdaClare the kindest, most generous woman she'd ever met, but beneath that plump, grandmotherly exterior beat the heart of a tungsten magnolia.

If IdaClare knew Hannah was interviewing replacements, she'd ask Jack for a second chance at dictatorship. Then she'd beg. Then threaten to cut her only child out of her will and bequeath her estate to Itsy and Bitsy, her grandchildren disguised as teacup poodles.

Or worse, she'd call in the two million bucks she'd loaned Jack to secure additional financing for the development. Real estate speculators whose net worth swung from Happy Meal to the Forbes 500 list were understandably hesitant to antagonize their wealthy, widowed mothers.

To stay off IdaClare's radar, classified employment ads hadn't run in newspapers within a hundred miles of Kinderhook County. Résumés were posted to Clancy Construction & Development in St. Louis, or e-mailed to Jack's executive secretary. Wilma screened the lot, ran background checks, then forwarded any survivors to Hannah.

Juline Shelton, the fourth prospect granted a personal interview, seemed impervious to air that would be easier to chew than breathe. Also to perspiration rings, mascara meltdown and the frizzies.

Her immaculate white chinos were wrinkle-repellant. A bright, cap-sleeved blouse, cubic zirconium studs, bead necklace and espadrilles personified summer business-casual.

Hannah, now stripped down to jeans, a silk tank top and straw slides, felt her hair volumizing into an atomic frizzball and her makeup congealing like forty-weight motor oil.

"It's beautiful here," Juline said, sipping her first glass of iced tea, while Hannah chugged her third. "Honestly, I can't imagine why you'd want to leave."

Honestly, Hannah didn't. If human cloning were possible, she could have it all, all at once, but that was beside the point. It wasn't her fault the hills weren't crawling with people eager to take on the responsibility of managing a retirement community. And David did agree—she couldn't jump ship before finding a new captain.

Who might be seated across from her right now.

"Believe me," Hannah said, "when I came here in April, getting married wasn't even in the deck, much less in the cards."

"You met your fiancé *here?*" Juline's tone suggested that Hannah had landed a kazillionaire geezer, à la Anna Nicole Smith.

"Not the first time. We met when he pulled me over for speeding and slapped me with a huge fine and court costs. Then a couple of days later, when a tenant—" Hannah interrupted herself, sensing that the murder of a Valhalla Springs resident probably wasn't a prime topic for discussion. "Oh, enough about me. Quite frankly, I'd like to hear why a single, attractive, twenty-six-year-old would want a job in the boondocks."

Juline's brows met at the bridge of her nose, as though the question were of the trick variety and algebra was required for the answer.

Strike one, Hannah thought. *Because it's there* isn't a logical reason to climb Mount Everest, much less apply for employment.

"The salary's okay," Juline said. "And the house is really cute. Two bedrooms would be better, but it's a lot larger than my apartment in Kansas City."

The wind swept a silky swath of hair across the young woman's face. As she pushed it back, she straightened in the deck chair, craning to see between the trees. "Gosh, look how weird the sky looks all of a sudden."

A dark wall of clouds loomed in the distance. The ominous, deep purple-cobalt layer compressing a dingy gray-blue layer resembled a second horizon. It was a sight Hannah had seen before: a tornado had flattened a quarter of Effindale, Illinois, her childhood hometown. Effindale hadn't been America's garden spot before the storm, but the speed and extent of the devastation were as vivid now as the day it happened. Instead of fear, the experience kindled respect for Mother Nature's power and a gut-level humbleness.

A tornado watch had been issued for central Missouri moments before Juline arrived. Watches and warnings were hardly rare between April and October, but the current bulletin included a weather-related job qualification that Hannah hadn't considered.

"Valhalla Springs has dedicated storm-warning sirens linked to the National Weather Service." Hannah pointed at the community center, visible through the trees. "The center's basement is a designated shelter, along with several others in the shops in the commercial district."

Juline picked at the buttons on her blouse, then at her beaded necklace. "If you're half as terrified of storms as I am, I'll bet you could get to one of those shelters in ten seconds flat."

"Not until I was sure our 396 tenants were safe."

"Are you serious?" Juline flinched. "Wait, that didn't come out right. What I meant was, how can you, or I, if I get the job, herd that many old people all by yourself—er, myself?"

Herd? Old people? Hannah decided to give her the benefit of the doubt. After all, when Jack offered her the job, she'd responded with a remark about bingo tournaments and Metamucil as a food group.

"Other staff members—paid and volunteer—assist in any type of an emergency, Juline. Longtime residents are terrific about escorting new neighbors to their block's designated shelter."

"Sounds like a kindergarten fire drill," Juline said, laughing. "'All right, children, quiet as a mouse, let's join hands with a buddy and form two lines at the door.'"

Strike two. Which could have been three, but Hannah was determined to prove her standards weren't too high for anyone to meet. Juline's interview had lasted longer than anyone's thus far, but not because the others were rejected without cause.

One man blithely disclosed a criminal record that Wilma's background check hadn't caught. Another smelled like a brewery neighboring a men's cologne factory. A fifty-two-year-old widow admitted she was on safari for a new spouse but couldn't afford to lease a residential cottage.

The most recent reject was about thirty, with full-sleeve tattoos, nose rings, a pierced tongue and a magenta mohawk. Poor Malcolm had slunk away from her with his tail between his legs, too traumatized to pee on her motorcycle's tires.

Still, Juline Shelton's kindergarten fire drill comment wasn't just inappropriate, it raised Hannah's antennae. A review of the application's personal information page found the box labeled Dependents was blank. On a hunch, she said, "So, how old are your children?"

"Six and—" Juline's nostrils flared. She tossed aside the necklace she'd worried like a talisman. "Think you're smart, huh? You don't even *have* kids, *do* you? Try having two, and finding a decent job and a safe place to live."

Tears welled in her eyes. "When I saw the ad, it was perfect. A dream come true. I could stay home with my kids *and* work."

She moved her iced tea glass aside and laid her forearms on the table. "I'm sorry. I really am. I shouldn't have cheated on the application, but if you'd known I had kids, you wouldn't even have given me an interview, would you?"

Hannah shook her head. "No, I—"

"See? How fair is that? Please, just give me a chance. You won't regret it. I *promise* you won't."

Hannah sighed and returned the form to the file folder. "I can't."

"Why." A statement, not a question, but it held not a trace of animosity. "Tell me how you can be so certain I can't do the job with kids, as well as you have without any."

The former ad executive that colleagues nicknamed Balls-to-the-Walls Garvey admired that kind of chutzpah. A lesson Hannah's grandmother mistakenly taught was that an unqualified no should be challenged. Whether a change of mind or heart results, it'll annoy the obstinate, the whimsical and relatives with mean streaks.

"Okay." Hannah splayed her fingers. "Live-in grandchildren aren't allowed in Valhalla Springs. Visits are restricted to one week. It sounds harsh, but people come here to retire and appreciate an excuse to not be a handy dump site for their children's children."

By Juline's scowl, she took exception to "dump site." If Hannah had a dollar for every tenant who'd used the term, Malcolm could dine on prime rib until Christmas.

"Apart from a manager's children contradicting that policy, a one-bedroom cottage is too small for a family of three. The great room is a quasi-reception area, not a place for kids and toys and Elmo videos blasting from the TV.

"Some prospective tenants tour by appointment. Plenty drop in and expect the manager to show them around. That isn't always easy for one person, and children aren't portable at a moment's notice."

Index finger hooked on her thumb, Hannah continued, "Add to that, handling commercial lease agreements and cancellations, tenant agreements, overseeing new construction, department supervisors, some social activities, promotion, direct mailings and responses, resolving tenant disputes, covenant violations…"

She gestured surrender. "I'm the one who's sorry, Juline. And disappointed. But I'm not being sarcastic when I say there've been days when taking care of a dog is almost too much to do along with everything else."

Juline might have assumed that Hannah was a fanatic zero-population growth advocate. Now her expression was a younger, prettier variation of Henry Don Tucker measuring Hannah for a straitjacket.

Itemizing the duties and responsibilities had boggled Hannah's own mind a little. Ye gods, she wasn't

Superwoman. Probably wouldn't rate an honorable mention in a Resident Operations Manager of the Year competition. But wouldn't the sum of any job broken down into its parts sound impossible?

Juline stammered, "M-my mom said this was too good to be true."

"Well, I wouldn't—"

"No, you're absolutely right. Nobody could juggle a family and all that…stuff. But how are you ever going to find anybody that *can?*"

Hannah was still deliberating long after Juline left, as thunder rolled like a muffled tympany, at once reverberating and retreating. She perused the sky, now a solid purpling bruise lanced with coppery flashes of lightning.

Wanted, she thought. *A mature, childless, reasonably intelligent person with excellent people skills and no felony convictions, neuroses, psychoses or substance addictions to manage retirement community. Housing and utilities provided; hours and salary commensurate with migrant farmwork.*

Peachy freakin' keen. Strike *retirement community* and it would read like an employment opportunity at Guantanamo Bay.

The phone ringing ended a reverie with no apparent future in it. She wasn't surprised when David told her he was going straight from the ice-cream-and-politics party to his office at the courthouse.

"We've got a long night ahead of us," he warned. "There's a whole covey of storms popping up in southern Oklahoma and central Kansas."

Hannah nodded, as though their phones had video-conferencing capabilities. "I'm headed for the porch to storm-watch, after I click on the TV and turn up the weather alert radio."

"An old boy here in Passover doesn't set much store in electronic gadgets. He said when his cows hunker in the field it means we're in for a heavy rain, but nothing dire along with it."

Hannah sincerely hoped the prediction was accurate, but she feared otherwise. "My great-uncle Mort was big on animal signs, too. After the tornado hit Effindale, he swore the dead horse floating in the mayor's swimming pool was thirsty and his hooves slipped on the concrete when he got a drink."

David laughed. "And you bought it."

"Hey, I was just a little kid." Hannah looked at Malcolm, flopped in the grass. "For whatever it's worth, the thunder isn't bothering Malcolm."

A pause and a "Yes, ma'am" cued her to David Hendrickson morphing into Sheriff Hendrickson. "Do keep me advised on that situation."

Judging from the background noise, his public had him surrounded. Because cell phones had revolutionized eavesdropping for busybodies and everyone else in a ten-foot radius, Hannah said, "10-4, Adam 1-01." Then, in a rush, whispered, "I love you, David."

"Yep, that's an affirmative, Zebra 3-28. Adam 1-01, clear."

Adam 1-01 was his official radio designation. The county's alphabetical identifiers stopped well short of Z for Zebra, aka Hannah, whose birthday was March 28. Either no one had picked up on him using ten-codes on his office phone and cell, or weren't inclined to comment on it.

Hannah listened to the dial tone, wondering what prompted that impulsive, "I love you." And resisting the compelling urge to punch redial and add, "Be careful."

Clicking off the handset, she supposed the threatening weather had her on edge. Just because she wasn't diving under the bed, didn't mean National Weather Service meteorologists were a bunch of nervous Nellies.

The yellow maintenance department van pulling into the driveway seemed like a good omen. For the air conditioner, anyway.

4

On any given weekday morning, the Short Stack Café, across from the courthouse, buzzed with lawyers, clients and locals catching breakfast, a cup of coffee or a bite of gossip.

The codgers nicknamed the Liar's Club held down a center table. If they didn't snag a fresh rumor to chew on till lunchtime, they'd improve on yesterday's, last week's, last month's, or last century's choice scandals and controversies. Failing that, they'd debate when and why the world started going to hell in a handbasket.

Ruby's Café was Sanity's other purveyor of homemade baking powder biscuits, sausage gravy to smother them with, and Grade A jumbos fried in bacon grease, as the good Lord intended. The storefront eatery was located in a strip mall anchored by Wal-Mart and a Price-Slasher supermarket.

A Liar's Club of a different kind frequented Ruby's on Monday through Friday mornings. The long-haul truckers', fishermen's, hunters' and route drivers' allegations were no more factual than their elders' across town, but they were less inclined to be-grudge the sheriff a table for one.

The aroma of fried apples, ham steaks and hominy grits swimming in creamery butter diffused the cig-arette smoke roiling above the café's larger, crowded seating area. David returned the men's waves, nods, and mouthed "Howya doin'?"s He also knew it was the badge folks acknowledged, not necessarily the person wearing it.

The far table in front of the coffee station was un-occupied, as usual. Dingy batting oozed from slits in the chairs' vinyl upholstery. The tippy, burn-marked tabletop was sun-faded and chipped. Old soldiers, David thought, still spry enough to march in the pa-rade, but demoted to its tag end.

His posterior hadn't met the seat before Ruby Amyx lumbered over with a brimming cup of coffee in hand. The diner's owner was in her early sixties, as tough as ten-penny nails, and never turned away a hungry stray, be it human or animal.

Her coal-black beehive, spit curls and lipstick rouge were a little…well, cartoonish, but Ruby was as likely to change them as she was to trade in her thirty-year-old red Caddy with fake fur glued to the dashboard.

"Hidey there, tall, dar—" Her customary welcome dissolved to a heaving sigh. "If'n you don't look like a cat done dragged you halfway to Half Way and back again, I don't know what would."

The Dallas County town named for its equidistance between Bolivar and Buffalo was outside David's jurisdiction, but the point was taken. He chuckled and said, "It's great to see you, too, Miz Amyx."

"Aw-w, you know 'twas meant for a scold, not a belittlement." The mother hen with no chicks of her own arched a penciled eyebrow. "Them storms woulda blowed through the same last night, whether you was out in 'em, or home like you oughta been."

David swallowed down a yawn. Piece together a string of naps and he'd grossed about nine hours' sleep in the past thirty-six, or so. And he'd felt pretty good, until Ruby reminded him how tired he was.

A faint, intermittent whine in his ears was escalating to a steady high C. Irritating, but he'd be sacked out in his own bed by noon, and sharing it with Hannah by nine that night. Still, the day couldn't come soon enough when His and Hers applied to towels in the linen cupboard, instead of whose mattress he stretched out on.

If it ever did.

Doubt crept in, as pernicious as cigarette smoke drifting from the room's far side. Contrary to Sunday school teachings, a weary mind is the devil's playground. David's wandered to last night's telephone conversation with Hannah.

He hadn't been shocked to hear another resident manager candidate had flunked the interview. Hannah then called herself a hypocrite for prejudging applicants' dedication to the job, while she shacked up with David at his house whenever she could. Said she felt guiltier and guiltier for sneaking around behind everybody's back.

David objected to "shacked up," but knew that was her conscience talking. He sympathized. Admired her honesty, with him and herself. He'd even laughed when she went on about Kinderhook County's ten political commandments starting with *Thine Sheriff can screw around with whomever he wants, as long as he parks his cruiser in her garage at night, instead of her driveway.*

"Screw around" rankled, too, but venting frustration was fine. Healthy, even. What bothered him was a nagging uncertainty that her legitimate-sounding reasons for rejecting one applicant after another were just excuses.

If it *was* more stall than substance, David couldn't fault her for it. Would he give up his home and his job to marry her? "Hell, yes" was a mighty easy answer for the guy on the catbird side of compromise.

And a lie, he admitted. Half of one, anyhow. He hadn't quit the Tulsa Police Department to save his first marriage. It wouldn't have, but he hadn't given it a second's consideration, either. He and Cynthia were classic examples of opposites attracting, then discovering their common ground was as solid as quicksand. Except his ex-wife wasn't wrong when she said, "A cop is my husband," instead of "My husband is a cop."

Hannah had no reservations about David's career choice. Oh, she fretted about him, sure. Wavered between monitoring the scanner Delbert bought her, and switching it off when an incident in progress frayed her nerves, instead of soothing them. But if anyone grasped how it felt to earn a paycheck for doing what you loved most, it was Hannah Marie Garvey.

As for the other half of his reflexive "Hell, yes"? Luke Sauers had promised months ago to buy David's land, if he lost the election. At the time, his campaign manager was a couple of bottles shy of killing a six-pack, and the offer was a duke's mixture of a bet, a reassuring gesture and a worst case scenario escape clause.

Luke *would* buy him out, though, circumstances be damned. He wanted the place for himself. Had, since David carved out a slice of Eden with a brush-hog, a bulldozer, a chain saw, a lot of sweat and a little blood.

With his property out of the equation, Hannah could keep her cottage and her job at Valhalla Springs. Hopefully, voters would let him keep his.

Ruby plucked at David's sleeve, startling him from the mental black hole he'd retreated into. The noisy diner, with its brightness and smells, crashed over him like a sensory ambush.

"I can see what you're thinkin'," Ruby said. "It's writ' all over your face that buttin' into your business ain't none of mine."

Evidently, his zone-out hadn't lasted longer than a few seconds. "Believe me, Miz Amyx. That was the furthest thing from my mind."

He passed a hand over his eyes, the heel grinding into the right one. The socket was so dry, it should have squeaked. Between blinks, he glimpsed a man swaggering by the window. The blurry profile was depressingly identifiable.

Jessup Knox wasn't a regular customer. Ruby was

wont to say he'd inspired the Right to Refuse Service sign taped to the cash register. To David's knowledge, she hadn't booted Knox or anyone else out the door. The privilege was reserved for the day she ran out of insults to hurl at the smarmy burglar alarm salesman.

"If you're what the cat dragged in," she told David, "then that there's the bull-footed peckerwood it hawked up."

He smiled. "Now, Ruby—"

"Gimme two shakes and I'll box up your usual, so's you can eat it somewhere else in peace."

He thanked her but declined. Running against Jessup Knox was one thing. Running from him was another. "Just a couple of scrambled eggs and wheat toast will do me fine."

Hearing Knox greet the Liar's Club like kin, which several probably were, David added, "And put whatever he orders on my check."

Second thoughts must have countered whatever argument she was poised to make. "All right, Sheriff." She backed away, saying, "But if that fool leaves afore you do, I'm tossin' a steak on the grill and you're gonna eat it."

Knox rounded the dividing wall and halted. Fists knuckling his hips, he bellowed, "Dave Hendrickson?

What are you doing hiding back in the corner, ol' buddy?"

In a dozen words, starting with a nickname no one else had ever used, David's opponent had him on the defensive and struggling not to show it.

The owner of Fort Knox Security mounted the chair across from David as if it were a saddle. He signaled for a cup of coffee and sloshed David's in the process. "Boy, if those bags under your eyes get any bigger, airlines are apt to charge extra to carry them on board."

David's expression was devoid of humor. "Like I keep trying to tell you, Jessup, this job you want so bad isn't eight-to-five."

"It would be, if you trusted your deputies to do theirs."

Ruby mopped up the spilled coffee, then banged a second cup on the table. It was filled from a nearly empty carafe. David's was topped off from a full, fresh one. "You eatin', Knox? Or jes' here to harass the sheriff."

Knox massaged the gut straining against his shirt's pearlized snaps. God help David if one of them gave. Picturing fifty pounds of blubber unleashed like a deployed air bag shriveled an already waning appetite.

"Much as I'd love to dunk a sweet roll in this cup of swamp water," Knox said, "I'm still digesting that fine breakfast the mayor bought me at the Short Stack."

Ruby sniffed and stalked off, muttering about pto-maine, botulism and birds of a feather.

"That gal's been funny-turned since Heck was a pup." Knox licked a fingertip and ran it along the chair rail above the wainscoting. "I wonder how long it's been since County Health dropped by for a look-see."

"Two weeks. She scored ninety-nine out of a hundred." David couldn't resist adding, "Seventeen points closer to perfect than the Short Stack."

"You don't say." Knox shrugged. "Could be, not all the tips she gets are in quarters and dimes."

Don't take the bait, David warned himself. Ruby doesn't need you to defend her, and she'll cuff your ears if you try.

"So, Dave. What's this I hear about that new squad car the taxpayers bought after you totaled the old one?"

Only a fool answers loaded questions. David swigged his coffee and gained a greater understanding of why restaurants with drive-thru windows became an overnight success.

"I hear tell, you wanted your cruiser painted black and white. Wanted the whole *county motor pool* re-painted black and white." Knox wagged his head. "Boy, it's so easy to hammer you for pissing away money, there's no sport in it at all."

Back when the wrongful-death lawsuit was still in the fiscal liability column, Luke told David not to requisition a box of paper clips until after the election.

He'd respectfully but adamantly ignored the advice. A sheriff who weighed ideas and decisions against a calendar wasn't protecting or serving the public. Of course, neither was Mayor Wilkes, whose son's body shop customized patrol units with expensive, ultra-blue reflective bands and pinstripes.

Police departments across the country had realized that black oversprayed on a predominantly white cruiser's trunk, fenders and hood cost far less than custom trim. A true two-tone paint job also enhanced recognition in low light, sunlight, in drivers' rear-view mirrors, and from air-evac and highway patrol helicopters.

"Why stop with the cars, Dave? Ask the city council to change Sanity to Mayberry, why don'tcha? Make deputies carry a bullet in their shirt pockets like Barney Fife."

Knox's jibes echoed the county commissioners' when David presented the idea to repaint the county motor pool. Not one of them glanced at the studies, surveys, testimonials and cost estimates he'd submitted.

Ruby delivered a heaping plate of eggs, toast and bowls of butter and homemade strawberry preserves. "You sure that's all you want, Sheriff?"

David nodded. Aromas wafting upward that should have had his taste buds slapping high fives, revolted him. Somehow, he had to choke down every bite.

"What's the matter, Dave?" Knox said. "I'm just funnin' with you. Can't you take a joke anymore?"

Thinking a swallow of coffee he didn't want might open his throat enough for the food he didn't want, David was reaching for the cup when his pager went off. He'd never doubted the Almighty's existence, but a little divine intervention now and then was a beautiful thing.

Marlin Andrik's badge number appeared on the LED screen. The chief of detectives wanted a return call, *stat,* and in private, not broadcast on the radio or out a cell phone's speaker.

"What's up?" Knox angled his head for a peek at the numeric message.

Marlin didn't send his personal bat signal just to

chat. David stood and pulled out his wallet. Three singles and two twenties. *Shit.* Ruby was in the back somewhere. There wasn't time to wait for change. Throw an Andy Jackson on the table and his unworthy opponent would happily report that David pissed away his own money the same as he did the county's.

His eyes flicked to Knox. Laying the three ones beside his untouched plate for a tip, David said, "Thanks for picking up the check, ol' buddy."

Someday, he'd feel bad for sticking Elvis with the tab. In his next life. Maybe the one after that.

"Good morning. Clancy Construction and Development. How can I direct your call?"

Another day, Hannah thought, another new receptionist. Considering this one's voice and eastern accent, she was younger than Hannah's bathrobe and a native St. Louisan.

"Jack Clancy, please," she said, and gave her name.

"Do you want to leave a message on Mr. Clancy's voice mail?"

"No, thanks. Anyone who knows Mr. Clancy knows better than to leave a message on his voice mail. He just hasn't figured out we're on to him yet."

"Then I have to put you on hold." The receptionist's tone suggested that Hannah was one of many stuck listening to a canned instrumental version of Streisand's Greatest Hits. She tipped back the handset, as though it would keep "People" from looping in her brain the rest of the day.

Chin resting on her palm, she surveyed the great room. Replacing the desk phone with a cordless model was supposed to enable multitasking during times like these. Dusting, for instance. De-humping the area rug where Malcolm played ostrich and buried chew bones the size of a brontosaurus's femur.

From this perspective, the leather couch appeared in need of a shave. She hadn't slathered conditioning cream on it since…well, never.

There were recipes to clip from the stack of magazines on the trunk used as a coffee table. Books, CDs, DVDs and videos on the shelves beside the fireplace crying to be alphabetized. The patched bullethole in the corner of the ceiling had a cobweb goatee. And look, just *look* at the—

"Hey, sweet pea," Jack said in her ear. "Sorry you were on hold for so long."

"No problem." Hannah slumped in the chair, exhausted. "It gave me the chance to do a little housecleaning."

"Mental? Or actual?"

She held out the phone and glared at it. Fifteen-year friendships were such a pain in the ass some-times. Clapping the phone to her ear again, she said, sweetly and sincerely, "Up yours, Clancy."

"So, this cottage you aren't cleaning. It's still in Missouri, I presume."

"Uh-huh. We stayed mostly on the southern edge of the storm front. A little hail, a *lot* of wind and rain. Nothing that me and Toto couldn't handle."

"Be glad Malcolm isn't a poodle. Mother said she had to double Itsy's and Bitsy's recommended daily dose of Valium."

"No offense to IdaClare," she said, "but teacup poodles aren't dogs. They're pot scrubbers with feet."

"They're Furwads from Hell. You're just their aunt Hannah. I'm even-Steven with them in the will. And I bought her the damned things."

"Live and learn," she said, grinning. "And speak-ing of Stephen, how's the best OB/GYN in St. Louis? Besides too busy to call me once in a while to dish about you."

A lengthy pause deflated her smile. She'd sensed Jack's relationship with Stephen Riverton had be-come less than blissful, despite their many years to-gether. Or because of them. Staying in the closet socially, purporting to be career-centric bachelors who lived in the same condo, not the same loft, must be emotionally equivalent to water gradually wearing down stone.

Jack cleared his throat. "He's fine. I'll tell him you said hello."

Hannah heard a No Trespassing sign being posted. Until recently, few ever had been, by either of them. Now the inflection was almost routine and it hurt.

They hadn't anticipated that her move to Valhalla Springs would affect their friendship. Why would they have? If a long-ago, impulsive, horribly failed attempt at being lovers hadn't destroyed it, nothing ever could.

Or so they'd believed. The first hairline fractures appeared almost immediately. Soon after, Jack's brief, impromptu visit mended them, only for a larger crack to emerge and branch into deeper, wider ones.

Once upon a time, he'd considered Hannah an equal. If asked, he'd say he still did and always would. She'd like to think when he was no longer her employer, they'd rekindle that platonic, no-holds-barred, two-Musketeers friendship they'd both taken for granted. Except what would a sheriff's wife and a resort developer have in common?

Hannah recognized the quiet creaks she heard in the background. The toes of Jack's Italian shoes, crossed on a corner of his desk, were tapping *impa-*

zientemente. Perpetual motion in some form came naturally to a man forever on the run from himself.

"We're still on for Saturday, aren't we?" she asked.

"Saturday?" Jack's voice rose, as if the conversation had suddenly veered into obscure territory.

"The day after tomorrow," she prompted helpfully. Then, "Last clue, Einstein. Your birthday."

"Thanks, but I know when my birthday is. The same day I finalize a golf course development in Michigan."

Wonderful. The timing of her planned face-to-face-off about employment qualifications wouldn't have been optimal, but David would have been there for the birthday cake cutting, and he always had a gun somewhere on his person.

"Spare me the guilt trip about the birthday party," Jack said. "Mother already laid a huge one on me."

Not huge enough, Hannah thought. She squared her shoulders, which would put them almost eye to eye, if Jack were a couple of hundred miles closer.

Rifts in their friendship aside, he was a silver-haired Irish teddy bear. One with nuclear capabilities, but a teddy bear, nonetheless. Her approach to compromise was key: a smooth, steady balance of experience, confidence and touch, like hitting the tarmac's black marks in a 757.

"Anything else?" he said.

"Nothing major," she stalled. "Wilma probably told you about yesterday's interview."

"First thing. She's still mad at herself for letting Ms. Mom slip by her."

"Well, I had a few reservations about Juline Shelton, even before I found out about her kids, but—"

"Fuhgeddaboudit, sweet pea." A scraping sound and a thump indicated two hand-cobbled shoes had hit the floor. "I won't authorize using a two-bedroom resident's cottage for manager's quarters." Jack chuckled. "And yes, I know you too well."

Hannah ducked down to examine the desk's knee hole, suspecting a bug had picked up last night's heart-to-heart with Malcolm, who'd taken refuge there until the weather calmed. No button mics were visible. Possibly because the desk's underside could use a shave, too.

"What if I'd had a kid, Jack? C'mon, one lousy kid. Old enough to feed and dress himself. Old enough to eat, dress and drive himself to school, even."

"If you did, you wouldn't have quit Friedlich & Friedlich."

"The hell I wouldn't have." She paced the narrow aisle between the desk and built-in credenza. "As much as I traveled? The hours I put in? Nights. Weekends. National freakin' holidays. How could I possibly have raised a kid—in Chicago, no less—in a condo where you had to squash your head against a window to see a damned tree?"

Aware she was ranting and enjoying it, despite Clancy's laughter, she went on, "If me having a child when you were desperate to hire a manager four months ago wouldn't have mattered, it shouldn't matter now that *I'm* the desperate one, trying after forty-three years to have a life, while you're free to fly off to Michigan on your birthday."

The swirling optical dots common to the oxygen deprived had dwindled by the time Jack caught his own breath. "Okay, all right. You win, as usual. I'll tell Wilma one child isn't an automatic out-skie."

"Oh, Jack." Hannah puckered and smacked a sloppy kiss into the receiver. "Thank you, I really—"

"*If* the kid's over ten," he said. "Make that twelve. And both kid and parent have to come to the interview. And Valhalla Springs' board of directors has to approve it. And if absolutely necessary, a two-bedroom cottage is a loaner, until an addition is built on the manager's cottage. Agreed?"

Before Hannah responded, he tacked on, "No pets, ATVs, motorcycles, scooters, go-carts, skimobiles or pubescent wannabe Paris Hiltons, either."

"That's it?" She leaned against the credenza and tipped back her head as far as her vertebrae allowed. "Gee, this widens the employment field so much, I can almost hear the organist tuning up for the Wedding March."

"Musicians. *Christ.* I don't want any electric guitars, keyboards, drums—"

"Goodbye, Jack." She pressed End, hesitated, then docked the handset. She hadn't talked to David since midnight, but the news of Jack's extremely conditional surrender could wait. By now, David was sleeping off one of Ruby Amyx's fabulous five-pound breakfast specials.

And life being metabolically sexist, he'd weigh the same when he wakened as he did before his head hit the pillow.

5

An electric utility bucket truck and a cable-TV repair van narrowed the mouth of the cul-de-sac to a single lane. David threaded his patrol unit through the aperture, then dodged a branch severed by last night's armada of thunderstorms.

None of the cloud rotations weather-spotters had reported had developed into tornados, but torrential rain, micro-burst winds and sixty-mile-an-hour gusts had downed power lines and caused minor property damage from the southwest corner of the county to the northeast.

Clear skies and the cool breeze blowing through the cruiser's open window lent a surreality to the shingles scattered across the pavement. Leaves and grass clippings plastered the windward side of a late-model pickup. On the opposite side of Greenaway Circle, a mature Bartlett pear tree was snapped off at the ground, smothering a flower bed.

Residents of the keyhole-shaped development clustered in their driveways and front lawns pretending to assess the damage. All eyes were riveted on the vehicles arrayed in the cul-de-sac's turnaround. David angled the Crown Victoria alongside Marlin Andrik's unmarked Chevy and behind the coroner's hearse.

On the right side of the horseshoe, crime-scene tape blocked entry to a split-level rancher. Uniformed deputies flanked the open garage to chase away those who couldn't parse Police Line Do Not Cross, or assumed it didn't apply to them.

David recalled the backyard barbecues he'd attended here, a holiday open house, the condolence call he'd made a few weeks afterward, then the number of times since that he'd intended to drop by.

Something had always cropped up and taken precedence. Nothing memorable. Just the stuff and nonsense that shifted today's list of priorities to tomorrow's. Before you know it, a month or two has flown by.

As David started for the house, Chase Wingate exited a minivan with Sanity Examiner in old English lettering on its doors. Before Marlin kiboshed radio transmissions, the county weekly's owner-publisher must have intercepted dispatch reporting a 10-18 at this address. Delbert Bisbee wasn't the only scanner-junkie who knew a dead body ten-code when he heard it. Far from it, unfortunately.

"Sheriff," Wingate said, "if you'll fax a personal quote about this sometime before Sunday, I'd appreciate it."

"Will do." David slipped Wingate's business card in his shirt pocket as a reminder. The newspaperman could be as persistent as his big-city brethren; he was just smart enough to know that anything he asked now, including the victim's ID, would foster a "No comment."

Veteran Deputy Bill Eustace directed David to the front door, saying, "They haven't had time to process the garage yet."

"You were responding officer?"

Eustace jerked his head at the rookie stationed on the other side of the garage. "It was kind of a tie between me and Vaughn."

"The garage door was up when you arrived?"

"Yessir. After the neighbor lady across the street couldn't raise anybody on the phone, she went in through the garage, then ran home and called 911. Me and Vaughn went in that way, too."

That meant at least three people had tracked in and out of the garage. If the killer had, as well, that portion of the scene was already contaminated. It couldn't be helped, but David's chief of detectives wasn't the forgiving type.

Eustace turned and waved at the garage's concrete apron and the white sedan parked inside. "Judging from the trash, leaves and twigs scattered around, I'd guess the door was open all night long."

David reserved judgment. Power outages and lightning can trip an older-model automatic garage door mechanism. So can a misaimed neighbor's remote control set at the same frequency. Or one from a burglar's private collection, often bought at garage sales for a quarter—battery not included.

Shaggy evergreens encroached on the home's curved walkway. The tips brushed David's slacks as he sidled past, toward a concrete stoop. Above it, the guttering sagged under a couple of seasons' debris. The wrought-iron handrail wobbled; a house number plaque dangled from a lone, rusty chain. The metal storm door's upper glass panel was sparkling clean, inside and out.

David peeled on latex gloves that proved the fallacy in one-size-fits-all. Anticipating the unmistakable stench of death, he thumbed the storm door's latch.

The outrushing air wasn't pleasant, but bearable. It was the foyer's refrigerated chill that raised the hair on the back of David's neck. Considerably colder than Hannah's cottage was yesterday. Enough that if he'd walked in blindfolded, he'd swear he was in a morgue.

To the right, the combined living room and dining room were as he remembered: as formal, uncluttered and spotless as a high-priced furniture store's showroom. Which, he admitted, was essentially what they were.

A carpeted stairway divided those company-only rooms from the family room at the back. The solemn voices, cryptic remarks and camera flashes revealed that the heart of the home was the primary crime scene.

Beginning just inside the archway, a field of plastic evidence markers resembled a miniature tent city. A coffee table had been overturned with enough force to crack one of the legs. Fanned across the carpet were magazines, a vinyl cigarette case, a paperback book, cork coasters, the TV remote. A filtered cigarette butt and ashes had spilled from a plastic ashtray. Mascara and lipstick streaked a wad of tissues.

Foreknowledge of the victim's identity and cause of death didn't prepare David for the sight of Beverly Beauford's corpse. The former sheriff's widow lay sprawled on her stomach. The exposed side of her face and neck were cherry red, and her chin slightly tucked. Impact with the floor had twisted her glasses upward. One lens magnified a bulging blue eye.

Junior Duckworth crouched beside her. The third-generation funeral home owner and three-term county coroner was shock-pale, his features taut. David knew Junior's wife and Bev Beauford had been high school classmates.

Opposite him, Marlin Andrik leaned in for a close-up photo of the lace scarf used as a garrote. The chief of detectives' customary emotional range went from inscrutably grim to inscrutably grimmer. Today, he looked as sick as David felt.

"I hate this fuckin' job," he snarled.

Marlin had said it before. Many times, yet never quite as savagely. Grief, rage and fear lacerated his voice. He took all homicides personally. This one hit too close to home.

Sheriff Larry Beauford had been an elected bureaucrat for whom crime scenes were photo ops, but Bev was still a cop's wife. Her murder crossed a blue line everyone in law enforcement wanted to believe was inviolate. Sacrosanct. An unalienable quid pro quo for putting their own lives at risk.

Marlin rocked back on his heels and looked up at David. "You need to hurl, go outside. Me and Duckworth already flocked the geraniums on the patio."

"If it'd help, I would."

"It won't." He wiped his mouth on the shoulder of his sport coat. "A smoke won't, either, but I'm gonna have one."

He passed off the camera to Josh Phelps. The trainee would assist the coroner when he rolled over the body, then commit that perspective to film.

Marlin was old school. Digital video and stills had their place, but in addition to, not in lieu of, traditional prints and Polaroids. A defense attorney who insinuated that court exhibits had been processed on Photoshop got their asses handed to them. Few things put the chief of detectives in a better mood.

David followed him to the front lawn, realizing the investigator was as eager to brief him as he was for a nicotine fix. They'd worked some horrific scenes together—a multi-fatality shooting sprang immediately to mind—but David couldn't recall Marlin's hand shaking when he lit a cigarette.

A deep drag was taken, held, then exhaled out his nostrils. "After all these years, shit's not supposed to get to me like this." The toe of Marlin's shoe eviscerated a clump of wild onion. "If you want Cletus Orr to lead this one, say the word."

"It's your unit. That makes it your call. No explanation necessary, either way."

David meant it, but hoped the case wasn't reassigned. Cletus Orr was a good investigator. He had seniority in years of service. There were reasons, though, that he'd twice been passed over for promotion to chief.

Cletus was also due to retire soon. If Jessup Knox won the election— David cursed himself. Hiring on as Orr's replacement hadn't occurred to him before, and damn well shouldn't have now.

"I'm just blowing off steam." Marlin's fingers raked his thick, rapidly graying hair. "I want this dirtbag. Want him about fifteen feet out and dead-bang in my sights, if possible."

He squinted at the sun, as though condemning it for shining at a time like this. "I thought it was a jolt when Larry Beauford kicked in the emergency room that night. Everybody could see, he was a coronary or a stroke waiting to happen, but *this…*"

He flicked ash off the Marlboro pinched between his gloved fingers. "Bev? Strangled to death in her own house? *Jesus.*"

The pause demanded and defied a response. Seeing wasn't always believing. A kid doesn't have to see the monster under the bed to believe it's there. Cops know monsters exist. If they lived under beds and had claws and fangs, instead of looking like everybody else, Bev wouldn't be lying dead on the family room floor.

"I haven't seen her around town since Larry's funeral," Marlin went on, "but the wife said Bev was volunteering at the hospital again, getting her hair done at the Curl-Up & Dye—that kinda shit." His eyes cut to David. "Who could have had a hate-on for that woman?"

A question he himself would answer, if it was humanly possible. God help the perpetrator, when he did.

"I saw the scuff marks on the carpet," David said, "and the smashed-up table. Do you think she walked in on a burglary in progress?"

"Phelps found the desk drawers ransacked in the spare bedroom Larry used for an office. The dressers in the master and Bev's jewelry box were dumped, too."

"Dumped as in interrupted, or staged?"

"You tell me." Marlin field-stripped his cigarette and dropped the mangled remains in his jacket pocket. "Bev's purse is on the kitchen counter on top of the mail. If there was any cash in her billfold, it's gone."

David asked, "How about her credit cards?"

"Still there, all nice and neat in their little slots."

Staged. A burglar cold-blooded enough to steal money from the woman he'd just murdered wouldn't balk at taking her credit cards. He might think twice about using them, but leave them behind? Not a chance.

A thief nicknamed the Basement Burglar was operating all over the county, but this didn't fit his MO. He'd left homes as neat as he'd found them—just a little emptier.

"What's Junior's best guess on the time of death?" David asked.

The coroner wasn't a certified medical examiner, but grew up in a funeral home, like his father before him. Duckworth's had phased out their ambulance service in the mid-seventies, but as a teenager, Junior had a second job transporting the sick, the injured and the dying to the hospital. He was also an assistant embalmer. Back then, it wasn't unusual for Junior to provide both services to the same person an hour or so apart.

Marlin's lips moved into what David alleged was a smile. "Notice how cold it was inside the house?"

David nodded.

"Notice the outfit Bev had on?"

"Uh-huh. A short-sleeved blouse and slacks." David thought back and frowned. "Not regular slacks. Those below-the-knee things."

"Capri pants." Marlin rolled his eyes. "My wife and daughter own about fifty pairs apiece. I keep telling 'em they look like they ripped 'em off a midget, but I'm a guy. What the fuck do I know about fashion?"

"More than I do," David said, grinning. The crude language he could live without, but not Marlin's droll sense of humor. To an extent, both were coping mechanisms and neither was intended for civilian ears.

Or eyes, David thought, noting Chase Wingate near the curb, speaking with a middle-aged woman dressed in cutoffs, flip-flops and a Silver Dollar City T-shirt.

David asked, "Where is Cletus?"

"Canvassing the neighborhood, starting with Sheri Watson, the neighbor who called 911."

"Is that her, talking to Wingate?"

"Uh-uh." Marlin chuffed. "Probably a lookie-loo from two streets over wanting her name in the paper." If cynicism was a country, he'd be the emperor. "Mrs. Watson's house has the only direct line of sight to Bev's. The family next door is bonding on a beach somewhere. That one with the For Sale sign is empty."

"What about the neighbors behind Bev?"

"We're working on it. Four uniforms—two of them, off-duty Sanity PD officers—are helping." Greenaway Circle was in county jurisdiction, but a Little Leaguer could punch a low-and-outside into the city limits.

Marlin said "Witness statements" as if it were an epithet. "I expect a minimum of nineteen different suspicious vehicle descriptions, three suspicious persons, seven gunshots and two tips about dudes who look exactly like fugitives on *America's Most Wanted*."

"About average," David agreed. "And it'll turn out nobody saw or heard anything until the neighbor found Bev."

As Jimmy Wayne McBride added another county car to the logjam at the end of the cul-de-sac, Marlin said, "Her prints were the only ones on the interior door between the garage and the utility room, too."

"By her, you mean Bev?"

"Sheri Watson's." Marlin poked another Marlboro between his lips but didn't light it. "The AC was cranked down as far as it would go, but the thermostat's clean. So are the desk, dresser drawers and the jewelry box."

David pondered a moment. Briefings with the chief of detectives were partly informative, partly figure-it-out-yourself. The methodology was like working a puzzle behind your back: ignore the big picture and focus on the pieces.

"Then the utility room door must have been standing open when Eustace and Vaughn arrived," he said. "Otherwise their prints would be on the doorknob."

"Not wide open," Marlin said. "Eustace pushed it the rest of the way with his baton."

"But Bev's prints *aren't* on it, or any of the other stuff. Not even her own jewelry box."

Marlin's eyebrow dipped. "Careful son of a bitch, our burglar. I didn't need Duckworth to speculate that the air was turned down to delay decomp, or make it a helluva lot harder to determine time of death."

Jimmy Wayne cast a lankier and slightly shorter shadow than David. "What're you doing here, boss? I thought you went 10-7 a couple of hours ago."

"I didn't get any farther than Ruby's." A full-size diesel SUV entered David's peripheral vision. Its gold shield decals on the doors and hood warranted a double take. "Thanks, McBride, for leading Elvis to the building."

Marlin said, "Maybe he's gone over to the dark side."

Jimmy Wayne started toward the SUV, pointing his finger at Jessup Knox, rocking and rubbernecking in the driver's seat. The chief deputy jerked his thumb sideward in the universal "Get outta here, *now*" gesture.

Marlin made throat noises. "Screw hand signals. How about I just shoot him?"

"It crossed my mind more than once after Knox

busted in on my breakfast," David said. "How about the three of us ignore him and get this scene processed."

To either rule out or confirm the possibility that Bev Beauford brought her killer home with her, Marlin told Jimmy Wayne to glove up and assist David with a preliminary examination of her vehicle.

Starting for the front door, the detective glared at Knox, now making a beeline for Chase Wingate. Marlin yelled, "Eustace—if that jackass sticks his nose past the tape, *shoot him.*"

The garage's concrete floor was littered with wind-blown debris, just as the deputy had mentioned. Assorted tools, brooms, mops and the like hung beside the door to the utility room. A lawn mower was parked in the far corner; plastic storage tubs and paint cans were stowed on plywood shelves nailed to re-cycled two-by-fours. David's half of his college dorm room had more junk in it than this.

Along the foundation, phantom outlines extending up the wafer-board walls alluded to cardboard cartons and claptrap stored for many a year. As far as he could tell, the few overlapped footprints on the floor weren't fresh.

Jimmy Wayne returned from the kitchen with Bev's key ring and a solemn look on his face. He issued a curt heads-up to the deputies outside, then pressed a wall-mounted button to lower the garage door. "Mother Andrik says, don't get in the car, and don't fuck up any prints when you're checking it out."

A bare bulb in the ceiling fixture exuded a meager forty watts of illumination. It was sufficient to avoid barking a shin on a shelf standard and note the absence of dusty black whorls on the vehicle's pearl-white doors and trunk.

"Marlin doesn't want it printed first?" David asked.

"You want to ask him again, be my guest." Contempt suffused Jimmy Wayne's voice and body language as he moved to the sedan's passenger side. You'd have to know him well to understand that the target of it had strangled a petite, fifty-one-year-old widow.

"Smells like a smoker in a pine grove in here." Jimmy Wayne shined a Mag-Lite on the carpeted floorboard. "Clean, though."

"Deluxe car-wash package," David said. "And wipe-down crews usually wear gloves." If the perpetrator had occupied Bev's vehicle, its recently detailed interior was a fingerprint tech's dream.

The garage door's remote control was clipped to the driver's-side visor. In the closed ashtray were several butts of the same brand spilled from the living room's ashtray. David left them for Marlin or Phelps to collect.

Leaning in to give the console a once-over, he saw

that the slender niche beside the seat held a postcard water bill, a women's clothing catalog and an opened number-ten envelope from the GMEI Group in Dover, Delaware.

Jimmy Wayne ducked, then reached over and pulled out a tri-folded flyer from beneath the driver's seat. "Sanity High's Booster Club is having a bake sale at the preseason football scrimmage."

"Same junk here, looks like." As David skimmed the postmarks on the empty envelope and the postcard's metered mail stamp, plastic evidence bags materialized on the seat.

"I'm bagging and tagging the soda straw wrapper I found under the floor mat, too," Jimmy Wayne told him. "Marlin won't be impressed, but he'll bitch if I don't."

"Yep. I don't see any need to mess with the contents of the console and the glove box, though. If Marlin does, I'll take care of it later."

On the back seat on the driver's side were three library books and a brown grocery sack. Inside it, a frozen Mexican dinner's carton bulged from its thawed contents spilling out of the compartmented tray. Under a loaf of bread was a package of chocolate candy, aspirin, two bottles of spring water and a blister pack of C batteries. According to the soggy receipt, the purchases were made at the Pump 'n' Munch at 5:47 last night.

It was nearer fact than speculation that Bev planned to microwave her supper before the storms hit. Water and batteries sized for a flashlight or a portable radio were bad-weather staples. The melted, silver-foiled candies wrenched David's heart.

One of Hannah's refrigerator magnets read, When the Going Gets Tough, the Tough Eat Chocolate. Picturing Bev hurrying through the store, gathering up the necessities, then impulsively indulging her sweet tooth was like a sucker punch to David's gut.

He gently placed the sack on the concrete floor, then flipped through the library books. A time-dated slip inside a Carol O'Connell thriller revealed that it, the Caribbean Island travel guide and a bestselling biography were checked out early yesterday afternoon.

Working a crime scene was like reading a diary, beginning with its final entry. Adding an approximate drive-time from the convenience store told David that Bev had arrived home at, or just before, six last night.

He'd gotten back to town from the ice cream social at about the same time, and it had rained on his drive home. The sedan's wipers were poised midway on the sedan's windshield. The control knob's position indicated they'd stopped when Bev turned off the ignition.

"Bev's keys," he said. "Were they with her purse in the house?"

"Yeah." Jimmy Wayne doused the Mag-Lite and weaseled backward out the rear passenger door. "On the kitchen counter."

"Doesn't that seem odd to you? This sack doesn't weigh more than three pounds at most." David held up the books. "These, I can understand leaving behind, but why didn't she carry in her groceries along with her purse and keys?"

Jimmy Wayne studied the door to the utility room, then the bag on the floor. "Maybe the phone was ringing." His eyes rose to David's. "Or maybe somebody in the car with her hustled her inside."

"Or was waiting for her in here." David nodded at the space between the side wall and garage door's metal track. "She wouldn't have seen him when she pulled in."

"But if he'd ambushed her inside the house, more than likely, the groceries would be in *there* with her purse and keys."

"You'd think." David edged away from the car. "Do what you want, but I'm not touching another thing until Marlin dusts this vehicle for prints."

6

Nellie Dunn's, the largest restaurant in the heart of Valhalla Springs' business district, was lively for the middle of a Thursday afternoon.

The late lunchers usually departed well before the little somethings arrived toting their shopping bags. They'd plop down for a rest, a chat, a cold drink and a little something from the dessert menu to tide them over until dinner.

Hannah assumed the two groups had overlapped because the golf course was closed. Last night's rain had flooded several greens and sand traps, and littered fairways with downed branches. It was doubtful the red flag waving above the clubhouse would be replaced with a green one before tomorrow morning.

The little something she'd ordered was a slice of lemon meringue pie and iced tea. To the man picking up the tab, she said, "I don't believe you."

Luke Sauers frowned and chuckled simultaneously. "Have I ever lied to you?"

"Probably." She nibbled a tiny sliver of pie. Free dessert this delicious was worth savoring. "You are an attorney."

His coconspirator said, "I wasn't there, but if I thought Luke was making it up, I wouldn't be *here*." Her nose wrinkled at the fresh veggie plate in front of her. "I've got a fridge full of this crap at home."

Claudina Burkholtz was Hannah's only female friend not receiving a social security pension. The single mother of three was also David's chief dispatcher, his original campaign manager and permanent fan club president.

After assisting with a murder investigation, Claudina aspired to becoming the county's first woman deputy. How she'd comply with the academy's height requirement hadn't been resolved. To meet the weight standards, she'd shed thirty pounds over the summer but still had fifty-some to go.

Hannah looked down at her pie and winced. "Fine friend I am."

Claudina waved a dismissal. "The world doesn't have to go on a diet just because I am. Get fat as a house, then knock off a couple of rooms and you start to get snotty about it." She winked. "That part, I like."

Luke fidgeted in place—guy code for "Let's can the girl talk, shall we?" He nudged a minuscule cell phone across the tablecloth. "Give David a call, if you don't believe me. He'll confirm the entire discussion."

"Yeah, right. I'm sure he wouldn't mind taking a break from working a homicide scene to discuss our wedding."

"Okay, this idea of Luke's is a little crazy," Claudina said.

"That, Ms. Burkholtz, is a major understatement."

"Not as crazy as getting married straight outta high school, popping out three rugrats in five years, then divorcing the sorry ass who's never sent them a birthday card, much less a child support check. It's within range, though."

Claudina folded her hands on the table. In a low honey drawl better suited for late-night radio than the police variety, she said, "But if it was me, and I thought for a second that marrying the man I loved in the park might—*might*—make a difference on election day, I'd do it."

Hannah's fork clattered on the plate. She sat back, astounded at what her friend was implying. "So you're saying, if I don't turn my wedding into a publicity stunt and David loses, it's my fault."

"Impossible to quantify," Luke said, "but yes, that's what I'm saying."

"Well, *I'm* not," Claudina huffed. "God help us if it happens, but David could lose either way. The way I figure it, you two have fiddle-farted around for months, so why not get it over with and maybe swing the election at the same time?"

Hannah laughed in spite of herself. "Jeez, that's so romantic."

"It will be. Claudina and I will take care of everything. Music, flowers, candles, cake—the works." Luke grinned. "Except the dress. That, we'll leave to you."

"You know my kids adore Sheriff David," Claudina added. "Polly and Lana are dying to be flower girls and Jeremy can be the ring bearer."

Luke chimed in, "David told me he'd take care of the tux, the minister and the limousine. What else do we need?" He hesitated, then answered his own question. "The marriage license." A reminder was duly registered in his BlackBerry. "Ten minutes at the county clerk's office. There's a three-day waiting period, so I'll put you down for no later than the Tuesday before."

Claudina's mop of curls quivered with excitement. "You can get dressed at my house. The girls will *love* it. We'll have to tie Jeremy to the sofa to keep him clean, but I'll let him pick out the video. Heck-fire, I'll buy him a spankin' new one."

They chattered about monogrammed napkins and birdseed bags. Hannah gripped the chair's armrests, panting as though a pillow was smashed against her face.

Luke had definitely discussed this with David. The tux-to-limo remark clinched it. He'd teased Hannah about grooms having it easy—two phone calls and a fitting and they were good to go. Which meant he'd sicced Luke on her for one of two reasons: To let her say no, in a manner even an obsessed campaign manager could perceive as final. Or to see if she might just say yes.

Given that David hadn't mentioned it at all, even as a joke, could be construed as a double-dog dare. And who, other than David, would assume the crass, arguably sacrilegious, politically motivated, hootenanny aspect of it might have a certain appeal. The buy-a-dress-and-show-up thing, for instance.

Particularly since the gumshoes knew David had proposed, but not that Hannah had officially accepted. The instant they did, IdaClare, Rosemary Schnur and Marge Rosenbaum would launch into manic, fairytale wedding mode, the likes of which had not been seen since Prince Charles took his first bride.

Risking the lake of fire for living in sin was preferable to listening to the three godmothers debate virginal white versus never-married-but-only-sporadically-chaste shades of beige.

They'd be crushed if Luke and Claudina took charge; David might be crushed if Hannah told her two tablemates to go ruin somebody else's wedding.

Then again, she hadn't left the starting block when it came to planning the happiest day of her life. Whenever she browsed through the bridal magazine hidden in a desk drawer, she had to grab a paper sack and breathe into it until the dizziness subsided.

Twenty-five years of seat-of-the-pants, multimillion-dollar corporate decisions were a breeze compared to selecting the one, the only, the *perfect* freakin' wedding invitations. Starting with ink color. If, of course, you cheaped out and didn't go for complementary pastel duotones. Or metallic. Or antique, airbrushed metallic.

How could she possibly slough off that—along with the ceremony's other eighty-four-thousand details—on anybody? No, the hell with how and who. Was *she* ready to take David Hendrickson for her lawfully wedded husband in three weeks?

Great-uncle Mort was fond of saying sometimes you've gotta take off the bridle, throw your hat in the air and let the panther scream. Mort Garvey wasn't a cowboy and wouldn't have known a panther from a saber-toothed tiger. But just because the old boy's wheel was short a few lug nuts didn't mean he was always wrong.

Hannah's brain spun inside her skull. If a paper sack had magically appeared, she wouldn't have known whether to breathe into it or throw up in it.

Luke murmured behind his hand, "She hasn't said no. Thinking about it's as good as a yes."

Claudina whispered back, "You don't date much, do you?"

Hannah picked up her fork. The cold stainless steel felt wonderfully solid. The pie, she polished off in one unladylike bite. She dabbed her lips with the napkin, then laid it on the table. "It was great seeing you both. Now, if you'll excuse me, I have to get back to work."

Startled, Luke shouted, "But what—" He gulped and lowered his voice. "But what about the *wedding?*"

Claudina stuffed a cauliflower floret in his mouth. "Don't call you," she said to Hannah. "You'll call me."

Hannah grinned. "Bingo."

Outside, the afternoon heat and mugginess had thinned pedestrian traffic. Awnings cast shady rectangles on the boardwalk, but seemed to trap the air, like striped canvas lids. Flowers in window boxes and stone tubs along the cobbled street looked as wilted as Hannah felt when she entered Valhalla Springs' postal substation.

The alcove housing the post office boxes resembled a bank's safety deposit vault with an arched oak trellis and a gate, instead of a door. Hannah keyed box number two; box one belonged to IdaClare Clancy.

Banded inside a large clasp envelope was the typical assortment of bills, handbills, winning sweepstakes notifications addressed to occupant and information requests from retirees seeking an alternative to Florida, the southwest and the Gulf coast.

Valhalla Springs couldn't compete with an endless summer. Hannah batted the hair off her neck, wondering why anyone would want a permanent July. Here, you had four seasons—sometimes a touch of two in as many days—plus a Victorian village atmosphere, peace, quiet and a genuine sense of community.

She dropped the mail packet into her shoulder bag to sort through later. On average, one in ten inquiries netted a personal tour. One percent of those added new tenants to the population.

"To see Valhalla Springs," she said wistfully, "is to never want to leave."

Thankfully, Luke and Claudina had. A scooter and a Miata were parked where his Beemer had straddled two spaces. Fearing that Luke might attempt a second offensive at the cottage, Hannah thought she'd do some casual window-shopping at Carla Forsythe's boutique.

Most of the shops, stores and eateries along Main Street had larger counterparts in Sanity. Carla's clothing store in town had a selection of wedding gowns, but aside from special requests and holiday wear, her annex catered to less formal ladies' attire.

Not that Hannah was in the market for anything long, lacy and *white,* by God. At least not in the next three weeks, as opposed to someday in the foreseeable future. After David was reelected. After a new operations manager was hired. After David's house was move-in ready. After his rottweiler, Rambo, bonded with Malcolm, instead of picturing him fried, fricasseed, roasted, stewed and barbecued.

After all those afters, *then* they'd get married and live happily ever…after.

Hannah groaned and started down the boardwalk to where her Blazer was parked, yielding to the deliveryman pushing a loaded handcart into the mercantile. Momentary inertia let thoughts she'd tried to outwalk catch up with her. She glanced over her shoulder at the boutique, then at her truck.

Eeny, meeny, miny… On *mo,* she shrugged, smiled

and headed back the way she came. "Just browsing," she'd say. And if Carla brought out the photo catalog with both stores' full inventory? Well, what was the harm in looking? A little virtual retail therapy, as it were.

When yet another bond issue to build a new sheriff's department met with defeat, the county commissioners leased a narrow storefront on the west side of the square for the detective division's headquarters.

The commission's generosity didn't include replacing the long-vacant storefront's fake walnut paneling, matted shag carpeting, water-stained suspended ceiling tiles and ancient fluorescent lighting. On the day of the detective unit's official ribbon-cutting, Marlin Andrik took one look at—and sniff of—his new domain and dubbed it the Outhouse.

A kindness, David thought, squirming in the molded plastic lawn chair on the visitor's side of Marlin's desk. It would be a small miracle if the seat defied physics and gravity long enough for Marlin to finish his progress report on the Beauford homicide.

David had left the scene around noon and gone home. Six hours later, he'd wakened with no memory of the drive, shucking down to his underwear and falling into bed. Blackouts were known to scare drunks into sobriety. All David could do was hope his luck held, thank God he hadn't had to drive clear to Valhalla Springs for some shut-eye, and vow for the umpteenth time to cut back on voluntary double shifts.

A long, hot shower and a home-grilled cheese-burger had him feeling almost human again—eager for anything besides half-listening to radio chatter on the scanner behind him and staring at the nascent bald spot on the top of Marlin's head.

"The fingerprints lifted from Bev's vehicle," David said, as though the conversational thread hadn't dangled for upward of five boring minutes. "You don't expect them to amount to much?"

Marlin looked from the photos on his desk to their corresponding documentation. "They're few, which helps. If Bev hadn't taken it through the car wash, we'd have eight thousand latents to run."

He tapped several close-up shots of Bev's sedan. "It's the far-between that doesn't have me juiced. The rear passenger door, trunk lid, back of the interior mirror…" Pulling off his reading glasses, he chewed on a mangled earpiece. "All different fingerprints. All in places that don't correspond to a perp along for the ride home."

Drivers adjusted rearview mirrors, not passengers.

There were no other indications that anyone aside from Bev had driven her car, since it was cleaned.

At the desk behind David, Josh Phelps was transmitting the latents to the Automated Fingerprint Identification System. AFIS's computerized database didn't read fingerprints, but numerically identified similarities. The more the markers, the higher the probability of a match. Phelps would then compare each of the system's mechanically selected candidates to the unknown one.

From Marlin's remarks, if AFIS did provide a hit, the follow-up was more likely to waste time than identify a suspect.

The phone rang, and Marlin snapped up the receiver. "Yo. Andrik." His eyes flicked to David. "Yes, Ms. Beauford. No, please don't apologize. I realize what a shock it was and appreciate you calling me back."

He listened a moment. Grimaced. "I know what I'm asking, but it really can't wait until morning." A pause, then, "Uh-huh. Yeah, we sure can. Thank you, Ms. Beauford. See you in a few."

He was on his feet before the receiver stopped wobbling in its cradle. "Interesting."

"Wild guess. That was Bev and Larry's daughter."

"Kimmie Sue Beauford, the never-was, never-gonna-be movie star." Marlin lifted his sport coat off the back of his chair. "She's meeting us at the house in fifteen minutes."

"I thought she lived in Los Angeles."

"She does. That's where I thought she was when I called to tell her about her mother." Marlin's jaw cocked as he tightened his tie. "Lo and behold, the contact number we had was a cell phone. Kimmie Sue was eating lunch in Joplin when she answered it."

"Joplin, Missouri?" David said, as though every state between here and the Pacific Ocean had at least one. "That's what, a hundred and twenty miles from Sanity?"

"Three hours travel time, give or take. About half interstate, half two-lane." Marlin lit a cigarette, in violation of city, county and state ordinance, but in keeping with the Thank You for Smoking sign on his desk. "She said Bev didn't know she was coming to town. Wanted it to be a surprise."

David leveraged himself out of the molded plastic vice clamped to his hips and thighs. "Helluva coincidence."

"Ain't it, though? That solo nuke-a-meal in Bev's grocery sack says she didn't expect company, but who drives cross-country to drop in on somebody?"

A detective adjusting a shoulder holster bears a striking resemblance to a woman adjusting a bra strap—an observation David thought was better kept to himself.

"My mom and dad sprang an unannounced visit on me a few months ago," he said. He'd answered that early morning pounding at his front door with a towel wrapped around his waist, a major league hard-on and Hannah wet and waiting for him in the shower. "But they never had before, and I kind of doubt they ever will again."

Marlin's expectant look eventually deflated. He was itching for the middle of the story. He did, in fact, scratch his neck, but he wouldn't ask and David wouldn't tell. Hannah might someday—when it struck her as funny, not near the top of life's most mortifying moments.

David glanced at his watch. Seven-forty. "Where's Kimmie Sue been since you reached her on her cell phone?"

"The Wishing Well Motel. We were still processing the scene when she hit town." He chuffed. "Jesus, you feel like a ten-pound turd telling the next of kin to relax, gimme a jingle when that migraine backs off, then we'll go to Mom's and figure out what the dirtbag ripped off, before or after he killed her."

"You're back to a burglary gone bad?"

"I'm not in love with it," Marlin said, "but I haven't ruled it out."

A press of a button disengaged the Outhouse's electronic lock mechanism. Access from the outside required a magnetized key card. The hole-in-the-wall detective division was also wired with interior and exterior surveillance cameras, silent alarms and motion-sensitive lights.

A similar system was installed at the courthouse to restrict access after business hours. Necessary evils, David allowed, but a can of spray paint would surely improve the can't-miss donor plaques that bragged: Protected By Fort Knox Security; Jessup Knox, Owner and Certified Specialist.

What Knox specialized in, apart from pissing off the sheriff, was open to speculation.

David lost the curbside who's-driving argument before he pulled his keys out of his pocket. Marlin's beater, gunmetal-gray Chevy smelled like an ashtray and decomposed French fries. By all appearances, a file cabinet had detonated inside, but it was the detective's mobile office and you just never knew when you might need a Brattleboro, Vermont, city directory.

While David settled into the passenger side, Marlin told him that Cletus Orr was witnessing the autopsy at the state lab in Columbia. Because Bev was a sheriff's widow, the assistant medical examiner had waived the standard first-come, first-served policy and moved her to the front of the line.

The ride to Greenaway Circle passed in silence, neither David nor Marlin being disposed toward small talk, or a verbal postmortem of a case laden with questions and precious few facts.

A block from the cul-de-sac's entrance, Marlin banged the steering wheel with the flat of his hand. "Damn it. We should have brought both cars."

David couldn't imagine why, was reluctant to find out, and doubted he'd like the answer.

"Kimmie Sue leaned on you pretty heavy after Larry's funeral," Marlin said. "If you had wheels, you could have asked her out for coffee after we finish at the house."

"And why would I do that?"

"Well, let's see, kemosabe. We've confirmed that Bev was strangled with her own scarf. Thirty-one percent of female homicide victims are killed by a family member, friend, lover—someone known to them. Bev's only child was conveniently two hundred miles from the scene. And when Kimmie Sue's dad died, it was obvious she was interested in more than your clean hankie and an arm to hang on to."

David reserved judgment. Everyone handled death

differently—sudden, or not. Kimmie Sue's clinginess and blatant flirting had made him extremely uncomfortable. Maybe losing the daddy she'd adored in the blink of an eye was no excuse, but David refused to condemn her, then or now.

"So," he said, "in your twisted mind, she's a suspect."

"It's automatic for next of kin. And she sees you as one of Papa's good old boys, not a trained, half-smart cop." Marlin looked sideways and smirked. "Five bucks, she'll ask *you* out tonight. Hell, she might even spring for dinner."

The unmarked's headlights swept a hard-shell Jeep with a California plate parked in front of 2208. "Then pay up." David pointed out the windshield. "It appears our next of kin didn't make the trip home all by herself."

Kimmie Sue Beauford's traveling companion had a couple of inches and twenty pounds of solid, gym-rat muscle on David. The deep-tanned, dark-haired Goliath dressed in a spandex wife beater and jeans introduced himself as Rocco Jarek. Two seconds and a snarl from Marlin elicited his real name: Rodney Windle.

In the months since her father's funeral, Kimmie Sue had transformed from a striking, green-eyed brunette to a blond, pouty-lipped Barbie doll. David's conservative roots might be showing, but a skintight halter top, denim miniskirt and high-heeled sandals weren't what grieving, overnight orphans usually wore to a walk-through.

"David?" Her aqua contact lenses glittered in the streetlight's halogen glow. Feigning disappointment, she said, "I've told Rocco so much about you, he's jealous, and you don't even remember me, do you?"

"Of course I do, Ms. Beauford. Allow me to extend my and the department's condolences about your mother."

She flinched, as if he'd slapped her. David had a feeling he'd be buying his own coffee with that five-spot Marlin owed him.

As they proceeded to the front door, Marlin angled his notebook, so David could read the line under Kimmie Sue's boyfriend's address, driver's license, social security and tag numbers: *Rocco Jarek—hired dick.*

David murmured, "He's a private investigator?"

Considering the source, he should have expected "Uh-uh. Porn star. Grade B, jumbo," Marlin grunted. "Don't ask how I know."

The air temperature inside the house was twenty degrees warmer than that morning. Most of the post-mortem odor had dissipated and the stench of stale nicotine and cigarette smoke prevailed. Despite the lights and lamps Marlin switched on, there was the perceptible, indescribable emptiness that four people, or four hundred, couldn't dispel.

Kimmie Sue hugged her bare arms tight to her chest and nestled against Jarek. "I've changed my mind. I can't do this." Peering up at him, she said, "Please, take me back to the motel."

"It won't be any easier tomorrow, Kim," he said. "Might as well get it over with, then we can kick back and relax."

Marlin and David exchanged a look. Any remark was open to interpretation. Trust two cops to hear implications where none might exist.

Kimmie Sue gripped Jarek's hand as they moved into the living room, then the dining room. As Marlin opened drawers and cupboard doors, she surveyed the contents and shook her head—no, nothing appeared to be missing.

From there, they trooped into the utility room, circled Bev's car in the garage, then backtracked to the kitchen.

"Everything seems like it always was," Kimmie Sue said. "Little things are different—the dish towels, that tacky compote over there. But gosh, you know, I moved to L.A. a long time ago."

David was watching her, gauging her reactions,

while Marlin concentrated on Jarek. So far, *detached* was the best description David could conjure. If it was a game face, Kimmie Sue's was the best he could recall. Evidently, fingerprint powder strewn on every horizontal surface and a goodly share of verticals didn't count as different, much less a *little thing*.

And he knew for a fact, that compote had belonged to Bev's mother. The first time he was a guest in this house, he'd told Bev that his grandmother had one exactly like it. Depression glass, she'd called it, because during the thirties, movie houses gave away all sorts of cheap knickknacks to help sell tickets.

Bev might have stored it away for safekeeping when her daughter was growing up, but if David had seen it, surely Kimmie Sue had, as well.

As she entered the family room, Kimmie Sue's eyes widened and darted from the damaged coffee table to the carpet flattened and trampled by gurney wheels and a dozen pairs of shoes. She shrank back against Jarek. "Oh, God. This is where Mom…" Her stiletto heels digging into the floor, she pushed against his chest. "No, please, I— Don't make me go in there. I can't. I *can't*."

Sobbing into her hands, she said, "Damn it, why are you doing this to me? Anybody can tell nothing's *gone*. She didn't have anything worth *stealing*."

Jarek glowered at Marlin. "This is bullshit. I'm getting her out of here."

The detective shifted his weight and the gentle, sympathetic tone he'd used on Kimmie Sue. "It's like you said, Rodney. It ain't gonna be any easier tomorrow." A shrug, then, "You'd think you'd want to help us find whoever did this to your girlfriend's mother."

"I do," Jarek blustered. "I just can't handle seeing Kim upset like this. First you hit her with the news her mother's been—uh, that she's passed on, then you expect her to take inventory? It's fuckin' cruel, man."

"I'm sorry, Mr. Jarek," said David, the designated good guy. "I realize how hard this is for both of you, but Ms. Beauford is the only one that can tell us what we need to know."

"Oh, yeah? What about neighbors? Friends?"

Bending down, David looked into Kimmie Sue's eyes. A trifle bloodshot but dry. He wanted to be surprised. "A few more minutes is all I'm asking for. Okay?"

Sniffling, she swiped the pad of a taloned finger along her lower lids. "Okay." A brave smile. "Thanks, David. For understanding."

Marlin smoothly separated her from Jarek. Cupping her elbow, he escorted her through the family room. Jarek stayed close behind, David now bird-dogging him.

They paused in the foyer where the stairway led to the second floor. Marlin said, "Go on up, while me and Ms. Beauford take a breather. Master bedroom's next."

David gestured *after you* to Jarek. The carpeted plank treads creaked under their respective weights. Beyond the landing were four doors, all of them closed. On the right, Kimmie Sue's old bedroom was now a guest room. The spare room nearer the end of the hall had been converted to Larry Beauford's home office and den. The first door on the left was a full bath.

Jarek strode directly to the second door. Reaching for the knob, he pulled back his hand, glancing at David. "I, uh, I almost forgot I'm not supposed to touch anything."

Not yet, you aren't, David thought. He took out a handkerchief and wiped off the powder residue smudging the knob. "All clear. You can go on in now."

Jarek hesitated, exhaled, then turned the knob. Once inside the master bedroom, David stationed himself at the door, forcing Kimmie Sue and Marlin to sidle past him. Nothing and nobody were going to lay a finger on that doorknob, until after she and Jarek vacated the premises and Marlin redusted it.

Kimmie Sue broke down for real at the sight of her mother's jewelry and clothing strewn across the bed and floor. Marlin recorded descriptions of a missing diamond cocktail ring, a pearl solitaire and earrings, a ruby brooch, a diamond pendant and Larry's horseshoe pinkie ring that he'd kept in Bev's jewelry box.

Kimmie Sue refused to enter her father's office. "I couldn't after he died," she shrieked. "I can't now. *I won't.*" She cut and ran down the hallway, stopping at the stairs just long enough to kick off her shoes, sending them flying into the foyer.

"Kim—" Jarek shot Marlin and David a hateful glare and chased after her. Seconds later, the door slammed hard enough to rattle the doorbell's chimes.

Marlin's mouth formed a lowercase O. "That went pretty well, don'tcha think?"

An engine roared outside. Tires squealed on the pavement. Chafing the back of his neck, David said, "I honestly don't know what to think about either one of them."

"Slick work on that doorknob." Marlin hitched a shoulder. "Could be, I'll be buying you a beer before the night's over."

Twenty minutes later, Josh Phelps greeted them back at the Outhouse with a grinning "Guess what?"

Marlin said, "You got a hit on AFIS."

"Yeah, but get this—"

"The print on the rearview matches Rodney Windle aka Rocco Jarek, current known address, Los Angeles, California."

Josh and David looked at each other, then at Marlin. He held up the tape strip lifted off the doorknob. "What the hell are you two staring at? Phelps said guess what, so I guessed."

Handing over the strip to the rookie, he said, "Well, what are you waiting for, Sheriff? Let's go pick up the drone."

David drove this time, his cruiser having an accessible back seat. "What about Kimmie Sue?" he asked. "How do you think she figures in?"

"Takes two to tango." Marlin lowered the window and hung over the ledge to smoke. "Jarek's been in that house. I don't know who shut all the doors upstairs after we processed it this morning. Phelps, probably. But when I said 'Master bedroom,' damned if Jarek didn't lead you straight to it."

"Bev's jewelry, though. It doesn't make sense that Kimmie Sue would say what's missing if she was in on the murder."

"Maybe she's stupid. Maybe the guilt got to her." Marlin drummed a rat-a-tat on the door panel.

"Maybe Jumbo Dick paid himself a bonus for doing her dirty work."

David didn't want to believe any of it; the burning sensation licking up his breastbone said one or all of the theories could be true.

The Wishing Well began life as a motor court, in an era when *motel* was synonymous with *sleazy*. Its age showed in the red shingled roof, clapboard siding and fieldrock trim, but for under fifty bucks a night, guests got a clean room, a pool, basic cable TV and free local calls.

"No Jeeps," Marlin noted.

"There's less traffic noise around the back," David said, and circled the L-shaped building.

The Wishing Well was his temporary home, after he took the chief deputy's job. The owner was delighted to have him and knocked a chunk off the weekly rate. The room he'd occupied was in the rear corner, so prospective customers wouldn't spot David's patrol unit and assume a raid—or a rendez-vous—was in progress.

Good ol' room 23 appeared to be vacant. Farther down were nine lighted windows with the drapes closed. Nine corresponding vehicles nosed the broad cement walkway. None of them was a Jeep.

Marlin hammered the window ledge. "Shit."

Pulling around toward the office again, David said, "Maybe Kimmie Sue's buying Jarek that cup of coffee."

"There're coffeemakers in the rooms" sufficed as the detective's exit line, before the cruiser rolled to a complete stop.

David didn't recognize the night-desk clerk. Marlin's yank on the office's glass door was anything but sociable. While he made a new friend, David did a one-eighty to survey the Wishing Well's street entrance.

Marlin stormed out of the office, his face redder than his necktie's diagonal stripes. Hurling himself into the passenger seat, he bellowed, "Fuckers checked out two hours ago."

Marlin snatched the mike from its hook. "Baker 2-03."

Dispatch responded, "Go ahead, 2-03."

"Get me a statewide APB, Tony." Marlin's finger inched down a page in his notebook, as he supplied the vehicle's make, model, description and tag number. "California registration, Rodney Windle, also known as Rocco Jarek. Probable secondary occupant, Kimmie Sue Beauford. Got that?"

Static, then, "*Larry's daughter?*" A lengthy pause. "What's the charge against them, 2-03?"

Marlin looked at David. His voice caught when he answered, "Suspicion of homicide, Tony. Both of them."

7

Malcolm whimpered as Cruella De Vil's henchmen loaded the dalmatian puppies into the truck. Hannah hugged his neck and set the popcorn bowl between his paws. Poor guy. He'd been depressed for days after she rented *Old Yeller.*

"It's okay, Malc. I promise this one has a happy ending."

A skeptical *moomph* averred that happy for a human could fall short of a tail-wagger for him. Even giant Airedale-wildebeests had trust issues, it seemed.

Malcolm was so riveted on the TV screen, he didn't twitch a whisker when the doorbell rang. Hannah zapped down the volume with the remote, as though the uninvited visitor might assume any overheard snatch of soundtrack was an auditory hallucination.

David wouldn't, but he was occupied with the Beauford homicide. The first forty-eight hours were critical. From what he'd told her earlier on the phone, the ten that already elapsed hadn't generated any revelations. Which was why Hannah was dressed for watching a kid flick with her dog, not for David, or for company. And honestly not in the mood for it, either.

Then again, the usual suspects never failed to bring refreshments along with them: ooey-gooey luscious refreshments that put the pie she'd eaten that afternoon to shame, let alone the bologna, mustard and crushed potato chip sandwich that sufficed as dinner.

Sure enough, the gumshoe gang stood in the glow of the porch's bug light. All five beamed at Hannah as though it were Halloween and word on the street was, she was handing out full-size candy bars.

To the first in line, she inquired, "What, did you leave the lock-pick gun in your other pants?"

The ones Delbert was wearing were solid navy-blue. His dress shirt, plain white. A braided leather belt matched his lace-up oxfords and attaché case. He pulled open the screen door, saying, "You told me not to use the lock picker anymore when you're home."

She'd told him not to use it, period. But concessions were rare, so must be appreciated while they lasted. As for Delbert's world's-oldest-Catholic-schoolboy attire, something was up and it wasn't his fashion-consciousness.

Marge Rosenbaum was the Mod Squad's recording secretary. A visor banded her cropped gray hair, as if a round of moonlight golf was planned after the meeting adjourned. She regarded her own white blouse and dark slacks, muttered, "I feel like a Bobbsey twin," and headed for the office nook to retrieve the extra chair they'd need in the breakfast room.

IdaClare Clancy's cotton-candy hairdo, jersey knit palazzos, tunic and the poodles hugged to her bosom were variations on her cottage's paint job and the lacquered baby grand in her living room. For Jack's mother, "in the pink" was an attitude, a lifestyle and her entire wardrobe.

She bobbled the Furwads, who appeared to be stoned out of their tiny, vicious minds. "Say hello to your aunt Hannah," she cooed, wiggling one of Itsy's, or Bitsy's, little paws.

Switching to a nonpoodle voice, she said, "I know I should have called, dear, but I couldn't leave them home by themselves. Good heavens, what if the house caught fire while I was gone?"

Jack would revert to an only child, but even he wouldn't wish a horrible, painful death on the teacup terrors. Just a sudden, natural, premature one.

Hannah waved toward the couch where Malcolm was lapping up unpopped kernels from the bottom of the bowl. "The snack bar's pretty much closed, but *101 Dalmatians* is now playing at Garvey's Bijou. He can fill in Itsy and Bitsy on what's happened so far."

The last two through the door were newlyweds Leo and Rosemary Schnur, whom Hannah had affectionately nicknamed Mr. Potato Head and the Vamp. Leo, a postwar German immigrant, bore an uncanny resemblance to the former, while Rosemary, his bride of three months, was a vision in plus-size lamé stirrup pants, huge gold hoop earrings and a cleavage-intensive, V-necked top.

Considering the massive baking dish lidded in aluminum foil Rosemary was carrying, it must have been her turn to bring the refreshments. Tonight's edible extortion smelled as fattening as ever, but wasn't the typical cake, cheesecake, cobbler, cinnamon rolls or cookies.

C-food, Hannah thought, as Leo held up a bag of tortilla chips. Talk about a revelation. Everything she loved most, apart from Malcolm, David and the gumshoes, began with a *C*.

"The eight-layer dip it is we're having." Leo's jowls quivered in anticipation. "Only the seven layers, my darling Rosemary used to make, but on the beans she put the spicy meat and now it is eight."

"More like a big taco," Rosemary said. "I just hope it isn't too greasy."

Two things were guaranteed to fog Leo's thick hornrimmed glasses: an unobstructed view of his beloved's bazooms and cuisine with a high sugar or grease content. In combination, the retired insurance executive's visibility descended to zero.

Hannah led him by the hand into the breakfast room, where Marge was brewing a pot of decaf. Hannah despised the stuff, but acknowledged her elders' caffeine sensitivity. Nursing a cup of weak, no-octane was preferable to letting the five of them loose after a meeting wired to the gills.

IdaClare was setting the table with a serving spoon, paper napkins and bowls. Physical therapy had restored dexterity to her right shoulder, but muscles and tendons ripped by a bullet wound mended, rather than healed.

She'd insisted that becoming a semi-southpaw had improved her golf swing and that she'd simply forgotten to sign up for this year's club championship tournament. "I was thinking about skipping it, anyway, dear," she told Hannah. "After coming in second so many times, Marge deserves that first-place trophy. What do I need with another dust catcher cluttering up my house?"

"For crissake, IdaClare. Quit fussing with the dishes," Delbert said. "We ain't having high tea at the Waldorf-Astoria."

"Ha. You wouldn't get past the doorman, Shorty."

"Ha, yourself." He removed six file folders from the attaché case and a tattered copy of *Trade Secrets from the Masters of Criminal Investigation*. "You couldn't get your rump through the goldurned door."

The serving spoon narrowly missed his nose, as Hannah seated Leo in his usual chair at the presumed foot of the square table. The presumed head, of course, was reserved for Sam Spade Bisbee. IdaClare was on Delbert's right and Marge in the desk chair on his left. Rosemary snuggled as close to her Leokins as the corner table leg allowed.

A bar stool was Hannah's regular perch, as much by default as by the five-to-one vote establishing her the sergeant at arms. In the past, their spirit of democracy encompassed nongumshoe motions, such as whether she should date the sheriff, then sleep with him, then accept his proposal. Abstaining from the voting process had been as futile as abstaining from David.

When the phone rang, Rosemary leapt up to unhook the receiver and pass it over to Hannah. On the other end Blanche Erlich said, in her adenoidal twang, "I'm sorry to bother you, but is Delbert there, by any chance?"

Hannah snapped her fingers at him and mouthed the caller's name. Delbert's reaction was electric. Only direct contact with 120 volts might induce the flailing, miming, head-shaking and hand-signaling that translated to "I don't want to talk to her."

"Go on, give him the phone," Rosemary whispered. "We want to hear him squirm."

Taking pity on the old fart, Hannah said, "Have you tried the community center, Blanche?"

A pause, then a snarky "Do you mean Carol Fogerty's house? Or the one that has the indoor pool?"

Click. Dial tone.

As the receiver made its way back to Rosemary, IdaClare sneered at Delbert. "So that's why you insisted on carpooling tonight. I've half a mind to call Blanche back."

"Oh, yeah? Well, get up off the other half and do it, then. The rest of us have a rip-snortin' new case to work on."

The file folders he distributed had gummed labels attached to their tabs. He'd titled their first "operation" Code Name: Alpha, followed by Beta, Gamma and Delta. Why the Greek alphabet had such cachet was never explained, but the fraternal order of Delbert ordained Code Name: Epsilon as the current topic of discussion.

Hannah knew she should slam on the brakes before the gang got rolling. And would, after she'd gobbled a fair share of tortilla chips loaded with Rosemary's fabulous dip before Leo shoveled in the rest.

Rosemary blushed pinker than IdaClare's hair at the barrage of compliments, and promised to bring the recipe to the next meeting.

Taking that as a cue, Hannah held up the unopened file folder. "I'm sorry, Delbert, but the Beverly Beauford homicide isn't going to be Code Name: Epsilon."

He peeled an antacid off the roll from his pocket and popped it in his mouth. Passing the rest on to Ida-Clare, he said, "Fine by me, ladybug."

She was prepared for an argument. Counterarguments. Another voting minority, and the prospect of holding the Mod Squad hostage, until Mrs. Beauford's killer was captured. Delbert agreeing had Hannah's mental alarm bells screaming a red alert.

"The Beauford case is a hot one," Marge said. "And—"

"Gruesome." Rosemary shivered. "Just this morning, I told Leo, since Delbert lost my .45 Magnum, maybe we should buy another one. You know, for protection."

IdaClare turned to Hannah. "Don't worry, dear. Like Marge was about to say, Delbert told us the case we're discussing today is a cold case. They're all the rage on TV and he thinks we need a change of pace."

"Tougher nuts to crack, they are, the cold cases." Leo tapped a temple. "To solve them, it is our noggins we must use."

They always had. It was the escalation from an intellectual exercise to active interference that David objected to. He'd threatened jail time more than once. Home in on Beverly Beauford's murder and he'd have a fistful of bench warrants issued as fast as a judge could sign them.

"How cold is this case?" Hannah asked, hoping it predated David's employment with the Kinderhook County Sheriff's department.

Delbert wasn't pleased to have his rip snorter upstaged. "I'll get to that when—"

"Now, Delbert."

"Twenty-three years. Satisfied?"

Hmm. By her reckoning, David would have been in eighth grade and living with his parents and three brothers in St. Joseph, Missouri. Hannah was already in Chicago, well into her second year of answering Friedlich & Friedlich's lone telephone line.

Gee, she thought, aren't you glad you asked?

Delbert rose to his feet. His head tipped back and his chin buckled as though he were about to address the top tier of an amphitheater. "At 1300 hours this afternoon, I conducted a CS&IGO for the purpose—"

"Hold it, Kojak." Marge's pencil lead pecked her steno notebook. "What's a CS&IGO? In English."

As if the acronym should be as familiar as others he made up on the fly, he replied wearily, "A Covert Surveillance and Information-Gathering Operation."

Hannah did her own CS on Delbert's outfit. Before she could inquire, he volunteered that a city public works' surveyor can't write as fast as people can gossip about a neighbor they don't like.

"You posed as a city employee?" she said. "That's gotta be illegal."

"Not unless you get caught." Either Delbert hadn't, or he'd posted his own bail. "Now, the *numero*-one rule any professional dick hangs his fedora on is that every case has a premise. Since I already had a beaut to work off of, going undercover was just to put the cherry on the cupcake."

His expression was as smug as a banty rooster in a henhouse. "Which is, that twenty-three years ago, with malice, aforethought and rat poison, Chlorine Moody murdered her husband, Royal, and buried him in the backyard."

The melody of "Woof on the Roof" filtered in from the living room. Delbert, Marge, Rosemary and Ida-

Clare looked expectantly at Hannah. Leo's back was to her, but if a bald head could project thrall, his did.

She stifled a laugh. Every fiber of her being wanted to. Notions didn't come more cockamamie than this one, but one unrepressed chortle and Delbert would be furious, or feel like a fool. But if she calmly, tactfully axed the idea, he'd relabel the files, Code Name: Zeta, aka the Beauford homicide.

"Wow, Delbert," Hannah said. "That's a whale of a premise you have there, all right." A gulp of decaf gave her pesky smile muscles something to frown about. "Except where did you get the idea that Mrs. Moody poisoned her husband?"

His woolly-worm eyebrows scrunched together. "From you, ladybug."

Astonishing, how a miniscule amount of liquid sucked down the wrong pipe could choke a person. Coughing hard enough to bruise a lung, Hannah croaked, *"Me?"*

"Well, I ding-dang sure didn't snag it out of thin air. What you told me about Chlorine a while back slid right by, at the time. I must not've been at the top of my game, for some reason. But soon as I saw her ugly kisser in the paper, the dots started connecting."

Hannah thanked Rosemary for the glass of water she'd fetched; Leo's offer to pound her on the back, she declined. "Dots? What dots? I talked to Mrs. Moody once—for ten minutes, tops—and you weren't there, when I did."

IdaClare read from a page in the file folder with the header, Preliminary Report. "Subject aided in the arrest and conviction of Rudy Moody for possession of illegal weapons. Subject later told P.I. Bisbee, Esquire, that something was fishy about Moody's father taking a powder, when Rudy was a kid."

Subject, meaning Hannah. Whatever. She thought back—months back, in fact—to David mentioning that Chlorine's husband, Royal, a traveling salesman for a Chicago novelty company, had abandoned his wife and then three-year-old son.

Shortly after Royal's disappearance, a major toy manufacturer bought the rights to a card game Chlorine had invented and named after her son. At the time, Hannah questioned how a woman who'd never been known as Mrs. Congeniality had mustered that kind of creativity.

To *herself,* she'd questioned it. Then something came up between her and David—so to speak—and Hannah promptly and completely forgot about the entire Moody family.

Therefore, Subject hadn't said a word about it to P.I. Bisbee, Esquire. The notorious conspiracy theorist had fabricated it himself and attached Hannah's name for credibility. "These dots of yours," she said. "Do any of them connect to a motive?"

"Aw, for crying out loud. Chlorine was *married* to him. Any half-decent criminologist knows that causes more murders than all the others put together."

Marge chuckled. "Then it's kind of a miracle that you've lived this long."

Delbert ignored her and the snickers making the rounds. "I got the same skinny from three different informants. Royal Moody was a good-natured, shirt-off-his-back type. He'd be on the road a week or two, come home for a couple days of Chlorine's nonstop nagging, then he'd light out again. Same routine for years, till he up and vanished off the face of the earth."

"But the unhappy people, they do that," Leo said. "The money trouble they got, or the life they got, they don't want, so *poof.* They run away and start over."

Like I did, Hannah admitted, though Leo was alluding to spouses who drain joint bank accounts, burn their bridges and their IDs, buy new ones and move to Barrow, Alaska.

"That man downstate did," Marge said. "Remember? I told you about him at a Code Name: Beta meeting. Or was it Code Name: Gamma? Whichever it was, he made it look like he'd been kidnapped and probably murdered. When the police finally tracked him down in another state, he was living with a girlfriend and said he'd had a psychogenic fugue and forgotten he had a wife and kids."

"He was a nut," Rosemary said. "Kidnappings and murders do happen for real, though. You hear on the news all the time about somebody going missing and the police suspect homicide, but can't find the body."

"They'd have found Royal's," Delbert said, "if they'd known where to look." He passed out enlarged duplicates of the original *Sanity Examiner* photo. "Judging by where Chlorine's standing, I'd say what's left of her husband is no more'n fifteen feet behind her and six feet down."

Hannah held her copy where she could have seen it a few years ago and studied Leo's over his shoulder. On the far left was a bulldozer and the trench for the new, municipal gas line. To the right of center, Chlorine Moody was prostrated against a flowering hedge that resembled concertina wire with leaves. With her face in partial profile and eyes magnified by trifocals, she did appear more frightened than angry about the urban renewal in progress.

Laying his copy of the photo on the table, Delbert said, "Those bushes she's protecting? They're on the outside and inside of a chain-link fence you can hardly see." A red felt-tipped pen circled offset rows of individual trunks emerging from the ground. "Not grown through it, mind you. *Planted*."

IdaClare gasped. "Oh, my stars and garters. He's right. That woman *did* kill her husband."

Rosemary clapped her cheeks. "It's as plain as day. Why else would anybody plant roses on both sides of a fence?"

"I know!" Marge said. "So they couldn't get to the other side." Pausing, she added, "Like why the chicken crossed the road? To get…" Her voice trailed away. "Okay, so it sounded really funny in my head."

Delbert was not amused. He could take teasing nearly as well as he instigated it, just not, as he termed it, when he was professionally ascertaining a modus operandi.

"Couldn't get to the other side," he repeated.

Glances were exchanged, then frowns, then Rosemary said, "It is sort of peculiar." She pursed her lips. "Why would you landscape the alley side of a fence?"

"Because you're crazy about roses," IdaClare suggested. "Maybe Chlorine bought more than she had room for because they were on sale."

Delbert rocked on his heels, whistling softly.

"The report, at the bottom, it says there are no roses in the yard anywhere else."

"Uh-*huh*. Keep goin', Schnur…"

The font Delbert had used was mercifully large and bold. Hannah didn't have to squint to read a bulleted paragraph on the next page. Her head jerked up. "Are you sure about the trash service?"

"Saw the truck myself, this afternoon, ladybug. Now, you tell me. Why pay a private hauler to empty your garbage cans at the curb, when city trucks pick up in the alley and the fee's on your water bill, whether you use it or not?"

He referred again to the photo. "It'd take a hacksaw to free up Moody's back gate, but the hedge wasn't that high or thick twenty-three years ago when she started lugging her trash to the curb."

"Approximately the time Royal Moody disappeared," Hannah remarked.

"And according to my sources, approximately the time Chlorine started mowing her own yard. When Rudy got old enough, she'd let him cut the front, but not the back."

Rosemary blanched and made the sign of the cross. "Sweet heavenly father. She didn't want her son to tend his daddy's grave." Her eyes widened. "Or *find* it."

Delbert's fingers curled like claws. With a spooky inflection in his voice, he intoned, "Years ago, somebody gave Rudy a puppy for his birthday. The day after, off to the pound it went. Time and again, that little fatherless boy'd bring home a stray and beg his mama to let him keep it."

He leaned closer, his narrowed eyes sweeping from Marge to IdaClare and back again. "But there'd be no dog for Rudy Moody to ever call his own. Uh-uh-uh. Dogs smell bones. And when they do, they dig—"

"Oh puh-*leeze.*"

Everybody jumped. "Gotcha," IdaClare said, laughing.

"Goddamn it, you old bat. You're about as funny as a crutch."

She closed her file folder and shoved it toward him. "Mrs. Moody's odd. Her son's odder than she is—big surprise. Otherwise, there's no proof at all that she killed her husband, much less that she poisoned him."

"But—"

"Oh, hush up and sit down. You've had the floor since we started."

Actually, Delbert seemed grateful for the excuse to retake his chair. Nothing like an afternoon's CS&IGO-ing to wear a guy out, Hannah presumed.

"No wife ever loved her husband more than I loved Patrick Clancy." IdaClare's raised, pink-polished finger served as a *but.* "I'd be lying if I denied looking forward to him taking cattle to market, or hieing off to buy 'em. Yes, I missed him. Worried about him. Prayed he'd come home safe and soon, but having the house to myself for a spell was as happy a time for me as it was a vacation for Patrick.

"That's one of two things wrong with Delbert's premise. Maybe Chlorine and Royal were miserable together, but he was gone more often than not. Why kill a golden goose who brings home the bacon and is scarcely ever underfoot?"

"Easy." Marge rubbed a thumb across her fingers. "To collect on his life insurance."

"The motive, yes, it could have been." Leo shook his head. "The collecting, she could not have done."

"Hey, that's right," IdaClare said. "The court won't declare somebody dead until he's been gone for seven years."

Rosemary said, "If Chlorine killed Royal for the insurance money, her sitting around twiddling her thumbs for years is my kind of poetry."

"Still twiddling she is, though," Leo said. "Not every state is the same. In Missouri, if the insured, he goes *poof*, no settlement is paid until a body is found and identified."

Hannah said, "Do you mean, if the body is never found, the beneficiary never receives any money at all?"

Leo nodded. "The insurance company, it may choose to pay some or all of the policy amount. A goodwill gesture. But that is at their discretion."

Rosemary burst out laughing. "Boy, wouldn't *that* be a kick in the pants. Pick the wrong state to murder your husband in for the insurance, then find out you can't collect a dime without a corpse. But you can't produce the corpse to get the money, or the cops will nab you for murder."

Marge said, "I guess that explains why Delbert's still with us."

A sly grin spread across his face. "What if there was a lot more money at stake than Royal Moody's life insurance policy?" He looked at IdaClare. "What if your scarcely underfoot goose was about to lay such a whoppin' golden egg, he wouldn't leave the nest till the undertaker carried him out?"

With a flick of his wrist, a worn slipcased deck of cards thunked on top of the marked-up photo at the center of the table. Malcolm, who'd crept up on the pile of people-food dishes Leo had set on the floor, skittered sideways, as if the bowls were booby-trapped.

Marge rolled back from the table. "Time out, while I put this mess in the sink to presoak."

"Good idea," Rosemary said. "I'll clear away the rest of the dishes."

IdaClare volunteered to help, after she checked on Itsy and Bitsy, then Leo excused himself for a trip to the powder room.

Delbert howled into the sudden semivacuum, "Where the hell's everybody going? I'm just getting to the good part."

Hannah absently scratched behind Malcolm's ear and studied the small box of playing cards. An illustration of a somewhat menacing-looking clown was juggling a bright-colored *R, U, D* and *Y*. Beneath his dancing clodhoppers, the copy read, "Come One, Come All! RUDY's Tons of Fun for the Whole Family!"

She was underwhelmed by the packaging and slogan, but the twelve-and-under market wasn't her realm of expertise. Still, the Ayer and Sons logo at the upper-right corner was familiar to anyone who'd ever been a child.

Delbert said, "As soon as I heard the name, the ol' lightbulb switched on. Along with every other game in creation, there's three more RUDY decks stuck back in a cupboard at the community center.

"None of the decks I found had the instructions," Delbert continued, "but it appears to be an Uno knockoff." He dumped the RUDY cards on the table and spread them out. "You match letters, instead of numbers, and the object's to get rid of all your cards."

"That game is another dot I didn't help you connect," Hannah said quietly, so the KP crew wouldn't overhear.

"Not directly," he hedged. "But the night of our caper at Moody's house, your impressions of Mama didn't jibe with one of Santa's toy-making elves. After Rudy went to jail on illegal weapons charges, I only half listened to the scuttlebutt in town. Nothing *allakazammed* till my peepers gandered at Chlorine's picture in the newspaper."

Hannah chuckled. "You're a smart old fart."

"Humph. You're just now figuring that out?"

IdaClare returned to the breakfast room, cradling the awake but groggy poodles. "The movie thingamajig's still on, dear, but I turned off the TV."

"I don't know about the rest of you," Marge said, "but it's getting awfully close to my bedtime."

Caressing Leo's forearm, Rosemary purred, "It's past ours, isn't it, sweetheart?"

Delbert made a gagging noise and fished out the roll of Tums from his pocket. "You want it short and sweet? Here 'tis. Rumor has it that Chlorine's made more off that dumb card game than she would've on Royal's life insurance."

"How much?" Marge asked.

"A cool million. By now, it's probably closer to

two with the royalties." Delbert held up the Masters of Criminal Investigation. "If any of you'd read this, like I told you to, you'd know motive, means and opportunity don't just apply to a murder."

He exchanged the book for the game's slipcase. "The original idea for RUDY had to be Royal's. Could be, either the toy outfit he worked for turned it down, or he knew they wouldn't pay squat for it and asked Chlorine to put out feelers. Or, she did it on her own, in secret. Whatever the case, she had the means.

"Opportunity knocked when a whopping offer to buy it came along. Cutting Royal out of that jackpot was a crackin' good motive to kill him."

"*If* she did," IdaClare countered.

"And if she did," Marge said, "after Royal disappeared and Chlorine got rich quick, wouldn't the police have gotten suspicious?"

"They probably were as soon as he went missing," Delbert agreed. "No body, no life insurance payoff, no arrestee."

"Okay," Hannah said, "let's assume Chlorine murdered him. According to your premise, you think she poisoned him—"

"I don't think she did, honeylamb. I *know* she did." He discarded the slipcase to count off on his fingers. "With a kid in the house, scratch guns, knives and blunt instruments for murder weapons. They're too noisy and she'd have all that blood spatter to deal with."

"Oh, eww." Marge smacked her lips, grimacing. "Skip the nightmare stuff, okay?"

"We've gotta have the whys with the wheretofores. Which is, that poison is silent and sneaky. No muss, no fuss. Except once Royal stopped twitching, Chlorine had a corpse to dispose of—also fast and quiet, so's not to wake up their son."

"Ach, the dead weight, it is heavy," Leo said. "That's why they call it that."

"Correct-a-mundo. There's no telling if Chlorine dug the grave before or after she offed Royal. From what I heard, he wasn't a big fella, but dragging a body out of a house and across a yard would've been a back-breaker."

Delbert spread his hands. "How she covered the fresh dirt, lest the cops see it, I don't know. Planting rose bushes on both sides of the fence is better than barbed wire for keeping out kids, cats and dogs."

"But not bulldozers," Hannah said.

"Chlorine's filed a lawsuit to stop them, but the city has a legal easement to that alley. It'll be a few days—the middle of next week at the latest—before her cease and desist order comes up on the court docket and a judge throws it out."

Leo said, "Then the premise of the Code Name: Epsilon, I don't understand. If the bulldozer digs up Royal next week, a cold case to investigate, we don't have."

"Yeah," Marge agreed. "Let the city do the dirty work."

"If a body's there and they find it," IdaClare said, "it'll be fascinating to hear how Chlorine explains it."

"For the love of Mike," Delbert bellowed. "Use your damned heads for something besides a hat rack."

Clenching the red marker in his fist, he circled Chlorine Moody's picture a half-dozen times. "After all these years, do you think she's gonna sit back and wait for the gas company to *prove* she's a thief and a murderer?"

8

Hannah was in bed, a nest of feather pillows cushioning her back, when a pair of warm, delicious lips kissed her awake.

Just like the prince who'd rescued Snow White. Except Royal Moody had eaten the witch's poisoned apple and was doomed to an eternal snooze in the rose brambles. And instead of seven dwarves, there'd been only five: Crabby, Pinky, Chubby, Naughty and Marge.

Hannah's tentative peek through her lashes found Prince Charming looming over her. Hooked on his finger was a hanger with a clean uniform and a plastic shopping bag with other minimum dress-code requirements.

"Hi," she said, scraping back the hair the fan blew across her face. "Don't take this wrong, but I didn't know I fell asleep, then I had this weird dream, but

I'm not sure I'm really awake, so would you mind saying something David-like?"

"I missed you."

"Good start."

"I couldn't stand another night without you."

She waggled her fingers, *keep going.*

He grinned. "Got anything to eat?"

Ah, yes. Her prince had really come. She stretched, then kicked back the sheet. The file she'd been reading before she nodded off fell to the floor, landing at David's feet.

"What's this?" he said.

"Nothing," she said. *Oh, hell,* she thought, and dove for the file.

A size fourteen-and-a-half boot attached to a sheriff with lightning reflexes pinned it to the floor.

David looked down at the label. "Code Name: Epsilon?" His chest expanded with the sigh of the persecuted. "I know I'll hate myself for asking this, but what's with all the asterisks?"

Whew, boy. Once upon a time, doodling was a harmless habit. Maybe if she whistled a happy tune, Crabby, Pinky, Chubby, Naughty and Marge would skip in for an encore.

"Hannah?"

"They're, um, supposed to be snowflakes."

"Okay…"

"Because—well, you know, it has to be cold to snow and that's a cold case, so…"

The boot lifted off the folder, as though it were soft, fresh and organic in origin. "Bisbee's at it again."

"Yeah," she allowed, "kind of. But aren't you glad it isn't the Beauford homicide?"

"Ecstatic." The gray in David's eyes blotted out the blue, like an ocular mood ring. "I thought he learned his lesson the last time he played detective."

So had she. Until tonight, there hadn't been any gumshoe meetings for more than two months. Seeing them out in force and in action was one of life's little oh shit/thank God moments. The *get it* part of *watch what you wish for.*

"Delbert has pulled some foolish stunts," she said, "but he isn't a fool."

"I never said he was. None of them are. If they were, they wouldn't be such pains in the butt." Aware that Hannah was a semi-willing conspirator, his informant and thus a present-company pain in the butt, he inquired, "How cold is cold?"

Finally, a question she could answer that might relax the nerve twitching at his jaw. "Ice cold. More than twenty years cold." She took the hanger he still held and hung it on the closet knob. "And way back then, it was a Sanity Police Department case, not the sheriff's."

"If you're expecting a hallelujah, you're in for a huge disappointment." David bent to pick up the folder. Thrusting it at her, he warned, "One complaint call from Chief Rhodes about the Apple Dumpling Gang and I *will* throw them in county lockup."

"But you don't even know what—"

He held up his hands. "Not another word. I don't have time to arrest myself for being an accessory before the fact."

So much for the Prince Charming-Snow White dream. Then again, David was currently dealing with the death of a friend and an investigation that wasn't going well—a gumshoe revival was the last thing he needed. If only she'd put that damned file in a desk drawer and curled up in bed with a book instead, he wouldn't even have found out about it.

He caught her arm as she started for the kitchen. "Hey. I'm sorry, sugar."

"For what?" Hannah smiled up at him. "No, that isn't your cue for a line-item apology, and God help you if you miss one, because that'll be what really pissed me off, which you'd know, if you loved me as much as you say you do, so it'll be obvious you don't, and maybe never did."

David's head reared back. It angled left, then right, like a satellite dish pivoting for a clear signal. The tic formerly at his jaw migrated upward to his temple. "This is just a guess, but what you're saying is, I don't have anything to apologize for?"

"Not a thing."

"Because your feelings aren't hurt, like most women's would be for going off the way I did, because you're not most women and you know me better than I know myself, sometimes."

"Bingo." She stretched on tiptoes and kissed his cheek. "God, we're lucky that communication has never been a problem for us."

"I reckon." As she left the room, he added, "Scary as it is for me, sometimes the crazy stuff that falls out of your mouth makes sense."

Malcolm stood in the shadowy breakfast room, body-blocking Hannah's path to the kitchen. On second glimpse, the four-legged barricade was shorter, burlier and wasn't wagging its tail. This was because what remained of it was stumpy and probably not inclined to express joy when it was intact.

Rambo's presence explained Malcolm's absence in the bedroom when David kissed away Royal Moody and the Five Old Dwarves. By a rhythmic thumping in the great room, her guard-mutt was leveraging the chair from the desk's kneehole, so he could crawl in and hide.

Hannah couldn't imagine why David had brought Rambo along. The rottweiler's purpose in life was terrorizing defenseless woodland creatures, fertilizing the meadow and patrolling David's land. One might presume a county sheriff needn't worry about trespassers, but smart thieves considered it a challenge and stupid ones were—well, stupid.

Rambo looked at her as though his own prayers for a midnight snack had been answered. She knew he was all bluff and no confirmed body count. Still, her heart went aflutter and not in a good way.

"Listen up, bucko," Hannah said. "This is my turf. And Malcolm's. Now cool it with the boogety-boogety rays, find some floor to lie down on and stay there. You got that?"

He hesitated long enough for her life from first memory through eighth grade to flash behind her eyes. Moving to the rug under the table, he hunkered down, then rolled over on his side.

"Good boy," she said, recanting all those snide remarks she'd made about assertiveness-training seminars.

Malcolm hoved into view. He looked at the recumbent rottweiler, then at Hannah, then strutted into the bedroom and returned, dragging his Scooby-Doo beach towel. Dropping it in the great room doorway, he circled twice, hunkered down and rolled over on his side.

Alas, a miracle in the breakfast room didn't beget another in the kitchen. After Hannah stashed the Code Name: Epsilon file in a drawer, she perused the cupboards, the refrigerator and its freezer compartment. All held pretty much what she expected—food, but nothing much to eat.

In fairness, that was less a result of crummy shopping skills, than the good stuff always ending up at one end of the county, while they foraged for crumbs at the other.

Living together separately. Living separately together. Either way, it sucked. And would, even if she didn't know there were marshmallow-fudge cookies, English muffins, hot dogs, a bag of salad greens, eggs, frozen waffles, lunch meat and bread to slap it between at David's house.

"Hannah," David called from the bedroom, "have you seen my cargo shorts?"

"You wore them home when you forgot your gray slacks. Remember?"

No audible response. Telepathy wasn't required to channel, *Sure, I remember now. Which doesn't help a helluva lot, when I'm standing in the bathroom in my underpants with nothing to wear, except the uniform trousers I just took off.*

While clothing outages were as common as grocery outages, Hannah knew the true test of a commuter relationship was personal-product outages.

Loaned razors that barely grazed a beard, or performed unscheduled kneecap surgery. David's discovery that mousse only foamed like shaving cream. Gender-bending deodorants that left her smelling like a jock and him like a botanical garden. Constantly regarding a large bottle of mouthwash with suspicion, and maintaining a running tally of the paper cups beside it.

Hannah listened to the water heater clack on and roar to life in the utility room. Outside the kitchen window, the moon cast more shadow than light and katydids skritched their eponymous song. Malcolm yipped like a puppy in the doorway, his hind legs jerking in his sleep. A few feet away, Rambo snored and slobbered on the area rug.

Across the county, the moon shone just as bright at the corner of East Jesus and plowed ground. Bugs serenaded there, too, the new house had a bigger water heater, *two* full baths and there'd be a king-size bed with a hot, handsome sheriff in it every night.

Okay, *most* nights. Duty would still call, but the A-frame's pantry was large enough for a case of marsh-mallow-fudge cookies. And for a price, every pizza joint in town delivered.

David had her heart. He deserved the home to go with it, and another four years as sheriff to keep it. Even if she had to hire Delbert, whose résumé was in the mailer she'd picked up at the post office. Or Marge, who'd snuck hers in Hannah's Code Name: Epsilon file when IdaClare wasn't looking. Or the Schnurs, who were piling into IdaClare's Lincoln when Rosemary said she'd lost an earring and scurried back inside to give Hannah the résumé tucked in her bra.

Or, about three minutes before "Here Comes the Bride" played in the park, Hannah could scratch out the felony clause in Valhalla Springs' employment contract, rehire Jack's mother, then make David promise to love, honor, cherish and buy her a Howitzer for a wedding present.

She shuddered and stared at the floor, telling herself to keep her options open and her mouth shut for the time being. Advertising was her game, not politics, but even Luke Sauers would agree: unless whoever killed the former sheriff's widow was apprehended and soon, the current sheriff taking a bride in a public ceremony would be like dancing on Bev Beauford's grave.

David spun the lid off the mouthwash bottle. As he raised it for a swig, the mirror reflected a column of paper bathroom cups on the counter. On the top one, an upside-down Quick Draw McGraw blustered, "Now hoooold on thar…"

"Hannah will never know the difference, podnah." David tipped the bottle, then lowered it. "But I will."

There've been strides, he thought, pouring mouthwash into a cup. He'd almost broken himself of drinking from milk jugs and orange juice cartons. Dirty clothes mostly went straight to the hamper, instead of piling up behind the door. And he seldom left toilet seats up, even in the courthouse washroom, despite Jimmy Wayne McBride saying he was whipped.

David watched the man in the mirror swish peppermint mouthwash around in his mouth. The same damn fool who'd needed to see Bev Beauford lying dead on the floor to remind him that life's too short, shit happens, and if you aren't part of the solution, then could be, you're the problem.

A partial truth. Doubts had always murmured in the background. Louder, at times, but never mute. They'd goose-stepped in hobnail boots through

David's brain at Ruby's, before he ever got the call about Bev.

He spat and raked a towel across his mouth. "I'm not the impulsive type." He cupped his hand under the faucet to scoop water to rinse the basin. "Never was. Never will be." He wiped splatters from the counter, then rehung the towel. "Slow and steady's just looking an awful lot more like stubborn and stupid."

Home was where Hannah was. The address didn't matter. What did was hearing, but failing to listen, whenever she teased him about not knowing how to be a wife.

David hadn't proposed to June Cleaver. He didn't expect gourmet meals or lifetime-guaranteed maid service. It had taken far too long to comprehend that wasn't what "wife" meant to Hannah, either.

The only security and stability she'd even known—financial and emotional—she'd provided for herself. She'd loved her alcoholic mother and Caroline Garvey had loved her, but had taught Hannah by example that dependence was a trap.

Valhalla Springs was her safety net. An income separate from David's was merely a token of it. Here, she'd remain Hannah Garvey, resident operations manager, who happened to be the sheriff's wife. Marry him, move to his house and take some marginally fulfilling job in Sanity, and Hannah would be Mrs. Sheriff, who also worked at XYZ, Inc.

The distinction was semantic and a trifle sexist for anyone other than a grown-up little girl whose sibling rivals were Jim Beam and Mom's boyfriend of the night. A grown-up little girl who joked about a childhood belief that the John Doe beside *Father's name* on her birth certificate meant she was somehow related to Bambi.

David splayed his hands on the vanity. He told his mirror image, "You can't *make* Hannah feel safe. Her mother yanked the net out from under her, time and time again. If you love her, sell out to Luke and leave her be."

A knuckle-rap sealed the deal. Someday, they'd find a place together. In the meantime, the cottage had all a man could ever need: Hannah, four walls, indoor plumbing and a roof. He'd convince her of it, as soon as a statewide APB on two homicide suspects wasn't threatening to yank him away at any minute.

"Problem solved," he said as he strode into the breakfast room. "I found the sweats you borrowed the morning you spilled maple syrup on your jeans."

Hannah jumped, turned, pulled her mouth into a smile. "Gee, and here I was, picturing you walking around in your underwear."

He hoped not, judging by the scowl she'd been aiming at the floor. "Oh, you were, huh?" He hooked a thumb in the elastic waistband. "I will, if you will."

The ornery grin she slanted had him wishing he'd crawled into bed with her, *then* kissed her awake. "I'll get back to you on that," she said. "When I'm wearing some."

David tripped over Malcolm's tail. A couple of yards to the left, Rambo was stretched out on the rug, as though his name was embroidered on it.

He stared at the rottweiler and the lamb, stifling an urge to go outside and see if the lake had parted in the middle. "I thought bringing Rambo here was worth a try. No way did I expect him to make himself at home."

"Thanks for warning me that the Terminator was patrolling the breakfast room," Hannah said.

"Plan A was to hang up my clothes, then bed down Rambo in the pickup for the night. Plan B started with kissing you."

"B was definitely better," she said, then repeated the little chat she'd had with his dog and its results. "I think Malcolm thinks I talked Rambo to death."

David grinned as he sat down at the bar. "Whatever works."

"How wise of you to leave it at that." She motioned

at the cabinets. "Tonight's specials are crunchy, smooth or frosted corn flakes."

"Okay."

Entrées decided, the beverage choices were cola or lemon-lime soda, orange juice, wine, water or her last can of beer.

"Milk," David said.

She groaned like a waitperson who'd already iterated a restaurant's no-substitutions rule. "Not unless you want dry cereal."

David smirked. "I'll have juice."

Hannah nodded. "Now that we're clear on what we don't have to eat, you vent about the Beauford case, because that's mostly why you're here, and I'll scrounge for snacks."

"I missed you, is why I'm here."

"Bull." A butcher knife that always made David nervous halved an apple in one stroke, which was why it made him nervous. "You called and said you'd be working too late to come over." *Whack*, a half split to a quarter. "I couldn't sleep." She shrugged. "Okay, I fell asleep, but I was sort of waiting up for you, anyway, with my eyes closed." *Whack*. "So whatever changed after you called was lousy enough for you to go home, get your pickup, a clean uniform and your dog, and drive all the way here to talk."

"Saying I missed you wasn't bull," David insisted. The butcher knife dismembered a stalk of celery. "But yeah, shortly after I called you, the investigation hit the skids."

While he explained, Hannah set their food on the breakfast bar and slid onto the stool beside him. "Sounds like a dead giveaway to me—no pun intended. If Kimmie Sue and Rocco aren't guilty, why would they skip town?"

David dunked an apple slice in the chunky peanut butter. "Why'd they go to the house for a walk-through, before they skipped?"

"We've discussed answering questions with questions, Sheriff. I won."

"That's all we've got, sugar, and mine was an extension of yours. If they are guilty, why didn't they skip the walk-through, too? Marlin pushed, but he'd have agreed to wait until morning if Kimmie Sue had pushed back."

Hannah scooped smooth peanut butter with a celery stick and licked it like an ice cream cone. David was dumbstruck with vegetable envy. "In the movies," she said, "the bad guys always return to the scene of the crime."

"They've been known to," he allowed. "That's why us good guys take scene photos of gawkers standing behind the tape line."

"But my guess is, if Kimmie Sue and Rocco were in it together, they went to the house to find out what you and Marlin knew."

David tore his eyes away from the X-rated peanut-butter show and focused on the food in front of him. He sniffed the milk carton's spout, then checked the expiration date—yesterday, it now being a couple of hours past Thursday. The milk smelled like Tuesday noon.

Hannah flinched. "I should have done that when I took it out of the fridge." The saucer of apples migrated closer. "All yours. Eat 'em before they turn brown."

"I'll share. I'm not that hungry, anyhow."

"No, thanks. After that dream I had, I'm off apples for a while." She took a cracker and bit off a corner. "I get the feeling you don't believe Mrs. Beauford's daughter is involved in her death."

By her tone, forbidden fruit and homicide were linked. How evaded him, so he said, "I don't want to believe Kimmie Sue's involved, but maybe she's a better actress than we think."

"Either way, if Jarek is the killer, she's a major liability." Hannah munched the rest of the cracker. "What if she didn't leave town with him, and he *took* her? Even if she didn't conspire in the murder, she'll suspect him eventually. Process of elimination, if nothing else."

Hannah's instincts and an analytical, logical mind had attracted David from the start. Not that he was blind to her womanly curves and bottomless brown eyes. Much as she professed to despise her long, curly-wavy hair, he loved to touch it, bury his face in it, see it tousled and tangled on her pillow while she slept.

Hannah Marie Garvey wasn't as tough as she wanted people to believe, more beautiful and sexy than she ever would admit, and a lot smarter than David, but thought the reverse was true. Stay on his toes, and he might fool her for the rest of his life.

He said, "The more time that passes without a stop on Jarek's vehicle, the more worried I am about Kimmie Sue's continued good health."

"So you do think he's involved." She'd dunked another celery stalk when David wasn't looking. Now he was coaching himself: breathe in, breathe out.

"They're, uh, they're both persons of interest." *And at the moment, not a fraction as interesting as what your tongue's doing...*

"I love it when you cop-talk." Her teeth severed the celery like Ginzu knives. "From what you've told me, I think Kimmie Sue's visit was a surprise. Mothers dream their daughters will hook up with captains of industry, not guys named Rocco."

She paused to dispense with the celery. "Since guys named Rocco already have a lot to overcome and usually for good reason, he decided to rip off his never-to-be mother-in-law. He cased the house on the sly, dropped off Kimmie Sue to shop or something and was tossing the place when Bev came home."

Hannah spread her hands. "At that point, he had two choices."

David nodded, wincing inwardly. Once that decision was made, if Bev hadn't been wearing her murder weapon, the killer would have used whatever else was handy. A recent homicide downstate involved a drug dealer who bludgeoned a deadbeat customer to death with a tree stump.

"Rocco grabbed his loot," Hannah said, "picked up Kimmie Sue and left town. They made it to Joplin before the storms forced them to stop. I assume Kimmie Sue isn't a morning person, or they'd have been halfway across Oklahoma when Marlin reached her on her cell phone."

She sat back and crossed her arms. "If Kimmie Sue—" She rolled her eyes. "Jeez, what were her parents *thinking?* If they'd had a boy, they'd have probably named him Rocco."

David chuckled and Hannah continued. "Whatever. *Kim* Beauford couldn't have known it was Marlin— all your phones block the name and number on Caller ID. Rocco had to bring her back, but just because they checked into the Wishing Well doesn't mean he unpacked the Jeep. Kimmie—Kim—might not have realized they were blowing town after the walk-through, until Rocco blew past the city limits."

David shook his head in amazement. "Not bad, Detective Garvey. If constituents wouldn't accuse me of nepotism, I might be tempted to put you on the department payroll."

"Then I'm right?"

"Well, that remains to be seen. I will say, you and Marlin think a lot alike."

She made a face, as though uncertain whether she'd been complimented or insulted. Comparisons with the chief of detectives had that effect on people.

"Same as I told Luke, all we can do is hang tight until those two and their vehicle are located."

Hannah tensed. A cracker she'd intended to slip to Malcolm the Mooch disintegrated in her hand. Glancing down at him, she stammered, "N-New rule, Malc. No more table food."

The mutt glared at David, as though he was a bad influence. He'd tried to be, with zero success. Table scraps in the dogs' bowls, not hand-fed on the sly, was David's house rule, not Hannah's.

The poor dumb dog whimpered and nudged Hannah's elbow with his nose, his heart obviously as broken as the cracker she was brushing off on a napkin. David said, "How new is this rule?"

"I, uh, pretty much since you were changing clothes." Still leaning forward, still chafing her hands over the napkin, she inquired, "So, you talked to Luke…recently?"

David sensed a change, aside from subject matter and the peculiar edge in Hannah's voice. Guilt about cutting off Malcolm's stealth panhandling, he supposed. "Luke called the house as I was leaving to come out here. He is *not* happy with me, but he'll just have to get over it."

Hannah sat back. She pushed her hair behind an ear, flipped it free again, then sighed. "It was a crazy idea, I guess. Totally inappropriate."

"Exactly what I said, right before I told him flat-out no."

"You did?" Her eyes widened, then narrowed. "When was this?"

"About a month ago, when Luke brought it up."

"Oh, yeah? And in all this time, you never said a word to me about it."

Confused, David said, "Why would I?"

She shot back, "Why *wouldn't* you?" A mirthless chuckle, then, "I already know the answer, but c'mon. Fess up."

David's mouth opened, then closed. A mental review of the previous thirty seconds didn't clarify a damned thing.

"Because I said no. Hell, I even spelled it. Then I forgot about it, till Luke pestered me on the phone again tonight."

Her face flushed as red as the apple peels. Clenching her teeth, she repeated, "You turned him down. A month ago."

"Of course I did. Even without Bev's murder taking priority, I can't think of a dumber way to waste a Friday night."

Slowly, Hannah tipped her head. The gears turning inside were visible. She said, "What are you talking about?" at the same time David said, "Why are you so ticked off all of a sudden?"

Their eyes met and held. "You first," he said.

"Uh-uh. You started it."

Started what? David blew out a breath. "Luke wanted me to help judge a toddler's beauty contest tomorrow night to get out the mom vote. I said no, and forgot about it. I didn't know till he called tonight that he'd signed me up for it, anyway. I told him to take a flying leap off a water tower and pray Jesus he landed on that concrete head of his."

Braced for a chapter and verse on whatever sin he'd committed, he gestured, *Your turn.*

Her color having returned to near-normal, she said, "Get out the mom vote, huh? Sheesh. The winner's maybe. All the losers' mothers wouldn't have been real fond of you." She glanced at the microwave clock, gasped, "Ye gods, will you look at the time?" and hopped off the bar stool.

"Hey." David grabbed a fistful of her Bulls jersey before it got away. "Aren't you forgetting something?"

Bowing back into his arms, she traced a fingertip down his cheek and trailed it along his jaw, his neck, the band of his undershirt. "No. I'm remembering what tends to happen after we've had a snack…talked awhile…relaxed…"

Her touch, the look in her eyes, and that low, sultry voice had an immediate effect. "We, uh, clean up the mess we made of the kitchen?"

"Sometimes."

"Make sure the doors are locked, then douse the lights?"

"Usually."

"Snuggle up in bed and drift off to sleep?"

"That, too." Hannah brushed her lips against his. "Eventually." The tip of her tongue flicked out, tasting sweet and hot and peanut-buttery. The images it conjured scrolled through David's memory, heightening his arousal.

Lost in her kiss, he was vaguely aware of her twisting in his arms, pulling them both upward, then to the floor. Her hair tumbling over his face smelled like crushed strawberries and he cupped her breast, feeling it swell at his touch. Her mouth never leaving his, she skimmed her hand across his chest, his belly, delving deeper, then her fingers closed around him, stroking, driving him out of his mind.

Falling back, panting, David struggled for control, missing her mouth on his, groaning as her tongue licked up the length of him and her lips parted to take him. The primal pounding ache for release near the breaking point, he freed himself and rolled her on her back.

He tugged off her pajama pants, then his sweats, eager to give, to feel her trembling rise to tremors.

Shuddering, she cried out, "Now, *now*," and when he slid inside her, the world exploded in bright, blinding white light, then faded to black.

An annoying clattering sound woke David—it was his pager vibrating like a wind-up toy on the nightstand. In the dusty gray light seeping in through the windows, he squinted at the glowing LED screen, grunted, then turned it right side up. The blurry numerals gradually coalesced into Marlin Andrik's phone extension at the Outhouse. A digital ASAP message, not a hit-the-gas-and-haul-ass one.

David slid from the bed, careful not to disturb Hannah, and clueless as to how or when they'd gotten there. He was naked from the waist down, a mite weak in the knees, and the left one had a bruise as big as a Kennedy half dollar.

If he was any happier, satisfied, and in love with the most amazing woman the Lord ever created, he'd just flap his wings and fly back to town.

After gathering the clothes he'd worn and those he'd brought with him the night before, he kissed Hannah's sleep-warm brow. He'd grab a quick shower at his house and trade the pickup for his county car.

In the breakfast room, Rambo and Malcolm had their noses pressed to the French doors, united in the urgent need to pee before their bladders burst.

"Quiet," David whispered, then let them out. A combined two hundred pounds scrambling across a wooden plank deck was anything but. He backtracked to peek in at Hannah. Grinning, he allowed that a hydrogen bomb in the backyard wouldn't rouse her for another hour or three.

He retrieved his sweatpants from the floor and pulled them on. Operating a motor vehicle barefoot was a misdemeanor. Wearing boots with sweats ought to be a felony. He folded Hannah's discarded pj bottoms on a bar stool, then loaded the coffeemaker and set it to start the brew cycle at eight.

David was giving the counters a swipe with the dishrag, when he paused and looked toward the bedroom.

"Not that I'm complaining," he said softly, as though Hannah were standing there, "but best as I can recall, you never did tell me what tripped that redheaded temper of yours last night."

9

In Realtor parlance, a neighborhood described as *established* often pertains to houses built when a spacious closet was an arm-span wide, and families whiled away summer evenings on the front porch, not in front of the TV.

Apart from its lifetime-guaranteed siding, the green AstroTurf glued to the porch, and a new storm door, the house where Chlorine Moody lived hadn't changed much in the decades since World War II.

A concrete driveway on the bungalow's kitchen side accessed the detached, single-car garage. Its heavy kick door had been replaced by a solid steel one with an automatic opener. Otherwise, what money Mrs. Moody lavished on her property's exterior was earmarked for upkeep and security, not beautification.

Behind that block of MacMillan Street, the property owner who'd fenced his yard first and without regard to easements and boundary lines had set the standard followed by neighbors to the opposite end of the block.

An uprooted hodgepodge of temporary enclosures, dirt piles and construction equipment impeded the view of the alley. For that Delbert was grateful, since broad daylight on a Friday morning wasn't an optimum time for trespassing on private property.

The exception to that rule was a mission that couldn't be undertaken after dark, on account of needing to see what the hell you're doing while you were doing it. Not to mention, when you were working with an operative such as Leo Schnur, who couldn't be trusted not to shine a dingdanged flashlight straight at somebody's window.

Amateurs, Delbert grumbled to himself, and glanced back over his shoulder. The same long-sleeved, one-piece coveralls that hung on him like Columbo's raincoat had Leo looking like the Pillsbury Doughboy with an untreated thyroid condition.

"Jehosophat, Schnur. Will you hurry up?"

"The hurry, I am," Leo wheezed. "The up I cannot any faster."

The alleyway's slope to street level wasn't much of a hill for a climber, unless he was a hundred pounds overweight, had a canvas bag full of equipment slung over his shoulder and was dumb enough to wear a pair of wingtips for a mission called Operation Tomb Raider.

A designation Leo wasn't aware of. Or what it entailed.

Keeping details on a strict need-to-know basis was critical. The less Leo knew, the less he could argue about—and the less inclined he'd be to panic, turn tail and waddle back to Valhalla Springs.

Delbert pulled down the bill on his cap, in the event a neighbor looked out to see what his idiot dog was yapping at in the alley. Flipping open his metal clipboard case, he gandered at the top page. A masterpiece, if he didn't say so himself.

The city's blue-inked logo and letterhead had been cut off a notice swiped from the public works' department's bulletin board. Pasted on a clean sheet of paper fed into a color photocopier loaded with watermarked stationery produced a dozen blank, almost perfect replicas of Sanity's official letterhead.

It probably wasn't used for work orders, but the one Delbert composed on the computer, then printed, looked gimcrackin' bona fide to him.

Beneath it was a handwritten list of dos and don'ts for removing and preserving hazardous materials. He

was refreshing his memory on the finer, more potentially fatal points when Leo scuffled up beside him.
"A bad feeling, I am getting," he said. He mopped his
face with a monogrammed handkerchief. "Ach, the
bad feeling I had before we got here."

"I know what you mean." Delbert pounded his
chest with a fist, then turned his head and burped.
"Tell Rosie to go easy on the black olives next time
she makes that dip."

"Last night's refreshments is not what the bad feeling is. The why we are here, I am afraid to ask."

"Good."

Delbert closed the clipboard. He moved to the
edge of an abbreviated culvert extending to the far
end of the block. Straddling it were utility saw-
horses rigged with flashing caution lights. Wired to
orange plastic netting were several Danger and Keep
Out signs.

A parked front-loader and a dump truck barricaded
vehicular traffic. The stench exuded by a half-dozen
garbage cans said their owners would sooner wait for
the city's alleyway pickup to resume than drag them
around front to be emptied.

Leo waved at a wall of climbing roses looming
nearly as high as the power lines overhead. "Worse,
it looks than in the newspaper picture."

"That's why we're tunneling through," Delbert said, "not going over."

From the duffel bag, he took out two pairs of leather gloves, hook-bladed loppers and a hacksaw. "If we free up that gate, we're in like Flynn. You start on the hinge side. I'll take the latch side and we'll meet in the middle at the top."

Leo surveyed the perimeter. "You are sure, the lady is not home?"

"A lady she ain't, but affirmative on the not-home part. If you'd read my scouting report, you'd know she cooks and delivers for Meals on Wheels every Wednesday and Friday morning."

Leo's scowl deepened. "A murderer, she takes food to shut-ins twice a week?"

"Yeah, and goes to church regular, and maybe hustles old folks cross the street when the Boy Scouts are off tying knots in a rope somewhere." Delbert shrugged. "So what? The vote was unanimous that she whacked her husband."

"Five to one," Leo corrected. "Not unanimous."

"Five in favor," Delbert recorrected. "Hannah didn't vote against it, she abstained."

"But no vote did we take on what Mrs. Moody did with the body."

"Didn't need to." Delbert jabbed the hedge with

the loppers. "I'm tellin' you, Royal's absotively po-silutely buried in the backyard. I already checked the cellar and—"

His mouth slammed shut about five words too late. Leo's dropped open as wide as the scoop on the front-loader. Delbert gagged him with a work glove before he yelled something incriminating loud enough to be heard clear to city hall.

Holding the glove in place, Delbert said, "What I'm gonna tell you is strictly confidential. Got that?"

Leo nodded.

"Between you and me. Not you, me and Rosemary."

Leo nodded.

"Because if you blab to Rosie, she'll blab confi-dentially to IdaClare, and she'll blab confidentially to Marge, and she'll blab at the Curl-Up & Dye, and lickety-split, Hannah and the whole damn county will know about it."

Leo nodded.

"Okay," Delbert said, reassured, but not enough to remove the gag. "When I was talking up the neigh-bors yesterday, I saw Moody's white Caddy back down the driveway. After she left, I slipped into the backyard for a lookie-loo and spied the door to the cellar.

"Lots of them had dirt floors, once upon a time, so

I picked the padlock on the doors and ventured in. No dice. Just wall-to-wall concrete as old as the foundation. No corpse in the cellar means Chlorine *had* to have planted Royal in the yard. *Capisce?*"

Leo nodded.

Delbert wrestled with an urge to tell Leo what else he'd left out of Code Name: Epsilon's report—and lost, mostly because he'd bust a gut, if he didn't brag to somebody.

"Since the cat was away," he said, "I figured the mouse ought to poke around a bit."

Leo's eyebrows shot up and disappeared under the bill of his cap.

"Hell yes, I was scared she'd come back and catch me, but the inside of that house?" Delbert whistled through his dentures. "De-ee-lux, amigo. All the woodwork's mahogany, the bathrooms are white marble, and the kitchen alone's worth more *than the entire house.*"

Realizing he was practically shouting, Delbert lowered his voice. "Now, why would Chlorine spend a king's ransom remodeling an old house, when she could've sold it and built a fancy brand-spanking new one?"

Leo said, "Uhtauautawnngmamawt."

Assuming he meant, "I'll tell you, if you'll take

your dirty, stinking glove out of my mouth," Delbert complied, albeit cautiously.

Leo spat, smacked his lips together, then rubbed them on his sleeve. "For that, I should punch you in the nose. Ever you do it again, and I will."

"Fair enough."

They shook on it, then Leo said, "The house she did not sell, because of the husband buried in the yard."

Delbert beamed at his protégé. "Correct-o-mundo."

"So the hole in the bushes, that, I will help you make. The digging up a corpse?" Leo shook his head. "That I don't got the stomach for."

"Neither do I, pal." Delbert clapped his shoulder. "I promise, all we're gonna do is get the dirt on Chlorine Moody."

As hoped, the thorny canes they bisected with the loppers and hacksaws were so enmeshed in the overgrowth, they dangled above their heads, instead of falling to the ground. Leo had struggled with hewing the branches snared between the gate's hinge straps and wrapped around the post. What he muttered under his breath might not have been obscene, but ordering a cheeseburger and fries in German sounded like blasphemy.

Their faces were scratched, their chins and noses dripping sweat, and rose petals caped their shoulders before brute force swung the gate wide enough to crawl through.

"The other side," Leo panted, pointing a trembling finger. "More bushes. Too tired, I am, to cut them."

Delbert swiped his face with his sleeve and yelped when an embedded thorn raked his brow. It was too hot. The job was too hard. Too big, even for the both of them.

No, damn it. They were too *old*. The spirit was willing, the mind as sharp as ever—well, his was, anyhow. But the body...

Funny how a man can remember being young, but can't for the life of him put a finger on when or how he got to be dadblasted *old*.

If he did, Delbert reminded himself. Royal Moody hadn't. He'd been cheated out of seeing his son become a man, just as Rudy had been cheated out of a father. Even worse, the boy grew up believing his father abandoned him.

He'd surely tried to pray his daddy home, then dared him, then sworn he'd slam the door in the bastard's face if he ever had the balls to show up. All the while, he'd likely watched fathers coach ball teams and lead Scout troops, and would've happily settled for an ordinary Joe who went to work in the morning and came home every night.

Hannah knew how that felt. So did Delbert. He dug through the duffel bag for a bottle of sports drink. It was half empty before the bitter taste washed from his mouth.

Yes-sirree. If sixty-nine years had taught him anything, it was that sparing the innocent was an excuse the guilty used when they lied to protect themselves. And even awful truths never did as much damage as the lies they hid behind.

"I can't quit on Rudy, too." Delbert finished his drink and tossed the bottle aside. "I won't."

David watched Rocco Jarek through the one-way mirror. The interrogation room's decor was as lovely as the rest of the Outhouse: flat, institutional-green walls and brown-speckled linoleum that had seen better days several decades ago. Recessed fluorescent light boxes added a greasy sheen and sallowness to the healthiest complexion.

Jarek fidgeted in the armless plastic bucket chair, worry lines creasing his forehead. He was dressed in last night's wrinkled shirt and jeans, and had a bad case of bed head.

Hard to say what he was thinking. David had a strong suspicion it wasn't *Thank God it's Friday*. Especially after a preliminary chat with Marlin Andrik, followed by an equal period of perceived isolation in that ugly, claustrophobic room.

Around dawn, a city patrol unit had spotted Jarek's vehicle in the Holiday Inn Express's parking lot. The patrol officer called for backup. It being a slow night and an even quieter early morn, half the Sanity PD, two deputies and a highway patrolman converged on the motel.

Jarek and Kimmie Sue were rousted like Public Enemy Numbers One and Two. It was professionally executed and not unwarranted for homicide suspects with an all-points order out on them. In hindsight, the sheriff's department would have preferred a smaller and less exuberant response than the D-day invasion on Normandy.

"Just because Jarek hasn't been charged with anything," David said to Marlin, "I'm surprised he hasn't lawyered up."

"The drone's living off Kimmie Sue," he said. "And she isn't paging an attorney for herself, much less for glamour boy."

David had remanded Ms. Beauford to a locked interview room at the courthouse. If separation anxiety didn't turn one of them, the lies cops told for leverage were easier to pull off.

He said, "I'm still trying to wrap my head around

them checking out of the Wishing Well and into the Holiday Inn because of a cricket in the bathtub."

"That's Jarek's story. Kimmie Sue already bitched about their room smelling like feet. When she saw the bug in the tub, she freaked."

"And you just couldn't resist asking if it had a top hat and answered to Jiminy."

Marlin sighed. "Try to be thorough and what do you get? A shitload of attitude."

"Imagine that." Usually his smart-ass interrogation techniques were worth a grin, if not a belly laugh. Maybe this would, too, someday, if the case ever stopped feeling like sand slipping through their fingers.

Slightly under twenty-four hours in, leads should have begun meshing with others into a discernible pattern of events. An investigation worked backward, starting at the scene and the estimated time of its occurrence. Reverse order didn't defy logic. Normally it enhanced it.

"Bug or no bug," David said, "moving from one motel to another is a pretty short flight to avoid prosecution."

"You want to rag me about it? Take a number and stand in line." Marlin stepped away from the glass and stalked toward the coffeemaker. "Seemed like common sense that a homicide victim's daughter would keep me informed of her whereabouts, unless she was involved. Of course, I'm just the asshole detective assigned to the case, so what the fuck do I know?"

He lofted the carafe at David, who waved a *no thanks*. "I'm not ragging you, Marlin. I was there, remember?"

David pushed aside photos and evidence bags and hiked a hip on the corner of Marlin's desk. "I've got no problem admitting that this one's felt hinky from the get-go and not only because the victim was Bev Beauford."

He took the cup of coffee Marlin handed him, as though he hadn't declined it three seconds ago. An oily skim congealed on the surface as the fumes cleared all eight sinus passages. Balancing the cup on his knee, he added, "It wouldn't have taken all night to locate them if they'd used that credit card again, instead of Jarek paying cash for their room."

Marlin grunted an agreement. "He says Kimmie Sue was too upset to get out of the Jeep when they checked in. He couldn't charge it on her card without her there to sign for it."

"*Her* card? Bev's name was on it."

"Kimmie Sue is allegedly authorized to use it. I'm expecting a court order any month now. Until I get it, the issuer won't verify the current time and temperature in beautiful downtown New Delhi."

David shook his head. "If Kimmie Sue's on the account, why wouldn't Bev authorize a second card in her name? Technically, Kimmie Sue is forging her mother's signature on every sales slip."

"If she did, we can charge her on it." Marlin jerked a thumb at the interrogation room. "Jarek the douche bag clammed up when I asked how his print got on Bev's rearview mirror. Him, we can hold for a while, but if we don't come up with something fast, I have to cut him loose."

"He could walk now, if he cared to."

"Couldn't stop him," Marlin agreed. "Fortunately, he's too stupid to know that."

David stood and set the untouched coffee on the desk. "I guess Kimmie Sue's been neglected long enough. Maybe her version of the truth will trip up the both of them."

"You're right about her being more receptive to you than me." Marlin swung side to side in the chair, his gaze leveled at David. "That's not a joke this time. Last night convinced me there's nothing funny about Malibu Barbie. Guilty or not, she's one spooky broad."

He glanced at Josh Phelps and Cletus Orr bent

over their respective desks. Lowering his voice, he said, "It's like I told the wife after I got home. It wouldn't surprise me to find out Kimmie Sue loved to pull the wings off flies when she was a kid. It also wouldn't surprise me if she didn't, but bragged that she did, just to screw with people's heads."

Take the fork to the left, a skosh past a fence post with an MFA Feed sign stapled to it. At the second rock cornerstone, go right, then left again at the third sycamore from the chimney where the old McGill place stood before it burnt. If you come to the trestle bridge over Turkey Creek, you'd done gone too far.

Hannah smiled, remembering the morning Ruby Amyx drew a map to David's house on a handful of paper napkins. They were still in the Blazer's glove box, though she now knew every dip and heave in Turkey Creek Road's concrete-slab surface.

Oncoming drivers had always raised a four-finger *howdy* and most smiled to back it up. Such was the literal passing acquaintance that native Ozarkers bestowed on everyone, yet familiarity had quickened the waves and broadened the smiles. Even though they wouldn't recognize one another on the sidewalk downtown, it was nice to be a member of the rural road-less-traveled club.

Along the shoulders, spiky purple blazing stars and blooming goldenrod mingled with taller, feathery Johnson grass—an allergy sufferer's second circle of hell. And a very short-lived bouquet, as Hannah learned when she was little.

Chiggers had feasted on her legs, while she'd hacked and sawed a butter knife through gobs of what she'd thought were wildflowers. A vase being as impossible to find in the trailer as a sterling tea set, Hannah had pawed through the trash heap underneath it. To a six-year-old kid, a bunch of flowers crammed in a rusty coffee can with wrinkled bits of aluminum foil glued to its sides was absolutely beautiful.

By the time Caroline Garvey had come home from the bar where she worked, Hannah had scratched her chigger bites bloody and her bouquet had wilted to a droopy "mess of goddamn weeds dirtying up the table."

Her mother had later apologized for yelling and said it was the thought that counted. The bleach water she'd dabbed on Hannah's legs had stung, but not as much as the sight of the beautiful vase and flowers strewn outside in the dirt, where her mother had thrown them.

"I still think they're pretty," Hannah told the dashboard. Particularly the tufts brushing the mailbox beside the lane to David's one-bedroom farmhouse. His temporary home was barely large enough for a bachelor sheriff, but many a memory had been made there.

The new house was gorgeous, but she'd miss hearing the rain drum on the farmhouse's sheet-metal roof, cuddling with David on the porch watching fireflies wink in the meadow, the deer grazing in the false dawn.

All that would change was the perspective. They would soon have a bluff-top vantage point, instead of being close enough to see horseflies pester a doe's flank and smell the vaporous ground fog that fell and rose with the moon's wax and wane.

Silver and gold, Hannah thought, humming the Girl Scout song about old and new friends. Her tenure in a troop had lasted maybe two meetings, but those tunes, "Kumbya" and "Gopher Guts" were ingrained in her brain.

Farther on, the narrow trestle bridge at the bottom of a hill that Ruby had warned was "too far" was now a landmark crossed before the turn into the A-frame's driveway.

Hannah lowered the window glass and breathed in the creek's loamy scent. The wet-weather springs that fed it were already slowing to trickles. In a day or so, the delicate minirainbows shimmering above eddies and near the banks would vanish and a toy boat would founder on the rocky bed.

Like the lane to the farmhouse, the new entrance was merely a break in the treeline bordering the unmown verge. Low-hanging branches snapped by bulldozers, well-drilling augers, cranes and concrete mixers would gradually reform a leafy arbor you'd have to be looking for to notice.

"Sort of like the Batcave." Hannah frowned and tried again, in a perkier tone of voice. "Sort of like the Batcave!"

Had Malcolm been along for the ride, he'd have rolled his eyes, too. Practice, she thought. That's all it takes. And a different frame of reference couldn't hurt.

Thinking of the places her personal superhero took her last night sent shivers tingling through every nerve ending. David never needed a map, or directions, to find them. Just as well, since most were gloriously uncharted territory.

From the first time they'd made love, the man had been like Magellan, constantly discovering, exploring and conquering worlds she hadn't known existed. Waking to a half-empty bed always dimmed the lingering afterglow, yet she knew a note beside the coffeepot would begin, "Good mornin', sugar" and close with "Love, David." Reading it was al-

most as sweet as hearing it spoken in that deep bari-
tone drawl.

The A-frame appeared before her, its steep-pitched
roof clad in shingles the color of tree bark. By day,
rows of skylights resembled elongated blue mirrors,
and after sunset, became a star-spangled observatory.
A wraparound deck widened at the rear where a field-
stone barbecue shared its chimney with the interior
fireplace. At the front, a prowlike wall of glass
seemed to stretch the view to the edge of the world.

The temporary parking lot that would become the
side yard ordinarily looked like McDonald's during
the lunch-hour rush. Since carpooling to a construction site hadn't caught on with the local carpenters',
plumbers', drywallers', electricians' and cabinet-
makers' unions, Hannah had seen as many as twenty
vehicles crowd the flat, once-grassy area.

Either today was a holiday she wasn't aware of, or
the spirit hadn't yet moved the crew. If nobody showed
before she left, she'd call David and tattle. In the meantime, she was happy to have the place to herself for once.

Acclimation was the intent. Taking and making the
leap from *David's house* to *our house* to *home*. Feeling it, not just thinking it and saying it.

Rambo emerged from the trees, his delight at seeing her again so soon masked by a steady amber stare.

"I come in peace," Hannah told him, loudly enough to be heard by any potential wild bears renowned for shitting in the woods. Or mountain lions, who'd pretended to be extinct in this area for decades.

To Rambo, she added, "If you ever tell David, I'll swear you're lying, but it's kind of nice having you around."

Sedge grass and joe-pye weed brushed her calves as she strode to the back door. Tucking her pant legs inside her boots repelled ticks and chiggers.

Nature was a great thing. There was just so much of it here, all at once. Everywhere you looked—nature, nature, nature. Trailer-park kids and condo-dwellers didn't know from nature. Was it her fault, she preferred hers…neater? Channeling her inner Laura Ingalls Wilder, Hannah ducked kamikaze June bugs and keyed the back door.

The A-frame's interior was light, airy and blessedly enclosed. Despite tarps, ladders, scaffolds and dangling electrical wires, its bones were the Ponderosa meets Ikea, with a dash of industrial chic.

Exposed beams and posts supported and traversed the cathedral ceiling. Above the hearth area, open galley kitchen and guest bedroom was the master suite loft. When needed, shoji-style screens would allow privacy, without blocking the light from the window wall.

David had asked her opinion on everything from the unsuited guest room's fixtures to the hardware for the kitchen cabinets. "This is our house, not just mine," he'd said, about eight gajillion times, which approximated the number of decisions attached to building a house from the foundation up.

Strange—or maybe not—that only once had Hannah's preferences deviated from his. That's why the bathroom basins were rectangular, rather than the traditional oval. Life, in her unspoken opinion, was already too complicated to obsess over switch-plate covers, doorknobs and the relative merits of Colonial Sage wall paint over Spanish Moss Sage.

"Besides," she said, moving to answer Rambo's request to patrol the front deck, "the man made stained plywood look like parquet, already."

Retrofitting a Brazilian cherry floor was negotiable, she decided. There'd be a fight for sure, if David ever tried to rip out the concrete countertops.

Compared to the interior coolness, Mother Nature was stoking up the sauna outside. The view from the deck truly was spectacular, though. It was kind of like being in a skyscraper, Hannah thought. With a view of treetops and a glade, instead of clustered billboards, neighboring rooftops and a six-lane freeway.

"A skyscraper," she repeated. Word associations

tumbled, then clicked. Her tentative smile widened to an openmouthed grin.

The Friedlich brothers had started their agency in a rented, two-room walk-up. Back then, Hannah's former employers had less advertising experience between them than she now did, by herself. Friedlich & Friedlich still managed the Clancy Construction and Development account, but it was hers for the taking. If Jack balked at the idea, she'd tell his mother.

A mental cheerleading squad yelled, *Go for it*. The stern voice of reason demanded research, a feasibility study and a prospectus. It also reminded Hannah of a Mod Squad assignment to complete, and the grocery list in her purse.

However, Reason assured, stupid as you've been not to have thought of going into business for yourself before now, maybe, just maybe, you can leave Valhalla Springs, physically, and still stay connected. From right here, at the corner of East Jesus and plowed ground. In David's—her—*their* dream house.

10

Delbert and Leo knelt beside the equipment bag they'd dragged into Chlorine Moody's backyard. Delbert handed his operative a face mask, plastic goggles with duct tape over the ventilation holes, and a pair of rubber dishwashing gloves. He then parceled out heavy-duty plastic scoops, prelabeled zip-top bags and his *pièce de resistance,* a folded grid map of the targeted terrain.

Numbered squares corresponded to those on the bags' labels. That way, each soil sample they took could be matched to a location and voilà—an *X,* or more likely, several of them would mark Royal Moody's grave.

If, Delbert thought, he was right about Chlorine's modus operandi. And if being right didn't kill them before they could prove it.

He struggled to contain the jump-out-of-his-skin

feeling he'd had ever since they'd breached the hedge. Before that, really. He'd nigh wet himself when that nosy kid on the bicycle had appeared in the alley out of nowhere. Then those bona fide public works department yahoos had scared his liver up behind his left ear.

"Quick, accurate and careful," he told Leo. "No shortcuts. No shillyshallying. Agreed?"

"Yes. What we are doing and why we are doing it, I don't get."

"Simple. Core out a plug of grass with the scoop. Dig down about six inches, then dump a good scoop of dirt in the bag and seal it. Fill in the hole, best you can. Cork it with the grass plug. Move to the next square and start over."

Leo's chins buckled. He looked from the goggles to the mask to the gloves. "Now tell me what it is, you are not telling me."

"Damn it, Schnur. We don't have time to—"

Leo sat back on his butt and crossed his arms. He glared at Delbert like a nearsighted Teutonic Buddha in muddy coveralls and a cap. When Schnur's stubborn side took over, a dynamite enema wouldn't move him.

"Promise you'll cooperate, if I tell you?"

Suspicion narrowed Leo's eyes. He shook his head.

Well, hell. On second thought, the truth would get him off the hook for feeling guilty about endangering his best friend. Mostly off the hook. If Leo got sick, even of his own free will, Delbert would never forgive himself.

He whipped off his cap to yank the goggles' elastic band over his head. "Gotta have these, the gloves and the mask for protection. Gotta have protection, because I'm betting Chlorine poisoned Royal with arsenic."

Pulling on a glove, he ignored a sound from Leo's position similar to air sputtering out of a birthday balloon. "If she did," Delbert went on, "arsenic doesn't degrade. Ever. What's leeched into the dirt may have stunted the roses on this side of the fence, too, but we can't prove diddly without soil samples to back it up."

"The poison," Leo squeaked, "it is in the dirt?" He scrambled to his feet. "And you want we should dig it up and for to put it in *bags?*"

"We don't have to," Delbert shot back.

"Thank God, for—"

"We could just cut to the goddamn chase and dig up Royal, instead."

Leo staggered backward, spouting gibberish and waving a frantic negatory.

"You're right about that," Delbert said, in a congratulatory tone. "If his corpse is loaded with arsenic, he's about ten times more toxic than the dirt ever thought of being."

And probably looked close to the same as he did when Chlorine buried him—a fact Leo didn't need to be apprised of, but that sent gooseflesh crawling up Delbert's arms.

From the Civil War to the early twentieth century, arsenic mixed with water was used as an embalming fluid. Delbert didn't know who discovered that the poison had an equally fatal effect on microorganisms that caused decomposition as it did on a spouse you wanted to shed. The embalming practice wasn't banned until somebody noticed that undertakers were expiring regularly due to repeated exposure to that deadly preservative.

"That's why I said we gotta be quick, accurate and careful. When we're done, every stitch we got on goes straight into the trash bags I brought, then into the biohazard bin at the hospital."

Leo aimed a mournful look at his wingtips. Delbert said, "Sorry, bub. Dig or don't, those are history. Till the lab tests are run, we don't know where the arsenic is, nor how high it's concentrated."

"If it is here."

Delbert put a fist on his hip. "Go ahead. Say it. You think I'm loco in the cabana, don't ya?"

Leo bent to retrieve his protective gear. "The bushes I have lopped and now the poison dirt, I will dig, so who of us is crazy, eh?" With that, he consulted the dot on the map and set to carving out a grass clump.

Delbert covered his mouth and nose with his face mask. It must be pitching those lace-up clodhoppers that had Leo all riled up. No problemo. On the way home, he'd treat Leo to a pair of Hush Puppies, like he'd been telling him to buy for months.

Delbert's excavation began at the spot designated Number One on the grid. Ground zero, in Delbert's estimation, which was why he'd assigned it to himself. If he were Chlorine Moody, he'd have plunked a corpse in the yard's least visible corner. Since the garage was on the south and the next-door neighbor's house was a two-story, Leo's half of the yard was less likely to be a one-salesman cemetery.

Residual irritation was expended on the hole he was digging. The sun had baked the moisture from the soil faster than he'd anticipated. A plastic scoop wasn't a shovel, either. He'd reckoned metal trowels were forbidden for sample collecting, since arsenic had some metallic properties. That, or the sons of bitches who wrote the rules had stock in a plastic scoop factory.

Progressing from Number Two to Number Three, Delbert gritted his dentures against the aches rippling from his neck to his knees. After the shoe store, he and Leo were hitting Wal-Mart for a case of Bengay. And a fifth of bourbon, for later.

The scoop's handle bent double, throwing him off balance. Wouldn't you know, a soft, sandy spot he thought he'd lucked onto had a rock smack in the middle of it.

He pecked and scraped at it to gauge its size. About to shift position a mite, he noticed reddish, flaky shards clinging to the tip of the blade.

His stomach lurched, then do-si-doed. He stared at the scoop in horror, swallowing down the bile rising in his throat. *Shallow grave…shallow grave* beat like a dirge in time with his pulse.

Get ahold of yourself, you old fool. That hole's not but an inch or two deep. And bad as these goggles are steamed up, you couldn't tell a splotch of clay mud from…well, from this gunk that *ain't* what you think it is.

Delbert had nearly convinced himself when his mind registered the significance of a droning sound. Sunlight glinted off the roof of the white sedan rolling up the driveway. He dropped the scoop and cupped his hands around his mouth. "Schnur! Hit the dirt! She's back!"

A clack, then the roar of an air conditioner's compressor revving the engine was as sweet as a lullaby. Chlorine wouldn't run the air with the windows down. With them up, she couldn't have heard him mayday Leo.

As the garage door rumbled open on its track, Delbert tamped the grass plug in place and grabbed the bagged soil samples and the scoop. On the opposite side of the yard, Leo lay as still as a beached whale. Chlorine likely couldn't see him for the side fence. Safer, though, to wait for her car to pull in past the driver's side window.

On five, Delbert mouthed to Leo. He pointed at the duffel bag, then at Leo, then at their tunnel. A gloved finger, then another ticked off the signal. At four, Leo panicked and scuttled for the equipment bag. By five, the duffel had popped out the far side of the fence. Had Delbert counted to six, it would have marked when Leo got stuck in the brambles.

"Go, man, go," he whispered.

Leo rocked forward and backward. Branches rustled. Rose petals fluttered down like a scarlet blizzard. "I can't, I can't."

The dull thump of a car door's slam almost stopped Delbert's heart. If Chlorine didn't see them, she'd see half the blessed hedge shaking like a palm tree in a hurricane. *Then* she'd see them. Meaning *him*. The old bat would have to run around the block and up the alley to put a face to the big, fat ass wedged between her gate and the gatepost.

Lowering his head, Delbert rammed Leo square in the rump...and bounced backward a good three feet. Digging in his heels, he rammed him again, pushing for all he was worth.

One second, Schnur hadn't budged an inch; the next, they were both sprawled on their bellies in the alley. Delbert glanced back at the tunnel, expecting to see Chlorine's kisser where Leo's butt had been. He had to blink a few times to believe it wasn't.

With his voice muffled by the mask still covering his mouth, Leo panted, "Thank you."

"Don't mention it," Delbert groaned. "To *anybody*."

It wasn't until they were transferring the soil samples and scoops from their coveralls' pockets into the duffel bag, that Delbert realized his cap was missing.

A morning that started with the ten-feet-off-the-ground feeling David always had after making love with Hannah was skidding downhill faster than a hog on ice skates.

The sense that Rocco Jarek was involved in the Beauford homicide was stuck in neutral. "The dirtbag's guilty of something" was Marlin's typical assessment pending direct evidence or a confession. Absent was the excitement, the growing anticipation of a hunt nearing a satisfying conclusion.

Circumstances wouldn't allow it. Doubtful, they ever would. It was his and Marlin's tacit agreement that if Jarek was guilty, he couldn't have acted alone. This precluded any feeling of retribution for the victim.

His mood didn't improve by the time he crossed from the Outhouse to the courthouse across the street. Apart from wanting to get it over with, David wasn't in a rush to interview Kimmie Sue Beauford. What put his molars on edge was the certainty that a hog in ice skates picks up speed before it hits bottom.

He shouldn't have been surprised when he opened the door to his office and found Kimmie Sue lounging in his desk chair, painting her toenails. Opposite her, Deputy Bill Eustace was flipping through a copy of *Field & Stream*.

The desk had been cleared to make room for a pedicure kit, a box of assorted doughnuts, paper napkins and lidded, take-out coffee cups. The radio on the bookcase was thumping a rap song. The air reeked of polish remover and perfume.

Kimmie Sue and Eustace glanced up and smiled,

as if they were happy to see him. David was nearly blinded by the scarlet mist descending like a veil.

A hand circled his wrist. Claudina Burkholtz tugged David back out the door and closed it behind him. "I tried to catch you before you went in there."

David couldn't recall the last time he was so angry he couldn't speak. This one, he'd never forget. *What the fuck are they doing in my office?* must have read loud and clear in his eyes.

"Breathe," Claudina ordered, turning his back to the outer office. "And keep looking at me. Everybody's watching to see what you'll do. Lose your cool, and it'll be all over town before lunchtime."

She was right. David knew it, as surely as he knew how lucky he was to have her for a friend and ally. The less rational, forever-fourteen side of him just wanted to haul off and hit something.

"This isn't the end of the world," Claudina said. "It's not insubordination, either, much as a by-the-book hunk like you believes it is."

David was miles from a smile, but managed an inquiring "Hunk?"

Claudina's laugh was a tad shrill, but a pretty good impersonation of the real thing. Genuine enough, that he could feel waves of relief diffuse behind him. She winked at him and drawled, "You're not bad lookin' for a country boy. Especially when you're mad."

"Mad, hell. I—"

"Listen to me. What Bill Eustace did was wrong, but Bill wasn't alone in being wrong. Inside that bull-head of yours, you're asking yourself if you'd have done the same thing."

She held up her hand. "Okay, maybe you're too cussed *fond* of black-and-white to see gray, but there's right, and then there's righteous."

Tapping David's upper arm, as though they'd agreed the Cardinals had a shot at the pennant this year, Claudina stepped from in front of the door and walked away.

David took in and let out another of those breaths she'd prescribed, before he turned the doorknob for the second time. The hen-party atmosphere was mostly gone. The breakfast picnic and claptrap were stowed in a grocery sack. His desk appeared much as he'd left it earlier that morning, and Kimmie Sue had moved to the chair beside Eustace.

Perfume and acetone still pervaded the air. Nobody spoke as David walked over and adjusted the radio dial to KSAN. The Dixie Chicks' "Not Ready to Make Nice" wailed from the speaker. David wasn't, either, but Claudina's lecture had struck a nerve. He might not make her proud, but damned if he'd disappoint her.

"Ms. Beauford," he said, "if you'll excuse us a moment, there's a chair just outside the door."

She chuffed, her arms falling into her lap, as though incredulous he'd suggest such a thing. "But, David, I've been—"

Bill jerked his head at the door. "Go on, hon. We won't be long."

Kimmie Sue flounced out, her platform sandals spanking the linoleum floor. She'd either rolled out of bed in full makeup, a miniskirt and a top, or the officers let her bring her luggage along with her.

Bill rose from his chair. His expression was paternal or patronizing, depending on your point of view. "I already know what you're going to say, Sheriff. Kimmie Sue was supposed to dally in the processing room until you got around to talking to her."

David sucked in another breath. If this kept up, he'd hyperventilate before he asked Kimmie Sue a single question. "That wasn't a suggestion, Eustace. That was an order."

The deputy chuckled and shook his head. "Look, I don't know how these things are done down Tulsaway, but here, we show the sheriff's daughter the kind of respect—"

"Respect? Strange you should mention that, seeing as how *I'm* the sheriff, and I don't have a daughter."

"Aw, c'mon. You know what I meant."

"Yep. I do." David yanked open a desk drawer. He shuffled a stack of Beauford crime-scene photos. "Putting me in my place, your affection for Kimmie Sue, her father, the chief-deputy appointment that Knox has hinted at…" He slapped a photo on the desk. "They're all more important to you than *she* is."

"That's not…" Bill's voice trailed off. His gaze riveted on Bev's lifeless body, he shifted his weight, as though his discomfort were physical. He looked up, but not at David. "I—uh, I dunno what to say."

David returned the picture to the stack and dropped it in the drawer. "No need to say anything. Just tell Ms. Beauford to come in, then get back out on the road."

"Yes, sir." Pausing in the doorway, Bill turned and said, "It won't happen again, Sheriff."

David slammed the drawer shut with his knee. Yeah, it would, he thought. Eustace wasn't the only one in the department with divided loyalties. Being stuck between Larry Beauford's cronyism and Jessup Knox's empty promises was a lousy place for a sitting sheriff to be.

"Les Williams." The Sanity police lieutenant shook Hannah's hand and motioned at a chair. He was about her age, married, and did a fair job of hiding his dislike for drop-in visitors. "What can I do for you, Ms. Garvey?"

"A favor, I hope." Her smile was business-friendly, assuring him that idle chitchat wasn't her forte, either. "I'm looking for information on the disappearance of Royal Moody. The desk sergeant said you were the man to see about a cold case."

"Is this a matter of personal interest?"

Hannah nodded. So far, so true, even though murder had never been among the causes she'd manufactured to explain her own father's total absence. The very idea that Caroline Garvey could have poisoned John Doe and buried him in a trailer-park lot was laughable, as well as depressing.

For one, the Garvey clan was Effindale's version of the Beverly Hillbillies, except they couldn't have struck oil in a petroleum refinery. And, if Caroline had killed her anonymous lover, Hannah's grandmother would have ratted on her in an Illinois second. Faster, if a reward was offered. For fifty bucks, Maybelline Garvey would have sworn her daughter conspired with Lee Harvey Oswald, kidnapped Jimmy Hoffa and broke up the Beatles.

Hannah would never know who John Doe was, or why he abandoned her. In a way, homicide would have been easier to accept. She'd have had someone to blame, other than herself, as children invariably do. She could also stop hoping, ridiculous as it was, that someday he might appear, saying how sorry he was and what a fool he'd been.

From her purse, Hannah took a photocopy of the first newspaper story regarding Royal Moody's unknown whereabouts. Passing it to Lieutenant Williams, she said, "I have copies of other articles if you'd like to see them."

Williams signaled for a moment to skim the page. "The guy never turned up again, huh?"

"If anyone's heard from Mr. Moody in the past twenty-three years, I'm not aware of it."

Williams swiveled toward his computer. Over rapid, two-finger key taps, he said, "The Cold Case Unit was just created a couple of years ago." He glanced sideward. "And I'm it."

He leaned nearer the screen, then pushed back in his chair and strode to a bank of file cabinets. "Unsolved homicides are the priority since there's no statute of limitations."

Riffling through a file drawer, he added, "DNA evidence and forensic technology may put away some bad guys who thought they were in the clear."

And gals, Hannah thought, but allowed that *guys* was pretty much a gender-neutral term. Which brought to mind two gender-specific *guys,* otherwise known as Sam Spade Bisbee and his trusty sidekick, Mr. Potato Head.

She frowned, realizing everyone had received assignments at last night's meeting, but couldn't remember what Delbert and Leo's were.

"I found Moody's file," Williams said, curtailing what might have escalated to a panic attack. "But there isn't much in it. Just the original missing person's report and a memo noting the case was transferred to the sheriff's department."

Peachy. There went Hannah's assurance to David that Code Name: Epsilon was a Sanity PD case. "Why would it be transferred to the county?"

The lieutenant shrugged. "Looks like it was at their request—whose, isn't specified. If I had to guess, I'd say a deputy, or somebody working at the courthouse was a relative or close friend of the Moody family."

He laid the file on the desk and sat down. "Don't quote me, but it's also possible that someone here shoved it off on the county mounties. Hard to speculate on what might have happened twenty-three years ago."

"Where Royal Moody's concerned, it's even harder to find out anything concrete." Hannah lifted her chin in an obvious attempt to read the typewritten report upside-down. "All I have is a batch of old newspaper clippings."

To her surprise, Williams chuckled. "No offense, but my eight-year-old daughter's a lot smoother at laying on a hint."

"Oh, I can be smoother if it'll help."

He rolled his eyes. "You want a copy of the report? I'll make one, but there's really not much to go on in it, either. Mr. Moody's wife initiated the report. She said her husband had set out for Kentucky—Nashville or Knoxville, she wasn't sure. Moody didn't call home much from the road, and she couldn't supply the names of the motels he frequented."

"Doesn't that seem odd to you?" Hannah asked.

"Sure, long-distance calls cost more then than they do now, but as I understand it, Moody was gone two or three weeks at a time."

"He took the sales job after he was discharged from the navy," Williams countered. "Ships can be out to sea for months. Just more of the same for her, maybe."

"Okay, but no idea where he stayed, either? What if she had to reach him in an emergency?" Hannah raised her hand in surrender. "Sorry. Curiosity gets the best of me sometimes."

"Understandable. And I will admit, if I'd been the

responding officer, I'd have made a bigger pest of my-self." The lieutenant stood, report in hand, evidently preparing to make the copy he'd promised. "This personal interest you have. Are you a family member?"

She'd been prepared for the question at the beginning. Lying would have been easy when Lieutenant Williams was just a nameplate outside his office door. But if she didn't fudge the truth now, he might retract his offer to copy the report.

"Well," she hedged, "I'm not a *blood* relative."

His hesitation was germinating her imaginary, marital branch of the Moody family tree, when he said, "Even so, I probably shouldn't say this, but there is some truth in all those jokes about sailors and traveling salesmen."

Yes, and Hannah had a feeling that Rudy Moody had heard every one of them, a thousand times over.

11

"Why are you being so hateful, David?"

"I'm not, Ms. Beauford. All I'm—"

"Would it kill you to call me *Kimmie Sue?* Or Kim? We've known each other for *years* and I practically grew up in this office."

David pinched the bridge of his nose, trying to stanch the pain receptors in his forehead. He'd seen the woman three times in his entire life—present ordeal included. Everything she said, her tone of voice, the tears she turned on and off like a spigot were as fake as her eyelashes.

A glossy platinum fingernail tapped the desktop. "See that little red heart with my initials in it? I drew that with a marker for my daddy after he was elected sheriff the first time."

"Will you *knock it off?*" David flinched, as though he'd shouted it but couldn't stop himself. "You're not sweet sixteen, haven't been for damn near two decades, and if you don't cut the teenybopper wannabe crap now, I'll lock you in a cell, until you do, *Ms. Beauford.*"

Lord Almighty. If he didn't know better, he'd think Marlin Andrik had wired his mouth for sound. David glanced at the video and audio recorders set up in his office. The deputy monitoring them flashed him a grin and a thumbs-up.

David expected a gush of tears or a demand for a phone to call her attorney. Kimmie Sue bolted upright in the chair, pulled down that place mat of a skirt and clasped her hands on top of it. "I'm sorry, Sheriff. Really, I am. I guess I was retreating from all the stress and didn't realize it."

Her about-face transcended spooky. On videotape, that chameleon routine might lay the groundwork for an insanity plea. David warned himself to be careful. His presumed receptiveness to her might be a web she'd woven for him.

"Back to this surprise visit to your mother," he began. "How long did you and Mr. Jarek plan to stay in town?"

"Long enough to talk her into selling the house before it falls apart. Dad was the king of putting off until tomorrow what needed to be fixed years ago."

"You and Bev discussed the house sale previously?"

"I mentioned it after Dad's funeral." She smiled. "You knew Mom. Decisions weren't her thing. Especially when money was involved. The trick was leading her in the right direction but letting her think she was in charge."

David's expression was impassive, his mind tracking the consistent past-tense references to her mother. Years removed from his grandparents' death, his parents were still known to say, "Oh, Mother *loves* that hymn," or "Grampa Hendrickson *has* a coat just like that."

He said, "I presume you wanted Bev to sell the house and move to California with you."

"What?" Kimmie Sue laughed. "Oh, God, no. You obviously have no idea how much it costs to live in L.A." She gestured dismissively. "That house was too big for them when they bought it, but Mom just *had* to have it. With Dad gone, all she needed was a one-bedroom apartment."

"A cozy little place," David said, "where she wouldn't have to worry about maintenance and upkeep."

"Exactly."

"And could give you the proceeds from selling the house."

"Not give it to me." Kimmie Sue's tone inferred that David was as obtuse about high finance as her mother. "A loan." She hiked a shoulder. "An investment, actually. Like a backer invests in a film production, or a play on Broadway."

Or, David thought, a gambler stakes his life savings on a sure thing at Churchill Downs.

Kimmie Sue held her forefinger and thumb a fraction apart. "My agent says I'm this close to a casting call for the second lead in the new Richard Gere movie they're shooting next spring. It's mine. I can *feel* it. But I've got to have new head shots, audition tapes, clothes, vocal training…" She touched the back of her hand to her brow. "After this nightmare, I'll need a month at a spa to get my cortisol levels back to normal."

At his inquiring look, she explained that cortisol is a stress hormone, then began itemizing its hideous, fat-boosting side effects. "You can starve yourself and still—"

"Let's back up to your homecoming," David said. "When did you and Jarek get into town?"

Either the change in subject or its abruptness annoyed her. "Why do you keep asking what you already know?" Her sandal tapped the floor. "Yesterday afternoon."

"What time?"

"Two-ish. Maybe a little later. The old hag at that filthy motel can give you the *exact* time."

"What if I told you a witness puts Jarek's vehicle in your mother's driveway Wednesday afternoon."

"You'd be lying. Or your 'witness' is."

In the manner of one poor lie being a feint before the knock-out punch, he said, "What if I told you we have proof that Jarek was at your mother's house prior to yesterday afternoon."

"Same answer. You're lying."

David placed Jarek's fingerprint-ident card and a crime-scene photo side by side on the desk. He pointed at the card's right index finger, then the close-up shot of the latent lifted from Bev's rearview mirror. "People lie, Ms. Beauford. Fingerprints don't."

When she leaned forward, her nostrils flared as she looked from one to the other. "That's *impossible*. Rocco's never been to Mom's house. I swear, he hasn't."

"Then how'd his print get—"

"It's a trick." Her hands balled into fists. "You, or that detective, planted it to incriminate him." Her eyes narrowed. "Dad talked about it all the time. How if you know what you're doing, you can frame somebody by transferring his fingerprint to evidence from a crime scene."

In theory, yes. In practice, forged fingerprints don't

withstand scrutiny. The one attempted forgery David was aware of made national news, when an expert noticed several latents introduced as evidence were absolutely identical.

Fingerprints are unique to an individual, but the impressions they leave will vary. Because of positioning and pressure, a burglar's latent lifted off a CD case won't be *exactly* the same as one from the big-screen TV he lugged out the door.

"Look at the time-date stamp on that photograph, Ms. Beauford. Now, I'd truly love to hear how you think we transferred that print to your mom's car, three hours before we knew Rodney Windle, aka Rocco Jarek, existed."

That knocked the wind out of her. She fell back in the chair, her aerosol tan appearing to hover an inch away from her face.

"He was there, Kimmie Sue. Wednesday afternoon, not yesterday. You *both* were. You were in the house, waiting for Bev when she got home."

"No!"

"Oh, you surprised her, all right. Didn't even let her unload her car before you started badgering her about money."

"That's a lie! I wasn't *there.*" A fist pounded the desk. "Will you listen to me? The first time I've been in that house since Daddy's funeral was *last night*—with *you*."

David sensed she was telling the truth, and said so. His interview skills weren't as honed as Marlin's, but he knew when to let a fish run out some line, and when to reel it in.

"Beg pardon, Kimmie Sue, for misjudging you."

"That's a pretty lame apology, but I'll—"

"Of course, you weren't at the house with Jarek. Gals like you get things done *for* them." David stood and walked around the desk. The brainteaser that confounded everyone at the scene was the key to the entire case.

"If this is the good-cop half of your act," Kimmie Sue sneered, "it's pathetic."

David leaned his backside against the desk and planted his hands on its shellacked surface. "Like you said, you were raised around cops. Picked up all sorts of interesting trivia about criminal investigation."

She rolled her eyes. "Bor-ing."

"Like how turning down the central air at the house affects determining a victim's time of death." Bending at the waist, he added, "Keeps down the smell longer, too, huh."

She recoiled, horror contorting, deforming her features. "Is that...oh, God, please, *stop*."

"You scripted it for Jarek. Drew him a floor plan of the house. Made sure he wore gloves and gave him pointers on how to make murder look like a burglary gone bad."

"No, no."

"I'll grant, that thermostat had me stumped till you mentioned fingerprint forgery. Lowering the temp was a smart move, except for pointing to a murderer with inside knowledge."

"Bullshit." The presiding judge in the courtroom at the building's far end must have heard her. "Everybody that watches *CSI* knows that."

David bent his head back and stared at the ceiling. His belly felt as if he'd eaten razor blades for breakfast.

To the white-globed fixture above him, he said quietly, "Everybody that watches television doesn't have a motive to kill your mother."

"I didn't hurt her. I'd *never* hurt her. I *loved* her."

"All those people watching CSI aren't Bev's sole beneficiary, either." David lowered his eyes. "And they don't have a boyfriend whose fingerprint was on the mirror in the car she had cleaned inside and out the day before she died."

Kimmie Sue looked at him, her face slack, her body limp, as though waking from anesthesia. She was thinking, though. Hard and fast. Weighing her options, David assumed. Demand counsel? Play innocent and shift all the blame on Jarek? Try to cut a plea bargain for herself by flipping on him? Or go mental again and let the psychiatrists duke it out?

Presently, she said, "Rocco and I had nothing to do with my mother's death. If we hadn't stopped in Joplin because of the storms, we might have gotten here in time to save her life."

"That's two hours—"

"I know how his fingerprint got on the mirror."

"Uh-huh."

"It was back in March. The sixteenth, I think. The date'll be on my credit card statement."

"Yours? Or your mother's?"

"The card is in Mom's name, but mine's on the account." She fidgeted. "It was just for emergencies."

David figured a manicure was an emergency to her, but Marlin probably had the account information and copies of the statements by now.

"Rocco had this calendar shoot in Miami Beach. I was between jobs, so I flew out with him. We were scheduled for a two-hour layover in Kansas City, but it started sleeting and they grounded all the flights out."

She paused, her eyes awash in tears. Wiping them away, she stammered, "I—I just realized, that was the last time I saw Mom."

David prompted, "What was?"

"That night, in Kansas City. I called her—you know, to tell her we were stuck at KC-I until morning. She insisted on coming up there to take us out to dinner."

"Let me get this straight. An ice storm grounded your plane, but Bev *drove* up there to meet you at the airport?"

"It was in the middle of the afternoon, David. The highways were fine. If it started to get slick, Mom was going to stay at the hotel with us."

"Go on."

"I know how this sounds, but it's the truth. Ice and snow didn't faze her. She's used to it, but city traffic made her nervous, so Rocco drove us to the restaurant, and—"

"When he adjusted the rearview mirror," David broke in, "that's how his print got on it."

"Yes! That's the only possible way it *could* have."

David ought to be insulted that she thought he was dumber than rocks and the box they came in. Instead, he just felt profoundly sad.

During business hours, parking spaces around the town square were in greater demand than the available supply. A mossy carriage block and a couple of surviving hitching posts beloved by the historical society had Hannah wondering how streets built for horse-drawn wagons and carriages could be too narrow to accommodate motorized vehicles. Dodge City never had traffic jams like this in *Gunsmoke* episodes.

On her fourth circuit, the parking gods smiled on her—about average on a sunny day. Rain brought out the Dramamine and her finger-happy inner bitch.

Hannah waved at the security camera above the Outhouse's exterior door. Annoying Marlin Andrik was always fun. It also beat confessing to David that Code Name: Epsilon was by default, a cold county case.

A buzzer extended an invitation to pull open the Outhouse's heavy, tinted glass door. Twice before, she hadn't responded fast enough and had to press the stupid buzzer again. Making it three would put Marlin in a good mood, but Hannah had her pride.

Even without the sudden switch from bright sunlight to gloom, entering the detective unit's headquarters was always disconcerting. She nodded at Josh Phelps and Cletus Orr, each involved in an apparent one-sided phone conversation, of which they weren't the active participants. Marlin was also on the phone, but cradled the receiver before Hannah reached his grotto at the back of the room.

"What's up, toots?" He stood, like the gentleman

he was, despite compelling evidence to the contrary. "You taking me to lunch?"

Hannah sneered at the nickname, as expected. If Marlin had a clue she liked it, he'd be crushed. "Sure," she said. "Why not? You pick the place. I'll pick up the check."

He sighed. "Thanks, but I'm babysitting Clyde in the interrogation room, while Hendrickson does the rubber-hose number on Bonnie at the courthouse."

She frowned, as did her stomach, which hadn't considered food until a second ago, but was now highly in favor of having some. "Well, if you can't go to lunch, why'd you even bring it up?"

"For the rain check you have to give me," he said, as though she was born yesterday and accidentally dropped on her head. "Otherwise, you'd get to bug me about God knows what for nothing."

While Marlin answered another phone call, Hannah sat down and pondered the Andrik Free Lunch program. She could have used the Garvey version in Chicago, but there are two sides to every promissory note. By Marlin's reckoning, she owed him lunch, but that obliged his cooperation now. She hoped.

He grunted monosyllables into the receiver and scribbled illegible notes on a legal pad, leaving her to peruse the anthropological study that was his desk.

Pencils and pens. Exacto knives and bullets. A magnifier, tissues and mutant tweezers. An accordion file's flap hung dangerously near his smoldering plant saucer-ashtray. A gnawed jumbo Butterfinger and a diet Coke can rested atop the two-volume L.A. County business pages atop a closed laptop computer. A five-by-seven studio portrait of his wife and two teenage children smiled out at enlarged crime-scene photos, photocopied bank statements and pawn shop stubs.

Near his elbow were a pile of clear-plastic evidence bags anchored by a clothing catalog and three library books. Their spines were considerably easier to read upside down than a yellowed Sanity Police Department missing persons' report: a Kathy Mallory mystery by Carol O'Connell, a Caribbean travel guide and a biography of the Duchess of Windsor.

Eclectic, to say the least. Hannah's eyes strayed to the logo on an envelope sticking out from under the bottom book.

"Jeezo-peezo," Marlin said, hanging up the phone. "Hey, Grasshopper," he yelled to Josh Phelps. "Take my calls for a while. Unless it's Hendrickson or my wife, I'm in the can reading War and friggin' Peace."

"Maybe I should come back another time," Hannah said.

"The hell. You're my excuse to slack off." He shook a Marlboro from the pack on the desk, saw that it was one of two remaining, then tamped it back in. "Fieldwork, I like. They should've executed Alexander Graham Bell when they had the chance."

"After they tortured him. Telemarketer calls 24/7, until he begged for mercy."

Marlin did the lip twitch she assumed was a smile. David attributed it to a muscle spasm, but admitted it happened more frequently when Hannah was around.

The first time they met, she'd topped Marlin's prime-suspect list in a homicide investigation. From that auspicious beginning, they'd gradually grown on each other. They weren't exactly friends and certainly not enemies. More like fraternal twins separated at birth making up for all that lost sibling rivalry.

Hannah pointed at the library books. "Thinking about a cruise to get away from it all?"

"Yeah, sure, toots. Being stuck in the middle of an ocean with a boatload of drones is just what I need to relax." He glanced at the books. "All this stuff's from the Beauford house."

"I'm sorry, Marlin. I know she was a friend."

"Uh-huh. The wife's pretty torn up about it." In other words, tough guys don't grieve in front of a witness.

"Funny, but I'm a Carol O'Connell fan, too," she said. "And I get that clothing catalog. At least I did, when I could afford the clothes."

"Expensive, huh?" Marlin tugged it from under the pile. "Like what, Victoria's Secret expensive?"

Hannah squelched a grin, imagining his horror at bras and panties that cost more than his favorite sport coat. "Closer to Saks Fifth Avenue expensive. Plus shipping and handling."

"No shit?" He set the catalog aside, rather than return it to the stack.

Leaning forward, Hannah indicated the envelope under the Windsor biography. "What's really weird is that years ago, GMEI was one of our clients at Friedlich & Friedlich. Rob Friedlich designed that logo on the envelope."

A hot, multinational advertising agency lured away GMEI, and F&F took a major hit in the accounts receivable department, after its CEOs spent their projected earnings before they were earned.

Marlin regarded Bev Beauford's personal effects with increasing interest. "So, what's GMEI stand for, anyway?" he asked, pronouncing it "Jimmy-I."

"Global Media Entertainment, International," Hannah said. "It's a conglomerate that distributes everything from retro hula hoops and video-game systems to LED stadium screens and surround-sound equipment."

"They do direct marketing?"

"It's possible, I guess. Like I said, it wasn't my account and it wasn't Rob Friedlich's for more than a few weeks. GMEI is the shark of leisure-time activities. They gobble small distributors and manufacturers as if they were minnows."

"Name a big company that doesn't." Marlin's nicotine lust got the better of him. He inhaled carcinogens and exhaled bliss. "Since I'm slicing another seven minutes off my life expectancy, you'd better tell me why you're here, in case that's all I've got left."

"Not funny, Marlin."

"Like I've told you before, toots, I'm a realist with a piss-poor attitude." He tapped the cigarette on the ashtray. "Plus, somebody's gonna blow the whistle on my recess any second."

For the second time in as many hours, she handed over a copy of the newspaper article on the Moody disappearance to a criminal investigator. "I realize this was before your time, but the Sanity police say the case files were transferred to the county. I thought maybe they're here, or you could tell me where to look."

"Why." It wasn't a question.

She gave him the easy explanation. "Something

David said the day you arrested Rudy Moody piqued my curiosity about his father. It's bothered me ever since."

"You? Or the wackos at Geritol Springs?"

"Let's call it a little of both."

"Here's a better idea. Let's call it nothin' doin'." Marlin started to return the photocopy, then squinted at the date. "Who told you the file was transferred to us?"

"Lieutenant Williams."

"Good man. Wish he'd promote himself to the sheriff's payroll." Marlin handed the copy over. "He's wrong about the files, though. Neimon Vestal was chief of detectives back then. He wouldn't blow his nose on a city case."

"I saw the memo noting the transfer. The lieutenant thought somebody in the courthouse had a special interest in it."

Marlin's chin buckled. "Didn't happen. If a friggin' meter maid had tried to moonlight it, Neimon would've heard, and then there'd have been two missing persons."

Arguing would trim minutes off Hannah's life expectancy and she wouldn't even get a nicotine buzz out of it. Puppy-dog eyes had worked in the past. Not today. Switching to an *I can be as stubborn as you can* glare didn't, either. Marlin owned the copyright and the patent.

"That file has to be somewhere," she said, her eyes cutting to the mismatched file cabinets lining the wall. "Twenty-three years old or not, it didn't vanish into thin air."

Marlin stubbed out his cigarette. "You don't really want me to look for it, do you?"

"Here's a tip. Try *M* for Moody."

"Cute." He yelled at Phelps, "Take the hold off my calls. The next one's mine, no matter who the hell it is." Pushing to his feet, he said to Hannah, "The file's not here, toots."

"But—"

"If by some friggin' miracle it is, I won't let you see it, and you'll go ballistic and try to grab it, and I'll have to arrest you for assault. So whaddya say we spare me, you and the bail bondsman the hassle. Okay?"

"Fine." Hannah grabbed her shoulder bag and started for the door. Spinning around, she said, "But you can forget about that rain check on lunch."

Marlin jammed his hands into his trouser pockets. "Call me psychic, but I had a feeling you were gonna say that."

* * *

Delbert sat hunched over in the waiting room's chrome-and-vinyl sling chair. His forearms were braced on his thighs. His lucky golf cap spun in his hands. A talk-radio program nattered from somewhere in the back of the cinder-block building. The joint smelled like fertilizer—chemical, not manure.

The girl at the counter understood *rush* well enough when she'd charged him triple in advance. Highway robbery—no question about it—but he'd paid it, knowing full well a lab test for a specific element is quicker and ought to be cheaper than a soup-to-nuts soil analysis.

Three hours. That's how long it'd been since he dropped off the bagged samples. He felt older than the dirt in 'em, too, but it hadn't stopped him from getting the job done. And he'd had Leo along for the ride, for God's sake.

From Chlorine's place, Delbert had chucked their gear down the hospital's biohazard chute and proceeded to the truck stop on the north side of town. Schnur balked at paying for a shower he could have at home for free, but he'd sung a different tune—awful German opera at the top of his damned lungs—after Delbert shoved him into the stall.

The truck stop's water pressure was double that at

Valhalla Springs. The scalding liquid massage was wonderful. Better than the magic-fingers kind Delbert had had at those motels with a coin box bolted to the bedframe.

Then Leo refused to walk sock-footed into the dingdanged shoe store. Delbert argued that it was the same as buying a raincoat when it was raining. Fortunately, he'd only shuttled three pairs out to the curb before one of them fit. A top-of-the-line Hush Puppy model, with a sticker price to prove it.

After that, Delbert dropped thirty-one simoleons plus tax at Wal-Mart for booze and Bengay, sprang for lunch at a fast-food place, gassed up the Edsel, then took Leo home and hied back to the testing lab.

By the time Code Name: Epsilon was stamped Mission Accomplished, Delbert figured he'd have enough change left from his pension check to buy a tin cup to panhandle with.

"Are you Mr. Bisbee?"

Delbert scowled up at a young jake with glasses as thick as Leo's, but a full head of curly hair. He glanced around at the room's other five empty chairs. "Good guess, picking me outta the crowd like that."

The jake introduced himself as Kerry Scott, the lab's head honcho, apologized for the delay, then gestured at an open doorway. "Step into my office, Mr. Bisbee. I'd like to discuss my findings with you."

Delbert made a show of checking his watch. "Wish I could, son, but there's someplace I gotta be in about five minutes. Just give me the report and I'll come back—"

"Sorry. I won't release it until you've answered a few questions."

"Whaddya mean, release it?" Delbert blustered. "I *paid* for it. Out the ying-yang, I don't mind telling you. Now, hand it over and I'll be on my way."

That's the problem with young folks these days, he thought a few moments later, taking a seat in Scott's office. No respect for their elders.

"I'm not familiar with the address you gave on the form. Where do you live, Mr. Bisbee?"

"In Valhalla Springs."

"Really." Scott consulted the huge topographical map taped to the wall. "I'm not aware that there was ever an orchard in that area."

"An orchard? You mean, like fruit trees?" Delbert shook his head. "Jack Clancy planted cherry trees here and there and around the golf course, but it's a far cry from what I'd call an orchard."

"And too recent." Still focused on the map, Scott went on, "Prior to 1947, growers all over the country sprayed pesticides with high arsenic concentrations on their trees. It was cheap and it worked, but it also saturated the soil. In some instances, the groundwater and nearby wells were tainted."

Hot ziggety. Delbert barely resisted the urge to toss his cap in the air. The lab jockey'd confirmed their samples contained arsenic and not just a pinch of it, either. If they'd been clean, Scott wouldn't be yapping about bug spray and fruit farming.

He turned away from the map. "Which means your samples didn't come from Valhalla Springs, Mr. Bisbee."

Delbert started, even though he'd confabulated a pip of a story, in the event he needed one. Contingency plans—no smart P.I. left home without 'em.

"Well now, Dr. Scott, I can see where the confusion derived from." Sitting back, Delbert crossed his legs and hung an arm over the back of the chair. "First off, that form didn't allow for a location that doesn't have a street address. I plugged in mine, instead of leaving it at 'out a ways on VV highway.'"

The lab superintendent appeared less than impressed by that reasoning.

"Here's the thing. Me being founder and president of the Valhalla Springs Treasure Hunters Club, I lead metal-detecting expeditions where nobody's tromped around for no-telling how long." Delbert waved at the map. "Unless you're familiar with what folks call the old Sandusky place, I can't narrow it—"

"I know exactly where it is," Scott said.

"You *do?*" Delbert cleared his throat and willed himself to stay calm. He'd gotten what he'd come for. All he had to do was stick to his story. "Then you know about the family plot north of the old home place."

Finally, he had Scott's attention. "No, actually, I don't. We soil-tested the property adjoining it."

A cough disguised Delbert's sigh of relief. Back in the spring, Walt Wagonner spied what he thought were gravestones poking up on the far side of a deep, brushy draw. Dusk was falling, leaves were rustling, and Walt scared the bejesus out of them with a load of hooey about the Sandusky Curse.

They'd never gone back. Delbert intended to—by himself, if Walt and the other nancies begged off. He just hadn't found the time, yet.

"Besides leadershipping the club," he said, "I ascertain and assess the hazard potential of a location vis-a-vis the possibility of somebody getting hurt."

Scott made a noise and covered his mouth with his hand. Odd ducks, these scientific types. Delbert continued, "When I found out arsenic's common to old cemeteries, I bagged up those dirt samples lickety-split."

"A wise precaution, Mr. Bisbee." Scott passed him a computer printout. "The accepted concentration standards for children frequently exposed to contaminated soil is thirty-seven milligrams per kilogram, or less."

"Humph. That works out to what, a speck in a little over two pounds of dirt?"

"Yes, if by speck, you mean virtually invisible to the human eye. Now, for occasional adult exposure, the ratio increases to one-hundred-and-seventy-five milligrams per kilogram." Scott's head tick-tocked. "Approximately a tenth of a teaspoon in the same amount of soil."

Still pretty skimpy, Delbert thought. A full teaspoon of arsenic in Royal's chili, or however Chlorine got it down his craw, would have hit him like a runaway Freightliner.

"Your club members," Scott said. "Have any of them complained of a red, itchy rash or skin lesions?" His fingertips grazed his neck. "A scratchy throat, perhaps? Watery eyes?"

"No, sirree. We had on coveralls, gloves, goggles, masks, the works." Realizing that was too much gear for a metal-detecting expedition at the tail end of July, Delbert hastened to add, "Leastwise, we will, next time we go metal-detecting out there."

Scott sucked air through his teeth. "I'd strongly advise finding another site, Mr. Bisbee. Judging from my analysis, the samples you collected show a concentration slightly above four hundred milligrams per kilogram."

"No sh—er, no kiddin'?" An involuntary shiver tracked down Delbert's spine. "Which ones?"

"Excuse me?"

"Which numbers," Delbert enunciated, "on which bags tested high for arsenic? They can't all be the same, coming from different parts of the yar—the graveyard."

Scott looked at him as though Delbert's ears needed a good scrub with a Q-tip. "This is a composite analysis, Mr. Bisbee. Contamination patterns vary too much for an accurate result on small, individual samples."

Delbert stifled a groan. He'd told that dingbat female clerk what he wanted when he brought them in. Composite, hell. All that gridding and numbering, scooping and bagging, and still no X marked the spot where Royal was planted.

He was there, though, by cracky. And they were a step closer to proving it.

As for the test results, they'd stay his little secret. He'd watch Leo like a hawk for any of the symptoms Scott mentioned, but knowing how much poison was in that dirt would make anybody break out in a rash.

12

Hannah swigged her iced tea. She swallowed and touched the glass to each cheek then her forehead. "The sign of the demented," she said, returning the sweaty glass to the table beside her chair.

The porch was too hot, even with the fan from the bedroom balanced on the railing. Inside, it was too cold. Malcolm, of course, was in dog nirvana, snoozing on the great room rug, but he had fur, and she was philosophically opposed to wearing a sweater with shorts.

Feeling herself slowly melt and mummify simultaneously did have its advantages. The computer's power cords wouldn't reach to the porch, and her side table wasn't big enough or sturdy enough to hold the components. Hence, the numerous e-mails with attached employment applications from Jack's secretary were logistically unavailable for review.

Besides, Hannah rationalized, during the summer months, nobody in corporate America did any actual work after noon on a Friday.

At the top of her legal pad was a list of titles for her nascent empire. One stood out, The Garvey Group. Granted, the agency would be a sole proprietorship whereas The Garvey Group alluded to—well, a group, as in two or more principals. But this was advertising and advertising was all about illusion.

It could be done. The numbers Hannah crunched assured that. Start small. Stay small. Don't reinvent the wheel. This time, she'd have a career *and* a life.

No, this time she'd have a life with a career. And if career intruded on Mrs. Sheriff David Hendrickson, she'd dump The Garvey Group and…buy a cow, or something.

Her gaze flicked to the doodle of a floor-length strapless gown. It was simple, elegant, and hid all traces of the hot-fudge sundae with mocha whipped cream she'd snarfed before daring herself to go into the dress shop.

Jonesing for chocolate was Marlin Andrik's fault. Her visit to the Outhouse had gone so splendidly, a hot fudge infusion wasn't just deserved, it was mandatory. If Mr. Personality wasn't a workaholic, his wife would probably tip the scales at nine hundred pounds. Or be his ex-wife. Or his widow.

At a rumbling sound, Hannah looked up and was instantly blinded by sunlight reflecting off a car's windshield. A turquoise Edsel's windshield, to be exact, with an old fart behind the wheel.

She froze, watching the aircraft carrier with white-wall tires drive up Valhalla Springs Boulevard. The porch shade is deep, Hannah intoned silently, and I am invisible.

The Edsel's front bumper passed the first leg of the cottage's circle driveway. *Yes, my liege. Return to Castle Bisbee, posthaste.* Delbert's profile in the side window was as fixed as a cameo's. Going...going...gone.

A tiny *ah* of relief escaped Hannah's lips. Delbert was home, safe from wherever the heck he'd been all day, and she was free to empire-build and doodle wedding dresses and toy with ideas for getting back at Marlin for being such an asshole at times.

By some auditory freak of nature, she didn't hear the Edsel's mellifluous motor before its front wheels rolled into the driveway. Yanking her feet off the rail, she crammed her notes and printouts at the back of the legal pad and flipped its pages forward to a blank sheet.

"The AC's broke again, huh," Delbert called, moving from the driver's door toward the trunk. His green, blue and red striped shirt tucked into yellow striped shorts resembled a TV test pattern after a bad hit of acid. "Lemme get my toolbox and I'll have 'er—"

"Oh, God, not the toolbox," Hannah said, as some might say, *Oh, God, not the bone saw.* "The air's working fine." She raised her hand. "Scout's honor."

"Then what the hell are you doing out here? Waiting on a bus?"

Yeah, she thought, to take me somewhere less infested with irritable and irritating geezers. "I'm communing with nature."

"Humph." Delbert pulled open the screen door. "I've had all the nature I can stand for one day."

So had she, but intuition and his gimpy gait said he hadn't been out bird-watching or netting butterflies. Hannah switched off the fan and followed him inside.

"How many holes did you and Leo get in today?" she inquired, knowing full well that he and his compadre hadn't been on the golf course, either.

"Holes?" Delbert plunked down in the chair beside her desk. "How'd you—" He blinked. "Oh. Uh, none. Lost our tee time." Mangling his golf cap as if it were a dishrag, he said, "What'd you get out of the Sanity PD?"

She stowed the legal pad in a bottom drawer, then took the copied police report from the Epsilon file.

She could tease him with it until he told her where he'd been and what he'd been doing. On the other hand, what she didn't know, she needn't lie about to David later on.

"The cold-case investigator gave me this," she said, holding out the report, "but it's pretty much a waste of toner. Supposedly whatever else was in Moody's file was transferred to the sheriff's department. I went down swinging there, too."

Delbert glanced up from the paper. "Why the sheriff's department?"

"Excellent question." She sat down in the swivel chair and repeated the answers she'd received, including Marlin's insistence that the transfer never happened.

"Thanks for trying, ladybug. I didn't figure on a jackpot, it being so long ago and just a missing—" Delbert leapt to his feet. "Yeehaw and hallelujah." He clapped her cheeks and smacked a kiss on her lips. "I've racked my brain for days trying to figure out how to get this, and holy comoglies, you did it!"

"I did?" Hannah cocked her head, delighted to have been so helpful, but how escaped her.

"People disappear. Cars don't." He tapped the computer monitor. "Now, get this thing cracka-lackin'."

While it booted up, he said he'd called Eldredge

Randal, the insurance agent named on the sticker on Chlorine's bumper, assuming Randal might have also written the policy on Royal's car.

"People didn't used to change insurance companies like yesterday's socks. A gal that poisoned her husband would be less inclined."

"Allegedly poisoned," Hannah said.

Delbert's grin had an elfin quality—adorable and devious. "Anywho, a neighbor had told me the make, model and year of Royal's car. From that, I knew the first part of its vehicle identification number had to be 1GN69. The tenth digit was D for the model year. The rest could be any letter or number, but the insurance dude wouldn't give 'em to me."

Hannah clicked the icon for the Internet provider. "Okay, you're champing to tell me how you knew *that* much."

"You would, too, if you'd read the *Secrets of the Masters of Criminal Investigation*."

Hannah had tried. She'd curled up on the couch eager to learn a few marginally legal tricks and techniques, mostly to stay a step ahead of Sherlock Bisbee. And might have gotten past the first chapter, if it hadn't read like a James Bond novel ghostwritten by William Makepeace Thackeray.

"The 1 is for cars made in the U.S. of A.," Delbert

said. "Moody's was a Chevy—a G for General Motors. Then there's the vehicle type code and body style."

He interrupted himself to dictate the Web site address of a subscription-only vehicle locater search engine. "Now the hitch comes in, with the codes for the engine type and series. Number 9 is a check digit—could be anything. Then 11 through 17 indicate the assembly plant and the car's production sequence. A man could spend ten years trying to guess them and still get 'em wrong."

Hannah stared at Delbert in amazement. "Wow. You're really something, you know that?"

Ever humble, he said, "Sure," then reached over her to type in his password to access the Web site's search function. Pointing at the police report, he said, "Put in Moody's VIN from the police report in that box, click on Submit and cross your fingers."

A dotted line zipped back and forth across the screen—a cyberspacial "Hold, please, for that information." Hannah watched it, thinking how shrewd she'd been to skip the vehicular part of the report, hoping to find a solid clue. That forest-for-the-trees thing; a Garvey ancestor might have coined it. Nearsightedness did run in the family.

A sense she'd missed something else bubbled at

the back of her mind but refused to migrate to the front. Borrowing the report from Delbert, she was visually scouring it when he cuffed her shoulder, scaring the crap out of her.

"Eureka! There 'tis, ladybug. In black and by God white."

The text was royal blue and the background gray, but Hannah didn't quibble. The four columns beneath the Detailed Vehicle History header revealed the Chevy's state inspection and registration dates and locations and its mileage readings. Three months after a "Title Issued or Updated" reference was sourced Missouri Department of Vehicles, Sanity, Missouri, a subsequent update noted a new owner and registration in Ottawa, Kansas. Delbert was prancing in place. "Scroll down, scroll down."

At the bottom of the next screen, the last of three triangular FYI icons referred to a dismantled title.

Hannah looked up. "What's that mean?"

Hijacking the mouse, Delbert initiated the computer's print function. "Could be, it was totaled in a wreck. Engine, maybe the transmission, went kablooey. The new owner might've junked it instead of fixing it."

Another mouse click evicted them from the Internet.

"Hey." She slapped his hand. "I was reading that."

Whisking the printouts from the machine, he put

the police report on top and picked up the cap he'd dropped on the floor. "Later, gator. I gotta copy these for tonight's meeting."

What meeting?

He paused at the door, adding, "Say, seven bells. Seven and a half, at the outside."

"But—"

Delbert waved at the breakfast room. "And turn down the air a mite, will ya?"

Hannah stared after him, then glanced down at Malcolm, roused from his nap by Delbert's hoots and victory dance. The pooch loved watching the computer screen, almost as much as TV.

Moomph. He cocked an ear. *I wanna see* couldn't have been clearer, if he'd clamped a pencil between his teeth and written Hannah a note.

"Sorry, big guy. We're both out of luck. I could bring up the Web site's home page again, but that's it. The sneaky old fart typed in the password himself, and I doubt it's 'open sesame.'"

Or even Leo's version, "the open says me."

Hannah swiveled around and grabbed the mouse. It was worth a shot, though.

What better place to hold a pity party, David thought, watching a roach stumble across the Outhouse's shag carpet. We ought to rent it out. Twenty bucks an hour. Could fetch thirty, after dark.

Josh Phelps had loaned him his desk chair, sparing David the discomfort of that plastic patio crap. The rookie investigator sat on his desk, facing Marlin's. Junior Duckworth had availed himself of Cletus Orr's swivel chair, after Marlin sent Cletus home to sleep off a sinus headache.

Kimmie Sue Beauford and Rocco Jarek had been cut loose. Marlin wanted to hold Jarek to the legal limit, essentially because he could. David demurred.

The detective's arms were winged behind his neck, his feet crossed on the desk. "Police work just doesn't get any better than this, gentlemen. Bust your ass for pretty much thirty-four hours straight building a case, then sit back and bond after it all goes to shit."

He grunted. "Present company excepted on the 'goes to shit' part."

"Don't let the mule drive the wagon," David said. "I didn't believe Kimmie Sue's alibi, either. Truth be told, it kind of pisses me off that it all checked out. That fingerprint, in particular."

"So they had dinner with Bev in Kansas City," Marlin argued. "BFD. It doesn't prove that's when Jarek left the print."

David planted a boot on the floor and crossed the

other one over it. "It's not logical that he wore gloves to toss the house, adjust the thermostat, strangle Bev and open her car door, then took one off to check his hairdo in her rearview mirror."

Phelps nodded, then caught himself. Rookies don't side with the opposition when the chief is looking. It tends to lead to evidence-recovery assignments in Dumpsters and crawl spaces.

"Okay," Marlin said, "it might be a red herring. It doesn't exclude Jarek from the crime scene, though."

David allowed that it didn't. Trouble was, it didn't put him there, either.

Junior Duckworth sighed and shook his head. "Bev pawning her own jewelry to pay her bills. That's just...wrong." He fiddled with his tie tack, as if it were a one-bead rosary. "I tried to dissuade her from that huge, expensive funeral she wanted for Larry. She wouldn't listen. Said she didn't care how long she had to make payments on it, he deserved the best money could buy."

"Seems she felt the same way about that worthless daughter of hers." Marlin leaned forward and riffled a pile of bank, credit card and loan statements. "Bev was sliding toward bankrupting herself, supporting Malibu Barbie—and her plastic surgeon. As far as we can tell, Kimmie Sue hasn't held down a real job since she flipped burgers during high school."

Phelps said to David, "Doesn't that contradict Ms. Beauford's statement? She told you she was here to talk her mother into selling the house and moving to an apartment." He spread his hands. "Between Bev's first mortgage and the second, there wouldn't have been enough equity left to pay the deposit and first month's rent."

"Kimmie Sue could have been lying," David admitted. "Or she didn't know the house was already mortgaged to the chimney cap."

"House or no house, Kimmie Sue still has a money motive," Marlin pointed out. "Homicide doubles the indemnity on Bev's insurance to fifty large."

"Follow the money." Phelps grinned. "I wish I had some for every time I've heard that."

"Damn right, Grasshopper. Name two homicides, since the day I started wishing you were never born, when the perp wasn't trying to keep his cash or was after somebody else's."

David mentally reviewed the recent closed cases and realized why Marlin asked for two examples, not one. The incident that had triggered the excessive-force lawsuit against David was in self-defense, not money-motivated.

A glare indicated how little David appreciated being included in the pop quiz. It missed its target, who was squinting up at the security monitor wired to the front door's videocam. "Screw that friggin' buzzer," Marlin muttered, and pressed a button to disengage the lock.

Nicole Ng, the department's summer intern, walked in carrying a file folder as though it might bite. The criminology major's white slacks were as dirt-streaked as her blouse. Her clean face and hands suggested she'd washed up in the ladies' as best she could.

"This is the only one I found," she said, handing the folder to Marlin, "and I looked through every carton in the basement."

His scowl softened. He may have smiled. "Good job, Nicole. I appreciate it."

"Is there anything else I can do?"

At the detective's curt *no thanks,* David said, "It's nearly quitting time, anyway, Nicole. Why don't you get a head start on the weekend?"

Junior Duckworth stood and said, "I'd better be going, myself. My brother's on a house call and I don't like leaving Mother alone too long at the funeral home."

After Marlin buzzed them out, he said, "Alone? From what I hear, LaVada Duckworth talks to dead people. And thinks they talk back."

David eyed the folder Nicole delivered. The stock

was thicker, brown and had a sheen to it, unlike the flimsy manila kind he was accustomed to. The label on its tab was so old, the edges were ragged where pieces had crumbled away.

"Who's R. J. Modine?" he asked.

"Damned if I know." Marlin flipped it open, scanned a page, snorted, then threw the file on the desk. "Some drone who went missing the day after Christmas, 1951."

He lit a cigarette and took a drag, like a thirsty man sucks water up a straw. The first, David noticed, since Junior Duckworth stopped in for a progress report. Why he ceased chain-smoking when the county coroner was present was a mystery. Or maybe not.

"You had Nicole grub around in the courthouse basement for a file you don't even need?" David said.

"No, I asked her pretty please to look for a file on Royal Moody, when she had time. This Modine dude must be the closest thing to it she found."

"And you wanted the file on Moody because…"

"Hannah tried to bribe me with lunch for information on Moody going AWOL. She'd already talked to Les Williams at the PD. I told her Moody wasn't our case, but she insisted we had the file. It got me curious."

David propped an elbow on the armrest, then his jaw on a fist. "Golf, fishing, clubs, a theater group, day trips, casino junkets… You'd think with all the stuff to do at Valhalla Springs, the Mod Squad would quit playing detective."

"Toots is as bad as they are," Marlin said, then conceded, "Okay, okay. It's five against one, and she doesn't know what they're up to most of the time." He flipped an ash worm in the general direction of the plant saucer. "But she was all fired up this morning."

Phelps chuckled. "Yeah, and she was torqued when she left, too."

Another effect Marlin often had on people, David thought. Usually not Hannah, though. She prided herself on getting in the last zinger.

"Just so long as Bisbee and crew stay away from Beauford." Marlin's tone inferred a warning to David, as if it were necessary. "Which is back at square one, if you take Jarek and Kimmie Sue out of the picture."

"They aren't out," David said. "At this point, she could be the killer as easily as him."

"Using Jarek as *her* alibi." Marlin snuffed out his cigarette. "Guilty or not, those two deserve each other. She leeched off Bev. Jarek leeches off her. Deduct the bills from the estate, and they may hit us up for gas money to get back to California."

David would give it to them, too, if they signed an affidavit saying they'd never step foot in Kinderhook County again. "Want me to start on Bev's telephone records? Luke isn't meeting me at the office for another half hour or so."

Phelps said, "Ma Bell is experiencing a system upgrade. No records available till late tonight, possibly tomorrow."

Bev had canceled cell phone service and landline Caller ID about the time she pawned her jewelry. Either one would have supplied contact info. Punching star 69 on her home phone at the scene had connected with Glo-Brite Dry Cleaners, but no date or time the call was initiated.

David rolled his eyes. "What ever did we do before computers were invented?"

"The same thing I'm gonna do after I reintroduce myself to the wife and eat a home-cooked dinner." Marlin folded his sport coat over his arm. "Meet you at the Beauford house about five o'clock and see if we missed anything."

He shoved the accordion file under his arm. "Look, I don't want it to be Bev's daughter. For a lot of reasons. But strangulation is personal. Kimmie Sue's got a major sense of entitlement. If she popped the question about the house and Bev told her about the mortgages..."

"I know." David grimaced. "The capability's there. It's the culpability I want sewn tight."

"That's why I'm recanvassing the neighbors,"

Phelps said, less than enthusiastically. "Marlin's convinced somebody saw something, besides the stoner who thinks maybe there was a white car in the driveway sometime that week."

"Aka Bev's sedan. I want a Jeep." Marlin caught the phone in mid-ring. "Yo, Andrik." He looked at David. "Lemme see if he's here." Receiver clapped to his shoulder, he said, "Chase Wingate's on hold, asking after the statement for next week's paper."

"He'll get it tomorrow, like I told him."

Marlin relayed the message. "Oh, really? Hang on." Receiver muffled again, he said, "Wingate's also e-mailing Jessup Knox's remarks about the homicide, in case you care to respond."

"Nope." David made a mental note to delete the e-mail without reading it. With advance notice, Chase knew he would. Darned decent of him to give it.

"How about letting Wingate quote me? 'Marlin Andrik, chief of detectives, suggested that Elvis stick his head up his ass and sneeze.'"

David laughed. "Thanks, but no thanks."

"You sure?" Marlin shrugged. "I'll save it till after the election. And say it to his face."

Assuming I win, David thought. Or maybe not. Even Elvis wasn't stupid enough to fire Marlin.

13

From the great room, Hannah heard IdaClare say, "I wish I could, Rosemary. Tomorrow is Jack's birthday and he'll be here by ten." A derisive snort, then, "Though it'd serve him right to spoil the surprise and be gone."

IdaClare looked at the doorway as Hannah walked through it. "Oh, *there* you are, dear. We were beginning to think we'd have to go on without you."

"Been trying to," Delbert grumbled, "for the past half an hour."

"Is everything all right?" Rosemary asked.

"Everything's fine and dandy," Hannah said. Which was true, now that Madame Rue, the supposed psychic medium who leased office space above Oliver's Apothecary on Main Street, had been evicted for an unauthorized séance. What began as a group reading had turned into something of a riot, with Mme. Rue the target of multiple deadly pocketbooks.

Doc Pennington had sedated the woman who was told that her beloved grandfather was a vicious horse thief and a hired gun, then revived the two participants who'd fainted, and dispensed cold compresses to the bruised.

Just another day in the neighborhood, Hannah thought, pulling on a cardigan and accepting the coffee and apple cobbler Marge offered her.

"I thought Jack had to be in Michigan tomorrow," she said to IdaClare.

"He fibbed so I couldn't throw him a surprise party. I called his pilot to ask if the jet was available, in case my friend in Tucson had surgery in the morning." IdaClare chuckled. "Just as I suspected, the plane's free till next Tuesday."

"I'll keep Itsy and Bitsy if you need to go," Marge said.

"That's sweet of you, but I don't have any friends in Tucson." IdaClare waggled her penciled eyebrows. "That boy thinks if he whispered in my ear, he'd hear an echo."

"Nah," Delbert said. "It'd blow out the other side."

Dipping into her cobbler, Hannah asked, "Have I missed anything interesting?"

"No," Delbert said emphatically.

Rosemary fingered a pixie-cut sideburn. "IdaClare and I got a shampoo and set at the Curl-Up & Dye this afternoon. The gossip about Beverly Beauford was thicker than the hairspray."

"Dixie Jo Gage thinks Cesar Montenegro did it," IdaClare said. "Everybody in town knew he had a crush on Mrs. Beauford, even before her husband died."

Hannah wondered if "everybody" included David and Marlin Andrik. By now, the latter had tattled to the former about her visit to the Outhouse. A tip about Cesar Montenegro might shorten another rant about running with the wrong crowd of senior citizens.

Rosemary said, "Cesar owns Aunt Chiladas and delivered take-out orders to Mrs. Beauford personally…if you know what I mean. Then a couple of weeks ago, she stopped ordering, but he kept going to her house, anyway."

"You know what they say about Latin men," Ida-Clare intoned. "Hot-blooded and hot-tempered."

"Oh, for cryin' out loud," Delbert howled. "Can we—"

Marge shuddered. "He's also fat, smells like taco grease and smokes those big, stinky cigars. *Ick.*"

"Maybe that was the attraction," Rosemary said. "Larry Beauford was fat and smoked cigars, too, and

Beverly must have been lonely. When she came to her senses and dumped Cesar, he was furious."

"The crime of passion, it would be," Leo mused. "Many of those there are, sad to say."

"Well, *I* think the woman was…" IdaClare paused, as though amending a harsher adjective. "A flake. Dixie Jo told me in confidence that Beverly begged her for a loan to go to cosmetology school. Then she was going to have a huge garage sale to pay her tuition. Next anyone knew, she'd up and donated everything to charity and was bragging about taking a cruise."

Hannah recalled the travel guide checked out from the library on Marlin's desk. Cash-strapped widow sails away from stalker plying her with free quesadillas? Consider the source, she warned herself. The Curl-Up & Dye's owner and clientele made supermarket tabloids look unimpeachable.

Delbert sneered, "Those gabby old hens are fulla bull. The likeliest scenario is a parolee from the Big House was after Sheriff Beauford for sending him up the river. When he found out Beauford had already kicked the bucket, he killed his widow, instead."

"Hey, I saw that movie." Marge snapped her fingers repeatedly. "The title's right on the tip of—"

"Leave it there."

"No, no. It was something like…"

Delbert commanded, "Zip it, and start taking notes. This meeting's about Code Name: Epsilon and by God, I'm calling it to order."

Rosemary's arm shot up. Leo whimpered at her bosom's tectonic shift. Ach, such a boob man, he was. "Question, please."

After Delbert confirmed it was pertinent, she inquired, "If the 'hens' at the beauty shop are 'full' of 'bull,' why did you send us there for gossip about Chlorine Moody?"

"Because," he replied, drawing it out, as if the answer were as elusive as Marge's movie title. "The truth is, a Sub Rosa Team Reconnaissance Deposition is tricky, and you and IdaClare are the best SRTRD operatives I've got."

"Really?" IdaClare blushed and touched three fingertips to her chin. "Why, Delbert, how sweet of you to say so."

Hannah and Marge looked at each other. They silently agreed that if the old fart put his mind to it, he could sell an extension ladder to a giraffe.

Rosemary was also smitten with her newfound status. "There are some ugly rumors floating around about Chlorine."

"Not a whisper about her doing away with her

husband, though," IdaClare remarked. "But everyone was shocked that she refused to hire an attorney or post her son's bail, after the sheriff arrested him."

Rosemary's hand pantomimed a bird's beak. "Cheap, cheap, cheap," she cheeped.

"Mean, is more like it," IdaClare said. "What choice did Rudy have but to plead guilty to the charges against him?"

Not much, Hannah thought. Rudy had been caught with a cache of illegal guns, days after David confiscated Rudy's sidearm for accidentally shooting out a florist's plateglass window.

Even before that, the unpaid reserve deputy hadn't had a future as a full-fledged law enforcement officer, regardless of how much patrol duty he assigned himself, or how many crime scenes he intruded on.

The spoon clinked in Hannah's spotless bowl as she set it on the bar. "I was there when Rudy confessed to every charge against him. He could have recanted and pled not guilty, but that usually doesn't work out real well."

"Rudy always was a brown-nosed, mealy-mouthed little shit," Rosemary said. Evidently noticing the sudden stillness in the room, she chuckled and waved a sheet of notepaper. "The manicurist's opinion, not mine. She also said Sheriff Beauford took Rudy fishing and riding around in the squad car when he was a kid, but Rudy and Chlorine were conspicuously and *unforgivably* absent at Beauford's funeral."

"That's a small town for you." Marge shook her head. "After my brother died, Mom never spoke to one of her closest friends again because she thought Linda hadn't attended the funeral. She *had,* but Mom was so grief-stricken that the whole day was a blur. She insisted if Linda was there, her name would have been in the guest book."

IdaClare polished her slender gold wedding band with her thumb. "More than four hundred people signed the book at Patrick's service. I felt guilty for not recognizing some names, took comfort in the familiar ones…and was hurt by the few I expected to see, and didn't."

A wistful smile, then, "It's silly that paying respects doesn't count if your name's not in the book. But to this day, I could tell you who they were, and I never quite believed them when they said they just neglected to sign it."

Delbert had the grace to pause several beats, then pointed at Hannah. "Okay, ladybug. Get to making your report, before we're all humming 'Weeping, Sad and Lonely.'"

In unison, IdaClare and Rosemary protested that

they weren't finished with their report. Startled, Leo jumped in his chair and blurted, "Amen."

Delbert ignored his crack operatives' incoming glares and aimed an outgoing one at Leo. "Criminitlies, Schnur. You sacked out all afternoon."

"But so tired, I am from the—"

"Heat," Delbert inserted.

Rosemary felt Leo's brow. "I told you it was too hot to play golf today, but would you listen?"

Hannah shot Delbert an "Oh, yeah?" look. He twirled a finger at his temple and nodded at Leo.

"No fever, but—" Rosemary squinted at her palm, sniffed it, then recoiled. "Why'd you put Bengay on your *head?*"

Delbert slapped the table. "All right, that's *it.* Chlorine Moody's got away with murder for this long, hell with it. Motion to adjourn—the meeting, the case, the whole goddamn ball of wax."

Hannah took the ultimatum as a variation on the ever-popular relationship Waterloo: "If you walk out that door, I won't be here when you come back." It assumed the walker truly intended to leave, and if so, had any intention of returning. In her experience, it further assumed the party staying put won't say, "Promise?" and summon the doorman to speed up the walker's departure.

True to form, Marge, IdaClare and Rosemary traded *Delbert's just bluffing* looks. Contrary to form, the gumshoes' female majority visually agreed to call him on it.

IdaClare gestured a willingness—not to mention, eagerness—to do the honors. With a snarky smirk, she said, "Motion—"

"Fails for lack of a second," Hannah finished.

"But that's what I was—"

"You guys voted me in as the moderator," Hannah reminded them. "I'm moderating." An eyebrow crimped in a decidedly authoritative manner. "Any objections?"

IdaClare's huff implied a major one, but none were vocalized.

"Excellent. Now, Delbert, stop pouting. Leo, drink your coffee and pretend it isn't decaf. Marge, get your pencil ready. Rosemary and IdaClare, do you have any specifics to tell us that date back to the time of Royal's disappearance?"

They didn't, so Hannah launched into the day's third recounting of her discussion with Lieutenant Williams, then the second and highly edited version of her argument with Marlin Andrik.

"The good news is, Eagle-Eye Bisbee found a clue in what I thought was a worthless police report." She delivered the afternoon's revelations about Vehicle Identification Numbers as effusively as a starlet with a pesky substance-abuse problem.

"Delbert didn't tell me the significance of what he found out from that Web site about Royal's car," she said, "but I wouldn't be surprised if it broke the case wide open."

Having at once flattered the old fart and primed the gumshoes, Hannah's arm swept up, like a game-show host's. "I concede the floor to P.I. Bisbee, Esquire."

Which he literally took, grunting and wincing, but also grinning, as he leveraged himself from the chair. Stapled copies of the Sanity Police Department report and the computerized search results were passed around the table. "First, feast your peepers on the date Chlorine filed that missing persons' report. Then, at the date she said Royal left home."

Marge said, "She waited fifteen days to report him missing?"

"Her excuse is in the report, too," Delbert said. "Now look at the date the title to Royal's Chevy was registered to a new owner in Ottawa, Kansas."

Hannah complied. "A month *before* Chlorine said Royal left town?"

"Thirty-two days, to be exact," Delbert corrected.

"My guess is, she didn't call the cops until people started asking why Royal hadn't come home yet."

"A risk it was," Leo said. "The neighbors, they could have remembered the car was gone before that and told the policeman."

"Not as risky as feeding him arsenic and hiding the corpse in the backyard," Delbert reminded him. "Chlorine counted on the neighbors being accustomed to Royal's comings and goings. His car being home longer than usual? That would've attracted attention. Being gone longer? Probably not."

Rosemary shivered. "If you're thinking what I think you're thinking, Chlorine Moody isn't just a murderer, she's a monster."

Frowning, Marge leaned sideward and whispered, "What's he thinking?"

"That Chlorine poisoned Royal, buried him, then drove his car to Kansas and sold it to cover her tracks."

"Like I told Hannah this afternoon. People disappear. Cars don't. Chlorine had to get rid of that Chevy for her story to work."

Marge asked, "Okay, but then how did she get home?"

"Twenty-three years ago, you could still take a bus to just about anywhere," IdaClare said. "And surely

Chlorine had her own car, with Royal being away that much. She could have parked it near the bus depot before she left town."

"Or walked home," Rosemary offered. "The old depot's boarded up now, but it wasn't far from the square."

A sickening thought occurred to Hannah. Chlorine hadn't made that trip to Kansas alone, either. Leaving her three-year-old son that long with a friend or neighbor would prompt questions beforehand, and be potentially memorable after the police were called in.

If Rudy had later remarked on what might have been an adventure to him, his mother would have insisted he'd imagined it. Or, from Hannah's impression of Chlorine, spanked the boy for lying and sent him to bed without his supper.

IdaClare pointed at a paragraph in the police report. "I realize that Chlorine told the police that Royal went to Kentucky, not Kansas." She looked at Delbert. "But isn't it possible that she told the truth? That Royal lied to *her* about where he was going? And that he sold the car, so he could disappear without a trace?"

"Sure," Delbert said. "But if Royal sold the car, that means he was gone a month before Chlorine notified the police, then told them it'd only been two weeks."

"That doesn't make much sense," Rosemary agreed.

"Neither does Chlorine selling a car with Royal's name on the title," Marge added. "Both owners have to sign it over, don't they?"

"Not the married people, no," Leo said. "A title in both the spouses' names, either can sign for the sale."

Rosemary laughed. "Do you mean I could sell the Thing without you even knowing about it, until it was a done deal?"

"Get rid of my Thing?" Leo recoiled in horror. "From the first date we had, you said you loved my Thing. Out now from the blue you say to get rid of it?"

Rosemary kissed his jowl. "I'm teasing, okay? I *do* love your Thing. You wouldn't be you without it."

That was true, Hannah thought. Leo without that vintage convertible Volkswagen would be like Delbert without the Edsel.

IdaClare sighed and shook her head. "It does make more sense that Chlorine sold the car. Otherwise, there's no logical reason to tell the police she hadn't heard from Royal in two weeks, when it was really over a month."

Marge blurted, "Unless he came home for a day or so, *after* he sold the... Mmm. Never mind. If he'd traded cars and Chlorine thought he'd abandoned her, she'd have given the police the description and VIN of the new one."

"As I was about to say," IdaClare went on, "what isn't in any of this paperwork is one single solitary iota of proof for Delbert to keep insisting that Chlorine poisoned her husband with arsenic."

"Oh, yes, there is." Delbert rocked on his heels and looked enormously pleased with himself. "Allow me to direct you to the police report, paragraph five, line three, sentence two, starting with, 'Mrs. Moody's face, neck, lower arms and hands were…'"

Hannah read the passage, then pursed her lips. No lightbulbs switched on. None glowed above Marge's, Rosemary's or IdaClare's heads, either, but Leo's right ear flushed as rosy pink as IdaClare's pantsuit.

Strangely, Delbert seemed to address Leo exclusively when he said, "Nasty stuff, arsenic. It's safe enough to be around, though, if you wear protective clothes, gloves, goggles and a face mask, then wash up real good afterward."

His gaze traveled from IdaClare around to Marge. "If you don't, and that powder gets on your skin, you'll break out with what appears to be—"

"The worst case of poison ivy I've ever seen," Hannah quoted from the report. She thought a moment. "Maybe that's why the officer went easy on Chlorine.

Lieutenant Williams told me, if he'd conducted that interview, he'd have pinned her down more."

Delbert's fist smacked his palm. "And anybody that says it's just another coincidence, like the rose hedge, the curb-side trash service, Moody's car, and the card game Chlorine took the credit for, I'll make you a helluva deal on some land I got down Florida-way."

Quiet descended for several long, ponderous moments. Then, IdaClare said, "A month." She reviewed the dated police report and the printout on Royal's car. "If you're right, her skin was still broken out from that poison a *month* after she murdered him?"

Rosemary chimed in, "Badly enough for the police officer to comment on it?"

A somewhat deflated Delbert admitted that he had no answer for why the aftereffect would've lasted that long. "Maybe it was on the clothes she wore and it didn't come out with the first couple of washes. Same could go for the towels she cleaned up with. There's no mention of the boy suffering likewise, but he could've, from the powder circulating through the ductwork."

"Or," Hannah suggested, knowing someone else would, if she didn't, "Chlorine just had a bad case of poison ivy the day she reported Royal missing."

* * *

Two hours later, Hannah squeezed the telephone receiver, wishing it was that lousy rat fink Marlin Andrik's neck. She almost said so, then remembered Bev Beauford's cause of death. Flipping off the great room ceiling was more compassionate, but less than satisfying.

"So," she said, "how long were you at the Outhouse, before Marlin told on me? Thirty seconds? Thirty-one?"

David chuckled. Or growled. Hard to determine on the phone, even when he wasn't thoroughly exhausted. "I'm not sure he'd have mentioned it, if an intern hadn't shown up with a file she'd found in the basement."

A file? Hannah stifled a *bingo* reverberating in her mind. After all, she'd already told Delbert she was resigning from Code Name: Epsilon. Life was happening, and she had other plans to make. The inevitable was now.

Delbert hadn't seemed surprised, disappointed or argumentative—a hugely suspicious reaction, if the meeting hadn't ended with a vote to surveil Chlorine Moody. Task Force: Hide and Wait would nab her red-handed, the instant she loaded Royal's corpse in her trunk to move to a safer burial site.

David went on. "The file was on a man named Modine, not Moody, but I do believe you got Marlin's antennas on alert."

"Not a chance. He just wanted to prove me wrong. And did, in his usual, snide way." She sighed. "But honestly, Delbert has pieced together a pretty compelling case against Chlorine Moody."

"Oh, he has, huh? Any facts to back it up, or just rumor, innuendo and too many *Murder, She Wrote* reruns?"

Behind that casual, slightly caustic tone lurked a lawman with no dearth of natural curiosity and a grudging respect for Delbert's instincts.

Hannah outlined the circumstantial evidence the gumshoes had collected. A few tiny prosecutable details, such as Delbert questioning Chlorine's neighbors while masquerading as a city employee, were glossed over, or left out entirely.

"I have a feeling that Delbert and Leo know more than what they've told us," she admitted. "And that Delbert hasn't let Leo in on everything, either."

"Women's intuition?" David asked.

"Sort of." Hannah slid a leg off the couch. Her bare foot rubbed Malcolm's belly, as if it were Aladdin's lamp and a genie would pop out to advise her on how much she should share with David. There was a fine line between being concerned for Delbert's safety and being a rat fink, like Marlin.

"It's like this," she said. "The gang was bickering and going off on tangents, as usual. All of a sudden, Delbert said to forget the whole case. Everybody— including me—thought he was bluffing, but I couldn't let them call him on it, so I stepped in and quashed the rebellion."

David drawled, "I do wish you videotaped those meetings. I'll bet they put Monty Python to shame."

True, Hannah thought, but the videotapes could be admissible as evidence in court proceedings—criminal *and* civil. "I assumed Delbert was mad because they weren't taking Epsilon, or him, seriously enough. Afterward, I wondered if it was a ploy to separate himself from the group and go lone wolf. Again."

There was background noise that didn't seem to be generating from the TV, unless it was tuned to *Animal Planet*. David said, "Why don't you call him tomorrow and tell him to bring everything he's got to my office Monday morning."

Hannah scowled at the vision of handcuffs forming in her head. Not that she didn't trust David. It was Sheriff Hendrickson, who had the bad habit of arresting the non-innocent. "Why?"

"For starters, to stall Delbert over the weekend. The Beauford case, you, and some campaign crap I can't get out of take precedence."

Hannah didn't mind being second on the priority list behind an active homicide investigation. Soon, these late-night catch-up phone calls would be conversations on the deck of the A-frame overlooking the valley.

"Second," David continued, "and I'm not BS-ing you, I think the old boy might have enough to justify a meeting with Les Williams about Royal's disappearance."

She bolted upright, scaring Malcolm right side up. Tensed and bug-eyed, his head whipped back and forth, searching for the bogeyman, so he'd know which direction to run away.

Hannah pulled down the receiver. "False alarm, big guy." Then into the mouthpiece, she asked, "Do you really think Delbert's on to something?"

"It's worth a look. Except tell him to make it Monday afternoon. Luke's signing—" Silence, then, "Just have Bisbee call me and we'll set a time."

"Okay, but next election, I've got dibs on being your campaign manager," she teased. "Luke sees way more of you than I do lately."

"Won't be for long, darlin'. Promise."

"10-4 on that, Adam 1-01." Hannah grinned and pumped her arm. *Yes.* It was all she could do to not tell him about the business plan simmering in the desk's bottom drawer.

Not yet, and not on the phone. She wanted to see his expression, the dawning realization that The Garvey Group could peaceably coexist with all that freakin' nature. After months of stalling, she had a plan.

A home-based agency was a start. There were several large *ifs* to resolve, but she dared herself to believe that finally, *finally* happily ever after had a date—Sunday, August 1—and a place—Sanity's city park—and a time...?

Two o'clock, Hannah decided, then amended it to one. Weddings. They're all about symbolism, right? Even those with a couple of weeks to go from an insane idea to "Oh Promise Me," and a sheriff's dispatcher and a lawyer/campaign manager in charge of pulling off the big day.

14

A reserved, tree-shaded parking spot in the driveway on the east side of the courthouse was one of the perks enjoyed by the Kinderhook county sheriff.

There were others. A new cruiser with a quiet air conditioner that didn't leak coolant, for instance. David felt reasonably certain he'd conjure a few more, once this poor excuse for wasting a Saturday morning was behind him.

A flick of the ignition key fired the Crown Victoria's engine. By year's end, the odometer would have racked up more miles than the average civilian vehicle logged in twenty-four months. David was copying the mileage reading in a spiral notebook marked Unofficial Biz, when Marlin rapped on the side window.

The tinted glass was a shade darker, but in the same spectrum as his naturally unhealthy skin tone.

Suck in another case or six of Marlboros and he'd be the Invisible Man, riding shotgun in the cruiser.

David lowered the window, just as Marlin said, "What's with the getup? You look like that lumberjack on the paper towel wrapper."

David regarded his red plaid, short-sleeved shirt and black jeans. Until a second ago, he'd thought the shirt was perfect for pressing the flesh at a bluegrass festival and barbecue, but no longer. Hell with the paper towel guy. As soon as he clapped on his Stetson, he'd look like Howdy Doody's big brother.

"Did you just mosey over to offer wardrobe advice, or do you need something?"

"I saw you going out the door when I came up from the basement. Thought I'd tell you to drive careful. You know. Arrive alive and all that shit."

The dashboard clock confirmed there was time to cat and mouse. God forbid Marlin should come out and say what was on his mind. "The basement." David nodded at a smudge on the detective's sleeve. "Did you raise anything besides dust?"

The detective shook his head. "Les Williams faxed me the report he gave Toots, plus a copy of the transfer memo. The to-and-from were interagency—no names, ranks, badge numbers."

A sloppy, accidental oversight, or intentional? "I

can't say if that was against protocol. Far as I know, there still isn't one."

"Not for an entire file," Marlin said. "I mean, did the uniform delivering it to the courthouse get beamed up to Mars, or what?"

"Might as well have, I reckon. Lost is lost."

"Who cares, though, right? Ancient friggin' history. That Moody drone goes *pfft*. The jacket on him goes *pfft*. Why it makes my head itch, I dunno."

It bothered David, too, and he knew why. The Beauford investigation was dwindling and they had no brilliant ideas to kick-start it again. A lead might develop if the phone company ever forwarded the records. In the meantime, poking around in something else was akin to not staring at a pot, waiting for the water to boil.

"From what Hannah said on the phone last night, Bisbee doesn't think Royal took off on Chlorine. He thinks she poisoned him with arsenic and buried him in the backyard."

"Bisbee's nuts." Marlin shrugged. "Okay, so maybe he's not the dumbest cluck at the nugget factory, but whatever he has, you know damned well he obtained it illegally, which makes it worthless to us."

"Not all of it." David told him about the out-of-state sale of Moody's vehicle. "Send me your fax from the PD. I'm going to make some phone calls before I meet with Bisbee next week."

"Sure you want to do that?" Marlin gave him a hard look. "It's a bad time to be rattling skeletons."

"Assuming there are any."

"There are. You know that as well as I do." Smoke streamed from Marlin's nostrils. "It's who they are, and the fallout…" His glance at the square's far side begot a whistle that ought to have drawn every mutt in town on the double.

An old-fashioned cannon's muzzle impeded David's view out the windshield. A wide-brimmed brown Resistol combined with a pair of long, skinny legs identified the figure loping toward them.

Jimmy Wayne McBride looked from Marlin to David, expectant, eager and a touch wary. A bead of sweat skidded down his cheek, but he wasn't out of breath. David wouldn't have been, either, five or six years ago.

"Got a lead on Beauford?" he asked.

"I wish." Marlin flipped his cigarette onto the ground.

"Then why'd you whistle me over?"

When Marlin didn't respond, Jimmy Wayne chuffed. "I just saw Junior at the Short Stack. Kimmie Sue wants the visitation for Bev on Monday evening and the funeral at two on Tuesday."

David guessed as much. Kinderhook Countians didn't live and die by the *Sanity Examiner*'s weekly publication schedule, but they did get buried by it.

Jimmy Wayne went on. "She also wants the three of us, Cletus, Bill Eustace and Marv Frazier to serve as pallbearers." He looked at David. "And you to deliver a eulogy."

"For Bev, it'd be an honor." For her daughter, it was undoubtedly intended as a public show of their contrition, her magnanimous forgiveness for suspecting her of murder, or a subtle proclamation of innocence.

"Marv Frazier can't walk without a cane, for God's sake," Marlin said. "That's why he took early retirement from the department."

"Junior says the casket will be on a trolley. We'll just walk alongside and the five of us can lift it on and off the bier, into the hearse and at the cemetery."

"Whatever." Marlin snorted. "Like you said, for Bev, it's an honor. It is whenever a guy's tagged for it. But even the wife agrees, women won't be liberated till they pull pallbearer duty as often as men do."

"It ain't easy," Jimmy Wayne agreed, "and I don't mean on your back muscles. It's the one upfront and behind your ribs that gets a workout, and you can't let it show."

Leaning against the Crown Vic's fender, he peeled off the Resistol and fanned himself with it. "Ninety-one in the shade already, boys. Misery loves company and all that, but I'm headin' for the bunkhouse."

Marlin said, "Aw, it ain't that bad, here in the shade." A fake casual note in his tone, he added, "Me and Hendrickson were doing some free associations before he takes off for the hootenanny. Want to try a few?"

The chief deputy seemed as bewildered as David. They both knew Marlin hadn't summoned him to play a parlor game.

"You know," he went on, "like if I say *banana,* you say what pops into your head, first. *Yellow,* or *fruit,* or what the fuck ever. Got it?"

Jimmy Wayne frowned. "I guess…"

"Okay—"

"Corral."

Marlin cursed under his breath. "Cute, McBride. Real cute. How about jailer?"

"Turnkey."

"Fat cats."

"County commissioners." He flinched and glanced around. "Make that Garfield."

"Reports."

"Paperwork."

"Case files."

"Too damn many."

"Missing files."

"Beauford." Jimmy Wayne stiffened. His green eyes strafed the detective with a glare usually aimed at scofflaws about to rabbit. "What are you getting at, Marlin?"

"Proving a point to the sheriff, is all." To David, Marlin said, "I thought of him right away when that file the PD allegedly transferred wasn't at the Outhouse or in the basement."

As he explained the gist to McBride, David considered the warning against rattling skeletons. On the night of Larry Beauford's stroke, any number of files and records disappeared from the sheriff's office, while emergency room personnel fought to stabilize their clinically deceased patient.

Throughout Beauford's tenure, rumors abounded that his cooperation was available for a price—either to make a charge go away, or levy one against an enemy. David never witnessed any collusion or corruption, but eventually sensed his hiring as chief deputy was window dressing. Beauford wouldn't have been the first crook to take cover behind an honest man.

Except dirty or clean, a sheriff's badge is a magnet for accusations of kickbacks, cronyism, graft, extortion and abuse of power.

There was a time, David allowed, when too many sheriffs let that power go to their heads, then slide south to their wallets. Others were figureheads who served at the pleasure of a political machine.

Corruption hadn't been cured. It just wasn't as easy to intimidate people as it once was.

"You're thinking Beauford was somehow involved with Royal Moody's disappearance," he said to Marlin.

Jimmy Wayne cut in. "Hey, I didn't shed any tears at his funeral, but he wasn't even the sheriff back then. Just a grunt deputy."

"Christ on a chariot." Marlin shook his head, a gargling noise escaping his lips. What sounded like bronchial spasms affirmed that he was capable of laughter, rare though it was. "I don't think nothin', except that the two of you are confusing me with that whackjob, Delbert Bisbee."

He hooked his fingers on the cruiser's window ledge and pulled himself to his feet. "Larry Beauford couldn't have done a murder for hire on a Yorkshire terrier. Five bucks says, he never flushed a dead goldfish down the toilet on the first try."

David squinted up at him, trying to read a face as

inscrutable as Lincoln's at Mount Rushmore. "Then why in the hell did we even have this conversation?"

"Like I said, I just bopped out to say drive careful." Marlin motioned at David's shoulder harness. "Click it or ticket, kemosabe. Sheriffs aren't above the law, and it's got a mighty long reach."

David shifted into reverse, feeling a deep, profound sympathy for Josh Phelps. Marlin was a top-notch criminal investigator, but a mighty tough, exasperating man to work with, even when he didn't talk like Yoda.

He took out a notebook and pen from his pocket, then latched the seat belt. If he could steer with one hand and compose a statement for Chase Wingate with the other, then the newspaper editor could shoulder his phone against an ear and take dictation.

The heel of his hand kept the notebook balanced on his thigh. Putting thoughts into words fit to print? To get that job done, David would need every mile between town and the bluegrass festival at Coffman Bend.

Hannah yelped and leapt into the handsome, silver-haired man's arms. Laughing, he hugged her tight and swung her around on the porch. "God, you look good. And you smell great. I've missed you so much, it was all I could do to keep it under a hundred, getting here."

A trial, no doubt, for an incurable speed freak with a Jaguar Mark II, who regarded an interstate highway as an elongated Indianapolis 500 with off-ramps.

As he set her down, his hands grazed Hannah's arms, then his fingers circled her wrists. "Oh, yeah, I forgot. Surprise!"

"And happy birthday to you, Mr. Clancy." She feigned disgust. "You big fat liar."

The cornflower-blue eyes he'd inherited from Ida-Clare crinkled at their corners. "Only in self-defense, sweet pea," he said, following her inside. "A guy has only one mother. Mine has pink hair, a pink house and thinks I'm forever six years old."

Malcolm gallumphed in from the kitchen and stuck his snoot in Jack's crotch to say hello. A series of enthusiastic snuffles left a lasting impression on his slacks.

"That's the only thing mom's Furwads have going for them," Jack said. "They're short."

"A mutt with chronic sinus drainage over two ankle-biters? No contest." Crooking a finger, Hannah led her employer into the breakfast room.

Streamers dangling from the fixture above the table danced in the breeze from the ceiling vents. A birthday-balloon bouquet was tied to a chair back. At its place on the table was a small, rectangular gift. On a saucer was a blueberry muffin impaled with a lighted candle.

Hannah burst out laughing at Jack's dumbfounded expression. "You are so busted, Clancy."

"Stephen blew it, didn't he? You called the loft to tell me happy birthday and he told you I was coming."

"Now, why would I do that, if I thought you were at cruising altitude somewhere between St. Louis and Michigan?"

"Oh. Good point. You'd have called my cell." Jack closed his eyes and shuddered. "That leaves what I've suspected for years. My mother is a witch."

"Wrong again. She's just a lot smarter than you are. But then, most of us already knew that." Hannah told him about IdaClare's ruse with his pilot. "If I had time this morning to buy muffins and decorations, I can't imagine what she's put together since yesterday."

Jack bowed his head and massaged his brow. "If you love me, you'll tell me how many old people are going to jump out at me when I get to mother's. If you *don't* love me, you'll still tell me, because I'm your boss and I'll fire you if you don't."

Hannah crossed her arms, contemplating her options. A zipped lip? Or the truth. One was tempting from an instant-unemployment perspective. Unfortunately, Jack wouldn't fire her if she stuck the birthday candle up his nose flame-first. Plus, there was his future as a ground-floor Garvey Group client to consider.

"I love you, needy though you are. If IdaClare's throwing a party, I wasn't invited."

"Meaning, no party." Jack's shoulders sagged in relief. "No hats, no horns, no confetti, no clowns, no pony rides. There *is* a God."

There was a time when Hannah prayed to Him for all those things, but would have been happy with a cake on the right day. Early or belated, a squashed SnoBall from Effindale's day-old bread store with a cigarette lighter held over it wasn't quite the same.

"Better make a wish and blow out the candle," she said. "The wax is melting like crazy, and a warm Flour Shoppe muffin is a terrible thing to waste."

So were four of them, evidently, since Jack ate three, as though he'd either returned from a desert island, or was about to depart for one. "Remind me to never retire here. Great place to visit, but I'd gain ten pounds a week if I moved in."

His eyes turned to the gift, wrapped in gold foil with a gold bow. "Really, you shouldn't have, sweet pea."

Hannah lofted her coffee mug. "To old friends. And you're the oldest one I have."

Chuckling, Jack clinked his mug with hers. "Can I open it now?"

"Rip away."

Inside, a red, enameled tin box was a miniature, remote-controlled replica of a Jaguar Mark II. By Jack's face, you'd think she'd bought him the one parked in front of the cottage. "Hannah Marie, you always buy the best toys a middle-aged boy could want."

"Thanks, but I failed miserably at finding the batteries for it. The jewelry store in Sanity doesn't carry them."

He shrugged. "Somebody in St. Louis will. I may even buy another one for Stephen, so we can race."

Spoken like a red-blooded, self-made Irish-American multimillionaire. "Gee, and to think IdaClare's in denial about your age."

"Nothing wrong with being young at heart. Especially when you get a cool car out of it."

"So, you really like it that much?"

"Are you kidding?" Jack ran the car up and down his trousers leg. "I love it."

Over the *vroom-vrooms* and tire squeals, she said, "Good, because it's also a bribe."

Errrrt. "Let's hear it." *Vroom.*

"Delete all promotion-related work from the operation manager's job description. Sign a standard agency agreement with The Garvey Group for Clancy

Construction and Development, et al, to commence on or before August 31. Give me a handshake agreement that I can freelance the account until then."

The baby Jag made a pit stop. "You're starting your own agency?"

"*Started.* Yesterday. I haven't filed for a business license, or any of that yet. In fact, you're the first to know, so you have to pinkie-swear to keep it confidential for a while."

"If I sign on as a client."

Keeping her tone light but firm, she answered, "Whether you do, or not."

"Who's the 'group' in The Garvey Group?" Jack pointed his toy at her. "And one of them better not be named Clancy."

"I said you're the first person I've told. Including David."

Hannah's fingernail tapped the table, as though in the throes of a dilemma. *Let him see you sweat* was strategic. Her board of directors consisted of Malcolm Garvey and Rambo Hendrickson, but she wouldn't admit it if her linchpin client relit his birthday candle and stuck it up *her* nose.

"Sorry, Jack. I'm not in the position to disclose that yet, either. You'll just have to trust in our fifteen-year personal and professional relationship."

His bright blue eyes riveted on Hannah's brown ones. "What if you don't find a new ops manager by the thirty-first of next month?"

Okay, God, she thought, if there is a You, I'll forgive You for all those birthday parties I never had, in exchange for a tiny, swift miracle. "With four qualified applicants to interview and a couple more from Wilma on the bubble, a replacement will be on board no later than the third."

Jack's gaze didn't waver, but he smiled out one side of his mouth. "Any of *them* named Clancy?"

Scooting closer, Hannah laid a hand over his, her thumb caressing his wrist. "I want it all, Jack. To be David's wife, to have a real home, a connection to Valhalla Springs and to you, and a job doing something I'm good at. Is that too much to ask?"

Setting aside his birthday present, he gently cupped her face in his hands. In a soft voice laden with affection, he said, "sweet pea, you don't, and never have fooled me for a second. All I've ever wanted is for you to be happy."

Hannah anticipated the *but* that often accompanies such sentiments. A professed foresight of what's *best*, what's sure to reap genuine happiness, as opposed to a misguided facsimile thereof.

"The CC & D account is yours. If you need start-up cash, that's yours, too, interest-free." He smushed her cheeks into a fish face. "But if you so much as *think* about hiring my mother, all Sheriff Hendrickson's horses and all Sheriff Hendrickson's men won't be able to put you back together again."

A mental instant replay affirmed that yes, he was signing on. The Garvey Group was *real.* IdaClare was permanently off the emergency-employee list, but if push came to panic, there was always Delbert, Marge and the Schnurs.

Hannah nodded. "Ah-ay, Yack. I'ss a 'eal."

He pecked a kiss on her trout-puckered mouth. "Gotta go *not* surprise my mother. Thanks for the car, and tell David the world's second luckiest guy says hi."

Removing his white fedora—the same, exact model that Matlock wore on TV—Delbert strolled into the First National Bank of Sanity's lobby at precisely 1158 hours. The lone weekend teller cut his eyes to the clock, as though willing the minute hand to snick two hash marks to the right, before he was forced to inquire, "May I help you?"

Delbert approached the counter and Clay S.—whose name was written on the gold plastic tag pinned to his shirt pocket—said to him, "That's, uh, some suit."

"Like it, eh?" Delbert flicked an imaginary dirt speck from his lapel. "This baby's a hundred percent pure seersucker with a gen-yew-ine silk lining. I guarantee, they don't make 'em like this anymore."

Clay S.'s head whipped sideward. He coughed loudly into his fist, making Delbert's ribs ache. "Hey, are you okay, son?"

The teller nodded, the flush gradually draining from his face. "Sorry. Something caught in my throat." Clearing it, he said, "Are you making a deposit? Need a check cashed?"

Delbert laid his hat on the counter, pulled his billfold from his pocket and fanned a wad of fifties and twenties across the counter. "Altogether, that's five C-notes. I want a cashier's check in exchange, payable to Chlorine Moody."

Clay S. counted the money, dividing it into equal stacks. "Five hundred dollars." He looked up, as though Delbert hadn't already told him how much was there.

"Uh-huh, that's the size of it. Now, about the cashier's check—"

"Do you have an account with us?"

"No, but that's cash, sport." Delbert removed another twenty and pushed it forward. "And here's another Tom Jefferson to cover the fee for typing nine words, four letters and some hyphens on a ding-danged blank check."

Clay S. peered down his nose, which didn't appear to have yet been broken. "May I see some ID, please?"

The expletives raging through Delbert's mind ended in *two-bit whippersnapper.* He savvied that the kid had jumped the gun on tallying the morning's receipts and disbursements, thinking it'd get him out the door by 12:01. A last-minute transaction bollixed things, sure enough, but that's the way the cookie crumbled.

Timing was everything for this caper. Arriving just as the bank closed for the weekend wasn't coincidence.

"Here's the situation," Delbert said in a reasonable, but *mano y mano* tone. "You want me outa here. Me, I got better things to do, myself, but I ain't leaving without that check. Now, are you gonna get with it, or am I gonna hail whoever manages this joint on weekends when he moseys out from the back to lock that lobby door?"

Five minutes later, Delbert tipped his fedora to the foxy, hazel-eyed blonde securing the door behind him. 'Twas a crying shame that phase three of Operation: Royal Flush had to deploy tonight.

Story of a P.I.'s life, he thought. So many dames, so little time.

The next female face that eyed him through a glass door wore a pair of steel-rimmed trifocals. Her finger-waved hair was a drab bottle-brown, then hair-sprayed as stiff as a cheap wig. Delbert assumed the lick of gray brushed back from the crown was supposed to look jaunty.

The aluminum storm door opened about a foot. The escaping air smelled the same as when he'd cased the joint a few days ago—cool, and a little stale, but not unpleasant.

"Good afternoon, ma'am. Are you Mrs. Chlorine Moody?"

She eyed his classic summer-weight suit, white side-buckle shoes, and the metal clipboard in the crook of his arm. "Who wants to know?"

A wave of nervousness slammed Delbert so hard he thought she'd smacked him with the door. If he faltered, Code Name: Epsilon would be scrapped. He'd have put himself and Leo in danger for nothing.

He pulled his shoulders back and pasted on a confident smile. "I'm Frank Larson, of the Sanity Public Works Department."

Borrowing the name of a real city employee cadged off the municipal directory was an agonizing decision. If Clay S., or the foxy blonde at the bank, or Chlorine knew this Larson fella, it was all over. An alias would be safer in that respect, but if Chlorine got on the horn to somebody in the know, he might smell a scam. It was, of course, but Delbert had five hundred big ones invested in pulling it off.

"I've got nothing to say to anyone with the city." Chlorine's fingers tightened on the storm door's handle. "Get off my property and stay off."

The shoe Delbert surreptitiously planted at the bottom of the door held it fast. Still smiling, he showed her the cashier's check—in view, but out of reach.

Her eyeballs jittered as she read the pay-to-the-order-of line, then the amount, then the signature. Delbert didn't notice before he left the bank that Clay S. had typed C.P.D.W. under Larson's name, not C.P.W.D. for City Public Works Department. If Chlorine spotted the typo, he'd have to convince her the official designation was City Public Department of Works.

So far, the five hundred dollars made out in her name had her complete attention.

"I'm authorized to compensate you for your shrubs and fence. They're encroaching on the city's easement, but the department feels it's the neighborly thing to do."

"Neighborly?" she sneered. "Taking me for a fool is more like it. You idiots at city hall think I'm too simpleminded to see this for what it is—a bribe, so's

I'll drop my lawsuit against you. Well, my attorney will be hearing about this and—"

"Excuse me," Delbert said, "but that's why I'm delivering this check, this afternoon." Which was true, in a manner of speaking. Banks, municipal and county offices, and Chlorine's hired shyster, judging by the answering machine at his office, were shuttered tighter than a convent.

It'd be Monday morning before she could contact anyone who'd pull the plug on his caper. If justice existed in this world, by tomorrow morning, she'd be eating breakfast off a foam jailhouse plate.

He continued, "I'm truly sorry to be the one to tell you, but right before court disconvened yesterday, the judge ruled your lawsuit null and void."

"What?" Seeing fear widen even an alleged murderer's eyes wasn't pleasant. Nor was it protracted. Recovering her wits in a blink, Chlorine pushed past him onto the porch. "That's a *lie* and you're *trespassing.*" She shoved Delbert backward. "My attorney would've told me—"

"He should have." Delbert stood his new ground. "Could be, Mr. Pratt thought he was doing you a kindness, waiting till Monday to tell you."

She started at his mention of her attorney's name. Lawsuits are public record, as any private detective knows. Well, those smart enough to do their homework at the clerk's office, anyhow.

Keeping the cashier's check in sight, but at arm's length, Delbert brandished a letter addressed to her printed on his gimcracking city stationery. "I'm further here to notify you of this alteration in the trench layout for the new gas line."

His fingertips underscored an indented paragraph. "As you can see, the project engineer is expanding the trench behind your property to install a K29-A Decompression Flange." Delbert tapped the bold-printed sentence declaring that construction would resume at 8:00 a.m. Sunday.

"You can't do that!" Chlorine blustered. "The city passed an ordinance years ago against construction work on the Sabbath. Any kind, shape or form." She pointed at the house across the street with the enclosed porch. "I've set the police on that godless heathen a half-dozen times for disturbing my peace." Her hand swept to the right. "And that one, the Sunday he started hammering a swing set together for those pickaninnies he's spawned."

Delbert struggled to contain his disgust. Except, Chlorine Moody was a human racist, not a garden-variety bigot. She hated everyone—herself included—so much that he almost tasted the bitterness exuding from her every pore. Maybe he was wrong about a crime unpunished equaling twenty-three years of freedom.

"You're right about the ordinance," he said, "but it can be waived for extenuating circumstances. Cleanup from this week's storm damage, for one. The interest of public safety's another."

He nodded in the direction of the alley. "If a house caught fire along this block, trucks couldn't get in to fight it." Clucking his tongue, he surveyed Chlorine's immaculate siding, the porch's cobweb-free ceiling and vacuumed Astro Turf. "It'd be tragic for a home this fine to burn to the ground. A spark on the wind, though, and she'd be a goner."

Chlorine looked sicker than she did when he told her the lawsuit was thrown out. She'd sunk tens of thousands of dollars in the place from that game her husband invented. The prospect of watching it go up in smoke had her groping for a wall to support herself.

He laid the check atop the letter on the clipboard. From his suit's coat pocket, he removed a sheaf of brochures he'd collected en route to the bank. Whether they were the frosting on the bamboozle, or just mean-spirited, he didn't much care.

"Seeing how fond you are of roses," he said, "here's a couple of nurseries that specialize in 'em and literature from some fence companies. I'd say most of your chain link can be salvaged and reset after the trench is filled in."

The brochures were arranged on top of the counterfeit letter, with the check on top. Keeping your mark focused on the money was a con man's motto.

"Have a nice day, Mrs. Moody." Delbert tugged his hat brim, exactly like ol' Matlock fixing to spring a trap on a murderer. "Come morning, just ignore those earthmovers firin' up. The sooner your fence is ripped up and the dirt's dug down about six feet, the sooner this'll all be over with."

15

Hannah listened to the phone ring at the other end of the line. And ring. And ring. For the past ten minutes, she'd listened to phones ring and ring and ring—each of them enough times for a senior citizen to hitchhike from Iowa to answer the damned thing.

She put the receiver in its dock and her chin in her hand. Delbertly intuition warned that a misdemeanor, or several, were planned, if not already in progress.

He hadn't uttered a peep last night when Hannah quit the Moody case. Nor had he called or dropped by today to coax her back into the fold.

IdaClare Clancy was another one she hadn't heard from. To resist bragging about outsmarting Jack on his birthday was as uncharacteristic as Delbert surrendering without a single *Jehosophat*.

Hannah turned her head and gazed out the window at the muggy, late-afternoon haze. None of the gumshoes had answered their phones. She couldn't remember calling each of them in rotation before, but a mass exodus seemed significant. They were, after all, the Mod Squad.

But she wasn't their nanny. They didn't need one. Armed guards, maybe, and a team of defense attorneys on retainer, but not a babysitter.

Everyone being out simultaneously was a coincidence, she thought. Just because I don't believe in coincidences, doesn't mean there's anything to worry about. Concentrate on tonight's dinner with David. How relieved and over-the-moon happy he'll be when I tell him I took months of bullshit by the horns. Stepped up to the plate and swung for the fence. Cleared the freakin' decks...

She cursed, picked up the handset and punched in the number for the community center, also known as activity central, particularly when heat or rain drove tenants off the lake, golf course, tennis courts and walking trails.

Naturally, the line was busy. She clicked the disconnect button. Idly wondered what she'd wear to David's. Decided on the usual jeans and a top, since a cocktail dress might be a bit of a tip-off. Drummed her fingers on the desk. Sighed and redialed the community center.

Well, hell. Still busy.

Of all people, Delbert should own a cell phone. Why he didn't was another impulsive unpredictability. Much as he loved any type of spylike gadget that lit up, made noise and ran on batteries, he hated to talk on the phone.

Third call to the community center, same result.

Hannah dropped the handset on the desk. "C'mon, Malcolm. Like Great-uncle Mort always said, why walk around in a circle when you can go straight and get somewhere else?"

The giant Airedale-wildebeest was always up for a ride in the Blazer. In his mind, self-propulsion should be limited to meals, drinks, potty stops and nap positions. Anything else was animal abuse.

Hannah had taken a few steps down Valhalla Springs Boulevard before she noticed that Malcolm wasn't following alongside. The poor dog with the apparently painted-on legs was slumped against the Blazer's rear bumper. He gave her a longing gaze, much like Ingrid Bergman's departing look at Humphrey Bogart in *Casablanca*.

Hannah whistled and patted her thigh. "It's a hundred degrees hotter in the truck than out here, doofus. No way will the air kick in that fast and cool it off."

The translation of his answering *burf* would probably get his mouth washed out with soap. Head and tail adroop, Malcolm slogged forward to join his tormentor.

Heat shimmers twitched above the boulevard and the lake's glassy green surface. Gnats whirled in the air like flickering orbs, but most of the birds, bunnies, squirrels and people must have been taking siestas.

Her tennis shoes *squitched* on gummy asphalt that smelled, oddly enough, like mothballs. Wrinkling her nose, she automatically squinted her eyes and surveyed the community center's parking lot.

A few cars and canopied golf carts ignored the dimensions and intent of the lot's yellow lines. Numerous residents who'd never played golf and had no desire to try owned electric buggies to zip around the development.

Malcolm had been forbidden entry to the building, since an incident involving the ladies' swim-therapy class, so he belly-crawled under a hydrangea bush to sulk while Hannah went inside.

"No, a *maybe* is *not* good enough," a woman in a polka-dot sundress said into the wall phone. "I'm not hanging up until you promise you'll be at the dance tonight."

Having solved the mystery of the center's persistent busy signal, Hannah wandered from the main room down the hall leading to the club rooms, smaller banquet rooms and the kitchen.

"Hey, Hannah," a male voice called from behind her. "Wait up."

Willard Johnson, the part-time physical fitness instructor, was dressed in workout clothes and toting a gym bag. "I've been trying to catch you at the office for days."

"You have?" She thought back. "I guess I have been in and out."

"I was going to stop by this morning on my way here." He winked. "Hoo-eee, that was one sweet ride parked in your driveway when I went by."

"Uh-huh. And you know darned well it belonged to your boss and mine, Jack Clancy."

Willard's grin wilted to an expression somewhere between dejection and resolve. "That's sort of what I need to talk to you about." He motioned toward a seating area in the main room. "How about we grab a coupla chairs."

Hannah frowned and shook her head. "Something tells me I'll wish I was sitting down when you tell me what the problem is, but I'll take it standing up."

Willard hemmed and hawed, then dabbed his glistening forehead with the towel draped around his neck. "Okay, it's like this. You knew when I took the job that myself and five others write science fiction novels under a pseudonym."

"Corey Percival Spoon." She snapped her fingers. "Ye gods. I am *so* sorry. I completely forgot all about that writers' workshop/retreat we talked about. Listen, it's a little late for national advertising, but not *too* late—"

"This isn't about a workshop I never wanted any part of in the first place." Willard shrugged. "No offense, but that was your brainstorm, not mine."

"It's still a great idea—"

"Except I'm not the guy to do it." His eyes rose to a spot an inch above her head. "I love this job and the people and you're the best boss anybody could ever have…but I've got to quit."

As predicted, a chair would be nice to have under her right now. Then again, if her knees buckled and she sank to the floor, she'd be in a better position to wrap her arms around his ankles and beg him to stay.

Still vertical but wobbly, she said, "Whatever it takes to keep you, just name it. A raise, more hours, new equipment for the gym—"

"I appreciate it. I really do, Hannah, but it's not—"

"You can't quit." She cocked a hip and rested a fist on it. "I won't let you. Hell, there'll be a riot if you leave, and I don't have the time or energy for a couple of hundred screaming senior citizens picketing my office."

The image must have flashed in Willard's head because he chuckled, then laughed out loud. "Thanks for making me feel guiltier about this than I already do."

"Here's an easy fix. Don't quit."

"I have a dream, Hannah." Rolling his eyes, he muttered, "Good Lord. Brother King's speech was our Sermon on the Mount, but it sure ruined starting sentences like that for the rest of us."

Blowing out a breath, he went on, "I want to write books with my own name on the cover. Make a living at it. I took this job because I won't freeload off my folks. They'd already evicted a paying tenant so I could move into the apartment over their garage. They didn't want me to pay rent, either, but twenty-six-year-old, divorced college graduates don't mooch off their retired parents."

That mature, responsible attitude is part of the reason I hired you, Hannah thought. And would have, even without his second-degree black belt in tae kwon do, Red Cross lifeguard certification, and experience working at Gold's Gym during college.

"Trouble is," he said, "the twenty-five to thirty hours a week I signed on for has upped to thirty-five or forty." He held up a hand. "Not your fault. All mine, because I can't say no to grandmas and grandpas wanting to swim extra laps, do a little more weight training, whatever. Add another ten hours drive time a week to that, and…"

He gestured in frustration. "My last Percy Spoon was two weeks late. I haven't worked on my own book in months. I thought I could do this and write, too. I can't. I just can't."

Hannah stared at him. She could scarcely breathe with her mind spinning a hundred rpms a minute. *Too good to be true* beat like a drum in the background. Never once had it occurred to her to offer Willard her job. He managed the community center like the proverbial well-oiled machine. As a result, she seldom had reason to think about it or him, and therefore, seldom did.

"Uh-oh, there's that look again." Willard angled his head. He backed up a step, then another. "Every time you get it, I end up in a world of hurt."

Hannah smiled. "There is a God. He doesn't do birthday parties, but ask for a payback miracle, and He's a heck of a horse trader."

Weight shifting to the balls of his feet, Willard appeared ready to bolt for the door. "Gee, wish I could stay and talk, but—"

"I accept your resignation, effective immediately.

Come by the office, Monday, and I'll have your final check ready."

That put his heels back in touch with the carpet. "You mean, I'm through? As of *now?*"

"Then we'll fill out the paperwork and I'll start training you to take over as the resident operations manager."

Willard's neck craned forward. His mouth opened and shut repeatedly, then he croaked, "Run that by me again?"

Laughing, Hannah closed the gap between them. "Imagine a gorgeous furnished cottage, utilities included, for free, versus rent and utilities for a dinky garage apartment in town. A full-fledged office with a computer, scanner, printer, Internet access and a fax machine, versus pecking away on an old laptop at a rickety card table. A salary and health insurance. No commuting. No time clock to punch. A very flexible schedule."

She grinned. "And I'll handle all the promotions, mailings, tenant inquiries and advertising. Plus, I'll be a phone call away if you need me."

At least ten seconds ticked by. "You're serious, aren't you?"

"Never been more."

Another ten seconds, then, "Okay, I'm interested.

I'd be an idiot not to be, but I need some time to think it over. How about I—"

"That's exactly what I told Jack Clancy when he offered me the job," Hannah said. "Want to know what his response was?"

Willard's arched eyebrows telegraphed, *Not really, but you're going to tell me, anyway.*

"He said, 'Now or never, Hannah Marie.' And it wasn't a bluff." She paused, smiling at the memory and how wise Jack truly was. "Gut instinct is a religion for him. He knew mine voted yes or no, the moment he said, 'Now or never.' Whichever it was, all time would give was a chance to talk myself out of the job, or talk myself into it. Either way, from Jack's perspective, the answer would have been the wrong one."

Willard considered that at length. "Gut instinct isn't a hundred percent, though."

"Maybe not. But I'll bet you've regretted way more decisions you talked yourself into, or out of." Extending her hand, she added, "And a minute ago, your gut said yes to being Valhalla Springs' new resident operations manager."

Willard closed his eyes, sighed, then shook on it. "I knew I shoulda made a break for it when you got that funny look on your face."

It wouldn't have done any good. She knew where

he lived, and had lunch with his mother, Benita, every few weeks or so.

Hannah and the new resident operations manager were at the front entrance before she remembered why she'd come to the center in the first place. "I don't suppose you've seen Delbert today, have you?"

"Bisbee?" Willard said, as though there could be two of them in all the universe, let alone Valhalla Springs. "No. In fact, I called his house a couple of times to make sure he was okay. When he didn't answer, I figured he'd gone on that bus tour down to Branson and Eureka Springs."

Hannah started. "Why were you concerned enough to call him?"

"Well, not concerned, as in worried. More like concerned he's given up on tae kwon do because he wasn't up to Jet Li speed yet."

Willard held open the door for her. "It's not like Delbert to miss class," he said, "but I haven't seen him since Wednesday, when he dug through the storage cabinet looking for some old card game."

RUDY. Which meant Sam Spade Bisbee had been on Chlorine's case sooner than she'd... Oh, my God. *RUDY.*

"Gosh, I hate to rush off, Willard." Hannah clattered down the steps. "But there's a phone call I have to make, pronto." Visually sweeping the hydrangea bushes for Malcolm's hideout, she blathered, "Why it's important, I'm not sure, but it is. I just know it is."

Assuming Malcolm had gotten tired of pouting and gone home, Hannah started into a jog, calling backward, "Congratulations on the new job. Don't tell anybody yet, though, okay? I'll explain later. Have a great weekend."

A forty-three-year-old woman who hasn't run since her mid-thirties, and then only once, shouldn't attempt an encore on a steamy July afternoon in the Missouri Ozarks.

The cottage being downhill from the community center was a major plus. And an adrenaline high must be as invigorating as the endorphin kind she'd read about. It was also good to know that Doc Pennington kept portable oxygen tanks on hand at all times.

Just as she leapt onto the porch, Willard's car cruised by at a speed usually associated with drivers gawking at a pileup on the highway. Hannah waved, let the still-sulking Malcolm inside, snatched the handset off the desk, then collapsed in the chair.

Chest heaving, she felt sweat stream from pores accustomed to extended periods of complete inactivity. By the time uncontrolled panting relented to normal breathing, she'd changed her mind about calling David. The reason couldn't be more selfish, but she hadn't almost killed herself just to blow a hole in their dinner plans and the surprises she had in store.

Hannah pawed through her purse for her wallet, then for Marlin's business card with his handwritten cell phone number on the back. What seemed like a lifetime ago, she'd loaned the card to Delbert for an emergency payphone call. That irony wasn't lost on her, either.

At Marlin's voice mail's cue, she said, "Marlin, Hannah. Something's nagged at me since I was in your office. I didn't know what until—okay, look. That GMEI envelope on your desk? GMEI bought out Acer and Sons several years ago. Acer and Sons produced and marketed RUDY, the card game Chlorine Moody supposedly invented. Mrs. Beauford and everybody else in town are probably in GMEI's direct-mail database, but—"

A click as rude as Marlin could be cut her off. "Oh, well," she said. "Mission accomplished."

Reaching across the desk to dock the phone, she hesitated, then sat back in the chair and punched in another number. Delbert's phone rang and rang and rang. So did IdaClare's. And the Schnurs'. And Marge Rosenbaum's.

"Fine," she snapped. "Obviously, Congress declared this National Don't Answer Your Freakin' Phone Day, and everybody forgot to tell *me* about it."

David made it back to town from the bluegrass festival just before Henry Beard's butcher shop closed at seven. Buying the last pair of thick, perfectly marbled steaks in Henry's meat case seemed like a good omen.

Now, setting them aside to marinate in his secret recipe, David cut slits in two Idaho bakers and stuffed them with braised onions and green peppers. A drizzle of butter, a dash of salt and pepper, and he reached into an adjacent cabinet for the aluminum foil.

Adjacent pretty well described the farmhouse's entire kitchen. All the cabinets, appliances, and a narrow pantry lined one wall. If the place hadn't been a temporary roof over his head, he'd have gutted the kitchen and started over. Turning away from the counter, he visualized the sink moved beneath the window and the stove where the sink was. Chuck the dinette, set back the wall for a side-by-side fridge, add a breakfast bar and…

Grabbing the shiny wrapped potatoes, he headed outside to the grill. Stop building sand castles as if you own the joint, he thought. The old house, the new one and the land they're standing on aren't yours anymore. They're Luke's. Or will be, on Monday when you sign over the deed.

He nestled the spuds in a coal bed reserved for them, stifling the urge to watch the gathering gloam fall over the meadow. As he covered the foil lumps with hot ash, he wondered if he should've been a tad more creative with the menu.

In the summertime, steak, baked potatoes and a spinach salad were as common as fried catfish and hush puppies. Sure, he'd bought the makings for an Oreo cheesecake, but this was a special dinner, even if Hannah wasn't aware of it. Hearing the phone, David shut the grill's lid and strode back inside to answer it.

"How was the hootenanny?" Marlin inquired.

David chuffed. "About time you called me back."

"Whaddaya mean, back? If you called me, I didn't get the message, as usual."

"That's why I didn't bother trying the office. I left one on your cell over an hour ago." David opened the refrigerator. "No big deal. I just wanted to touch base."

A pause, then a curse. "The battery's dead on my cell. Guess I forgot to plug it into the charger last night."

"Likely story." Bricks of cream cheese slapped the counter. The eggs, David laid on a wadded kitchen towel. "So, anything exciting happen while I was charming voters?"

"That's why I called. Cletus is on the way back from the courthouse with Bev's phone records. Like everything else, the fax machine here is a piece of crap."

"You're just now getting them?" David glanced at the clock on the stove. "Jesus, did they chisel them on stone tablets or what?"

"A miscommunication." If the rattle on the line was a chuckle, it sorely lacked humor. "With the phone company, if you can imagine."

As David cut open the cookie package to lessen the cellophane racket, Marlin went on. "Aw, to be honest, the gal I got the sixtieth time I called was a doll. Name's Stephanie Michaels. Tattoo it on your arm, boss, 'cause she's the go-to person from now on."

David transferred handfuls of cookies to a plastic bag. "She comprehends the words *homicide investigation.*"

"That she does. Bev's records were on the wire before we hung up. Ninety days' worth." A slight change in tone preceded, "Soon as Cletus delivers them, I'm sending him out on a call. It looks like our basement burglar hit another house last night while the owners were out of town."

David eyed the rolling pin he'd use to crush the

cookies. Excellent therapy, cooking. He'd been itching to smash something for days. "How many robberies does that make? Four? Five?"

"Five. Assuming he didn't go for a daily double we don't know about yet."

"Where'd he hit this time?"

"Tuscumbia," Marlin said. "Same MO. Busted a basement window for access, backed a vehicle into the garage, loaded 'er up, and drove off."

The Outhouse's door buzzer was audible over the line. Cletus Orr must have returned with the telephone company printouts. Marlin confirmed it when he said, "The reason I called is, Phelps was wondering if your offer to help look over Bev's call records was still good."

Phelps was? *Yeah, sure.* David clenched his teeth as guilt's spidery tentacles crept up his breastbone. Marlin had put in close to fifty hours since Bev's body was found. Phelps, almost as many. David had worked a goodly chunk, but had been off most of the day eating country barbecue, listening to some damned fine music and shooting the breeze with the kind of people usually referred to as the salt of the earth.

Hannah would understand if he postponed their dinner on short notice, given how late it was already. She always did. Or, even more wonderful, if his job taking precedence did irk her at times, she never let on. And wasn't keeping score to bust his chops about it later, either.

. "No can do, Marlin," he said. "Sorry, but—"

"Toots comes first." Marlin hastened to add, "And should. At least, until you get a ring on her finger. Then you can treat her like a wife."

David laughed. "Like you do yours, right? Foot massages, breakfast in bed on Sundays, bringing her flowers for no reason in particular—"

"My *ass*. I don't know who laid that crock of shit on you, but it's a—it's a—well, it's a crock of shit, that's what it is."

"Uh-huh," David said, grinning. "Let me know if you and Phelps find anything interesting."

Delbert slithered onto the garage roof. He winced at every scraping noise on the rough composite shingles. He'd smell dirty tar and bird droppings for a week, too, but so far, Operation: Royal Flush was proceeding without a hitch. Well, none he couldn't handle, anyway.

The sun beating down all day had softened the shingles, giving the golf shoes he'd spray-painted black better purchase than he'd expected. On the other hand, the roof hadn't cooled off after dark as much as he'd hoped.

Sprawled at a belly-down slant near the peak was like lying in a tanning bed with the lid up. Without that touch of a breeze floating by, his goose'd be cooking, for sure.

The black, long-sleeved turtleneck, slacks and sock hat he wore didn't help. Neither did the camo face paint concocted from shortening and black shoe polish. The last time he'd smeared on the goop was for an inside job back in the spring. That night, the temperature had been in the mid-to-high fifties. Now it felt like his forehead was slowly melting into his shirt collar.

Rolling to one side, then the other, he carefully pushed off his backpack's shoulder straps. Holding on to one, he fumbled for the wallet keeper attached to his belt. The hook at the end, he clipped to a D-ring on the backpack. If it took a notion to skitter down the roof, he could grab the line and reel 'er up again.

Contingencies, he thought. Any you don't think of in advance, you sure as hell can't prepare for. And he was prepared, for nigh anything, apart from the operation being a bust.

He took a slug from the sports bottle strapped to the backpack, then licked his lips. Cold water had never tasted any sweeter, but he had to ration it. Hydration was critical, but he sure as sixty didn't want to climb down that rope ladder to take a leak, then climb back up it again.

The backpack's zippered interior yielded two toy walkie-talkies—a red one and a blue one. They were cheap plastic sons of guns, but the fancier, expensive models made cricket noises when you keyed them and lit up like a dingdanged Sputnik.

He thumbed the button on the side of the red one. "Team one," he whispered. "This is command central. Do you copy?"

IdaClare's drawl blasted out the speaker. "Delbert? Is that you?"

Who the hell else would it be? "Jesus criminy, woman. You don't have to yell."

"Oh." She lowered her voice. "I wasn't sure you could hear me if I didn't."

Delbert scowled in the direction of her Lincoln, parked two houses down from Chlorine's and on the opposite side of the street. He couldn't see it, or the crazy old broad behind the wheel, which might be a good thing. "You and Marge stay in the car and keep your eyes peeled. Copy?"

"We won't." A duet of snickers wended from the speaker. "What I mean is, we *will* sit tight and we *won't* take our eyes off—"

"Press the button if you got something to report.

Clear," Delbert groaned. Amateurs. Female amateurs at that.

Hannah was the exception. She'd done a pip of a job getting that police report. He wished she could have deployed with them tonight, but being the rope tugging between him and Hendrickson wasn't fair. Besides, no telling what might slip out, pillow-talking with the sheriff.

After jamming the red walkie-talkie into his left hip pocket, Delbert keyed the blue one. "Team two. This is command central. Do you copy?"

Silence. He peered at the front loader in the shadowy alley. He knew Leo and Rosemary were squashed inside the cab. After he lock-picked the door, they'd made so goldurned much racket climbing in, every dog within three blocks had barked itself hoarse.

The ruckus drowned out their clumsiness, but it was a wonder half the neighborhood didn't converge to see what in blazes the fuss was about. Delbert smiled in spite of himself. How private dicks managed covert surveillance before TVs and central air made every house a blind, semisoundproof vault, he couldn't imagine.

"Team two," he whispered again. "This is command central. Do you copy?"

Rosemary, thank the Lord, had sense enough to whisper back. "Sorry. Leo dropped the talk-thing, and it's so dark, we couldn't tell where it went."

Delbert bit back a snide remark. "Can you see the target area okay?"

"Yes. I can see you, too."

He gasped and ducked down.

"Better, but I can still see the top of your head. The roof looks like there's a pimple sticking up from the peak."

Dentures clenched, Delbert said, "Can you see the ground where I showed you?"

"Sort of. It's darker out there than it is in here." A pause, then, "Leo wants to say hi."

"Surveil the perimeter, team two. Alert command, if the quo changes status. Clear."

Delbert stowed the blue walkie-talkie in his right hip pocket, then delved into the backpack for his night-vision binoculars. With his eyes riveted on Chlorine's back door, he sent a silent prayer to Giles, the patron saint of beggars.

A P.I. with four knuckleheaded amateurs for backup damn well wasn't a *chooser.*

16

Marlin held the remaining third of a double deluxe cheeseburger in his left hand. In the other was a cheap plastic pen with its barrel chewed down to the ink cartridge. A Marlboro smoldered in the ash saucer.

He was aware of the burger grease, tomato and pickle juice trickling down his wrist and dripping onto his desk. He just didn't give a shit.

The Beauford homicide was whipping his butt. He knew there had to be a pattern—a flashpoint, with trails leading up to it and one going out. He simply couldn't find the maypole for all the damned streamers flying every which way.

He'd give his right nut for a bull session with Hendrickson. The sheriff wasn't a trained criminal investigator, but had street smarts and instincts to spare. He asked the hard questions and didn't let ego squelch the dumb ones.

Declining that opportunity was a first. Tonight must be some special occasion for him and Toots. Anniversary of their first date, or something equally gag-worthy. Or he was just horny.

Marlin could relate.

Around the French fry he was chewing, he said to Phelps, "Gimme the quick and dirty on Montenegro, again."

The rookie gestured with his pork tenderloin sandwich. "Second interview, same as the first. Cesar admitted he had a thing for Bev Beauford. He thought it was mutual, then all of a sudden, she broke it off. No reason given. She just showed him the door."

Marlin swallowed the fry and took a puff on his Marlboro to keep it lit. Phelps's mother, Winona, the manicurist at the Curl-Up & Dye, pointed them at the taco pusher. That's how desperate they were—following up on tips from old broads with curlers in their hair and plastic bibs around their necks.

"The drone's got a couple of common assaults on his sheet. That makes my neck itch."

"They're old, though. And so's Montenegro. Both prior charges involved troublemakers at the restaurant." Phelps half smiled. "Cesar's a little rougher when he shows somebody the door."

"His alibi's weak."

"There's a six- to fourteen-hour window on Bev's time of death," Phelps argued. "I'd be suspicious of anybody who could account for that much time, any day of the week."

So would Marlin. The storms knocking out the electricity at Bev's house for approximately two hours further complicated the M.E.'s determination. She was alive to call the dry cleaners Wednesday evening, and dead at the time of the E-911 report, the next morning.

Evidence at the scene alluded to the time of death as within an hour of that last phone call. Speculation wasn't proof.

"Maybe the basement burglar altered his MO," Phelps said. "He wouldn't have to case Bev's house long to figure out she lived alone. She caught him in the act, and he panicked."

"I love how you think, Grasshopper." Marlin dropped his burger on the wrapper and wadded up the whole mess. "Let's see, our perp is a burglar we can't catch, who's entered every house before and since by busting out a basement window—except at Bev's, on account of there's no basement.

"His specialty is boosting electronics, but hers weren't touched. He operates at night, but hey, maybe he had a hot matinee date and needed extra cash. And instead of bailing out Bev's patio door when he heard the garage door go up, he stuck around and killed her."

The wadded dinner hit the trash can like a dull ta-da. "I like it. A two-for-one."

Strangely, Phelps seemed to have lost his appetite, as well. The tenderloin and his order of onion rings went into the take-out sack and into the garbage. If neither of them remembered to dump it, the rats would think Thanksgiving was early this year.

"I'm just trying to think outside the box," Phelps said.

"Uh-huh. Well, the paradigm synergy is analogous to the hypotenuse squared." Marlin shook his head. "We *wear* suits. We *think* like cops."

Not, he added to himself, like a close friend of the victim. That had been the smoke screen he'd thrown up for himself since the start. Like Junior Duckworth more or less said yesterday, their perceptions were limited to what Bev chose to project. Anything that didn't jibe with the woman they knew was subconsciously discounted, if not rejected.

Bev Beauford was a stranger. Marlin exhaled the last drag from his cigarette. Christ, his wife was a stranger to some extent.

People don't know themselves as well as they believe they do. What they're capable of, what their limitations are. If they did, there'd be fewer homicides and fewer family members that put their lives on hold to care for terminally ill or handicapped relatives.

Marlin stood and moved to the dry-erase board on the wall behind him. Wiping it clean forced a fresh start. "This is the box, Grasshopper." He divided the board into thirds. "Examine the contents."

Under Unknown Subject, he dictated as he wrote. "Some inside knowledge of police procedure and forensics. UnSub wore gloves, turned down the thermostat. Was almost certainly acquainted with vic. Was either at the scene when Bev arrived, or she let him in—time indeterminate. Premeditation, probable."

"And afterward," Phelps said, "UnSub staged a burglary to make it look like the motive."

"That's one theory." Marlin added it to the board. "What if the Unsub staged it to cover a search? Distract us from something removed from the scene?"

"Except nothing was stolen. The missing jewelry's been accounted for." Phelps wagged a finger. "Oh, I get it. Not merchandise. Something incriminating."

"Possibly," Marlin said, with completely disguised pride. The kid could think when he put his mind to it. "Make Bev the target, instead of a wrong-place, wrong-time victim and it alters the perspective."

The list he wrote under Vic bothered him, but not

as much as letting his wheels spin for three days. "Bev was all about appearances. Larry couldn't keep his dick in his pants, but divorce wasn't on the table. He's dead, Bev's finances are in the toilet, but if she stops being her daughter's sugar mommy, Kimmie Sue won't love her anymore."

"Whoa." Phelps sucked his teeth. "That's harsh."

"Also logical. Nobody's perfect, kid. Die in your sleep and the cops won't autopsy your life. Bev didn't, and I'm just warming up."

He went on. "Okay, she hooks up with Cesar Montenegro. He's eligible. He's loaded. He's also moving too slow to plug the leak in her net worth. She peddles her jewelry to stay afloat. When that's gone, she starts cleaning the closets for a yard sale."

He rolled his eyes. "God forbid, she get a job. Appearances, again. Folks might think she was hurting for dough because Larry was a lousy provider. That trumps adultery to people. Have your fun, but take care of your family."

Phelps pushed up from the chair and walked over. "Then Bev dumps Montenegro. Then she gives away the yard-sale stuff to the First Baptist resale store." He scratched his head. "That doesn't compute."

Marlin ignored the verb. Grasshopper wasn't Hendrickson, but he was learning. "It does, if she stumbled over a gold mine." He returned to his desk and hoisted a library book. "Cruises aren't cheap, and Hannah was right about that mail-order catalog. Maybe Bev was angling to snag a rich dude on the ship, but it smells more like hers was about to come in."

He lit another cigarette and flipped through the call records again. Fingertip skating down a page, it stopped at Chlorine Moody's number above the one for Glo-Brite Cleaners. "Chlorine said Bev called her about another donation to the church?"

"Uh-huh. Mrs. Moody's the cochair of the committee that runs the church's resale store. Mrs. Beauford wanted some furniture picked up as soon as possible."

"Did she say what? A couch, mattress…"

Phelps hesitated. "I, uh, I didn't ask. I can call her back and—"

"You dumb *fuck*." Marlin threw the cigarette at the ashtray and dug through the papers on his desk. "Not you, kid. Me." Grabbing his reading glasses, he compared the convenience-store receipt with the call to the cleaners. "An hour and six minutes."

He whirled on the rookie. "Bev came home and left a frozen dinner in the car, called Chlorine, didn't unload the groceries for another hour and six minutes, called Glo-Brite, and then somebody strangled her?"

Phelps looked from one time notation to the other. "I should've caught that."

"*I* should have caught it, for crissake. Bev was dead before that last call was made. I can't prove it, but I'd stake my retirement fund on it."

"But—" Phelps held up his hands. "Okay, bust me down to traffic for being stupid, but why would the killer call Glo-Brite? I mean, really, that's—"

"How you'd make sure it comes up as the last number dialed, when a nosy cop punches star 69 at the scene," Marlin finished.

Phelps pondered a moment. "I see where you're going. What I don't see is a connection, let alone a motive."

"I don't, either, but the trail's been in front of us all along. I've got a hunch it's a long, twisty son of a bitch, too. But if we can find the flash point, the pattern will snap into place."

The rookie seemed skeptical. Dubious was nearer the mark. Might be, Phelps just wished he hadn't trashed his dinner, because the fat lady wasn't quite as ready to sing as he'd hoped.

Marlin motioned at the power strip screwed to the wall above Phelps's desk. "Unplug my cell from the charger, will ya?"

The rookie lobbed it to him, then sat down at his

desk. Frowning, he reviewed his copies of the case notes and call records—a confused young bloodhound in search of an alleged trail.

Marlin keyed the speed-dial code for Hendrickson's home phone, then ended the call before it connected. If and when his hunch solidified was soon enough to alert the sheriff. As he switched to his voice mail box, his eyebrows rumpled at the Valhalla Springs office number being among the string of missed calls and messages.

Hendrickson probably told Hannah about the intern searching the courthouse basement for Royal Moody's file. Later was also soon enough to listen to Toots give him grief about it.

"Divide and conquer, Grasshopper. Get me the registration on Chlorine Moody's vehicle. Next, back in May, could be June, Bev placed three calls to this GMEI outfit, whatever the hell it is. Google me up a corporate pedigree. I want to know if it's public or private, who's on the board of directors and shareholder info."

"Follow the money," Phelps said.

"Damn right, whether it's coming in or flushing out."

Marlin pushed aside a file to uncover a phone number and an extension written on the blotter. "After my new best friend at Ma Bell answers a couple of questions about traffic on Moody's line, we're going to her house to ask a few more, in person."

David grinned as he presented the cheesecake as if it were a culinary sacrifice to the gods. The crust visible through the glass pie dish was made from Hannah's favorite cookies, crushed as fine as sand. Chunkier bits were sprinkled across the top, contrasting with the luscious creamy filling.

She moaned and shook her head. "You're evil and that's the eighth deadly sin."

"You know you want some."

"This is true. And if you'd told me it was in the fridge, I wouldn't have eaten so much of that fabulous dinner." To the *Aw, c'mon, just a bite* look on his face, she held up her hand. "Death by cheesecake is a great way to go, but it isn't what I had planned for tonight."

"Okay…" He, who had eaten twice as much as she had, levered out a huge slice and tipped it onto a dessert plate. "I'll just have to be satisfied with torturing you by eating mine in front of you."

"That, I'm used to." Hannah pushed back from the dinette table a bit, as though a lack of breathing room was the furniture's fault. "One of these days, those million-calorie meals of yours aren't going to vaporize on contact with your stomach."

David topped off her wineglass with one hand and set down a mug of fresh coffee with the other. The man was the world's best kisser, the world's best lover, a gourmet cook and ambidextrous. What more could any woman want?

"How many times do I have to tell you?" he said. "This is a diet compared to how much I ate in high school and college." Sitting down across from her, he added, "Don't worry, I'm not going to get fat. Whenever the scale tips over two-forty, I cut back from thirds to seconds."

He'd be down to halved firsts when she became Betty-Crocker-in-training. Claudina's advice on that subject was to serve Hamburger Helper as an entrée, a canned vegetable and a salad on the side, then lick David's tonsils the instant he walked through the door.

If that didn't work, she could always resort to peanut butter, celery sticks and sliced apples.

David cut the point off his cheesecake and waggled the fork at her. "Taste?"

Lips pressed together, she shook her head again. If she held in what she had to tell him for another second, she really would explode. How and where to start…those, she hadn't rehearsed on the drive over.

Actually she had, but every intro sounded like Kathy Griffin on crystal meth. Getting in touch with her cool, sophisticated inner Meryl Streep was a washout, too. Evidently, she didn't have one.

"Are you okay, sugar? That's a mighty strange look on your face."

"The wedding is August 1."

He stopped chewing. He blinked, then swallowed. "The wedding."

"Ours. In the park."

Hannah's tongue didn't simply loosen, it went into convulsions. "I haven't told Luke and Claudina yet, but I found a dress. The shop's altering it for me. Claudina's daughters are the flower girls and Jeremy's the ring bearer. Willard's taking my job, starting Monday—"

David's fork dive-bombed the saucer and bounced off. His fingers stayed curled, as if flash-frozen. "Taking your job?"

"I hired him on the spot this afternoon. Okay, I put him on the spot, too, but sometimes you have to take charge."

"Hannah—"

"No, wait, wait. Just listen, I haven't even gotten to the best parts yet." She laughed, intoxicated with the wonder of it all, how everything had come together so fast, so perfectly.

"I'm launching a new ad agency. It *is* launched,

pretty much. The Garvey Group. Sounds kind of like a stock brokerage, or an insurance company, but that's a plus—gives a subliminal Old Guard respectability."

Excitement racing her heartbeat, aware her voice was escalating, feeling as though she'd levitate any second, she went on. "The group is me, Rambo and Malcolm, but that's our little secret. Jack Clancy's my first client—the construction company *and* Valhalla Springs—so I'm out, but I'm still in."

"Clancy knows about all this? You told him—"

"And he's behind me a hundred percent. He even offered a no-interest loan, if I need it."

Fists pummeling the air, Hannah all but shrieked, "Can you believe it? It's like my fairy godmother's finally back from vacation and got with the program. I'm working from the new house, so when you're home, I'll be home. After all these months of limbo—*shazam*—everything's ready, set, go."

David's expression went from none whatsoever to comprehending to rigid and pale. Not exactly the reaction Hannah had hoped for, but jeez, in one huge lump, it was a lot to process. She was reeling a bit herself from the aftershock.

Leaning back in his chair, David blew out a breath that sounded as though it originated at his toes. "All of it, one more time. Take it slow. Complete sentences. Chronological order. Please."

Laughing, Hannah raised her wineglass, toasting her own surprise. So what if the delivery had been a teensy bit garbled? The pressure was off. *Salud,* and let the happily ever after begin.

"Take two." She paused for a healthy drink of wine, then another, because it tasted wonderful and she was thirsty. Arms crossed on the table, she began with meeting Luke and Claudina at Nellie Dunn's, the lightning-bolt inspiration at the new house and ended by saying, "I could have reviewed applications and done interviews for years and not found a better person for my job than Willard Johnson."

She shrugged. "Forest for the trees, I guess. That's my excuse, anyway. Then again, if I hadn't had to dodge IdaClare, the help-wanted ad would have run in the *Examiner* and Willard might have answered it weeks ago."

David stared at her, stone silent. His jaw worked, yet seemed welded shut. What he was thinking, feeling, was as impossible to read as a message encased in a block of marble.

Hannah's eyes locked on his. Emotions tumbled and flooded through her. Bewilderment, fear, anxiety, despair, anger—the complete opposite of what she'd expected.

"What's *wrong* with you? I thought you'd be happy!" She raked her fingers through her hair. "I thought you'd jump up and pull me into your arms and dance me around, shouting, 'I love you, I love you.'"

His tone sliced the air like a chill draught. "Why didn't you tell me any of this before now." It wasn't a question. An accusation, at best.

"Because—" Disbelief leavened Hannah's chuckle. Was she dreaming this? If she went outside and came in again, would it be David Hendrickson in that chair, or this grim, hostile stranger?

She ticked the reasons off on her fingers. "This is Saturday night. I haven't seen you since Thursday. You've been busy with a homicide investigation and campaigning. I thought it'd be next week before I could talk to Jack. I didn't know until last night that he'd be here for his birthday. I was too dense and distracted to even think of Willard until this afternoon."

Resentful at being put on the defensive, she sneered, "Ridiculous as it seems now, I wanted to tell you all this in person, not on the phone."

"Oh, yeah?" David pressed his tongue against his teeth, his head moving side to side in utter, horrified amazement. "We've got us a bona fide coincidence, sugar. That's why I waited till tonight to tell you I sold out to Luke. The earnest money's in escrow. We close the deal, first thing Monday morning."

He was joking. Teasing. He had to be. Why, Hannah couldn't fathom, but sell out? Just like that? Impossible.

"I was gonna surprise you," David said. "Tell you I was moving to the cottage, so you wouldn't have to quit your job."

"You just up and sold the place. Yeah, right."

"It'd come between us for too long already. I was sick and tired of showing up at the cottage at midnight and hauling out again at dawn. And of you driving way the hell out here and hauling out at dawn."

"Everything," she said. "The new house—your dream house, for God's sake. The land you worked so hard to clear. All of it, without saying a single, solitary word to me about it?"

"Oh, that's rich." David bolted from the chair. He slapped the refrigerator, then gripped the back of his head and spun around. "You're pissed because I sold a house you never liked, out in the middle of nothin' and nowhere, which you hated, but it's fine—it's goddamn *fantastic* for you to plan a wedding, quit your job, start a business, get Jack on board—shit, you can't sneeze without Clancy around to say 'Bless you'—all behind *my* back and all without saying a word to *me*."

"I didn't do *any* of it behind your stupid back." Hannah was on her feet, fists balled and primed to punch a hole clear *through* the damned refrigerator. "Luke talked to you about the wedding first—"

"Yeah, and I told him, forget it." David glowered at the ceiling, then grimaced. "Then, when he whined at me again, I told him to talk to you." He lowered his evil eye to her. "Because I was absolutely positive *you'd* tell him to forget it, and maybe beat him up a little, so he'd leave *me* the hell alone."

A smile twitched at Hannah's lips at the thought of being a six-foot-four-inch sheriff's one-woman goon squad. It vanished instantly. "Okay. Fine. The wedding's off."

"What?" David's arms dropped to his sides. "Why? You want to get married in the park, you'll get married in the park."

"*We're* getting married. Not just me. If you hate the idea—"

"It's cheesy, it's a lousy publicity stunt, it's got *disaster* written all over it." He gestured conciliation. "I should've known you'd go for it."

"Yes, you should have." She pointed in the

A-frame's general direction. "And I didn't hate that house. I *love* the house and I *love* the land, and for the record, I'm pretty fond of *this* place, too."

"Love? C'mon, darlin'. Be honest."

She *was* being honest. "Okay," she said, "that's a fairly recent leap, but I *do* love it, and I never hated any of it. I just kept wishing it was closer to Valhalla Springs."

Hannah looked away, more sad than angry. "When I was on the deck the other day, I pretended it was winter and imagined how incredibly beautiful it would be to watch the snow falling down into the meadow."

"It is. I could hardly wait for us to see it together."

"But you didn't wait. Worse than that, you didn't trust me."

"Where the hell does trust come into this? I—"

"Months ago, you listed it with a real estate agent, because you thought you'd need the equity to pay a defense attorney. I knew then, this place was more than an address to you. I told you that. I *showed* you, the day I yanked up that For Sale sign and threw it in the back of your pickup."

"I remember. And it meant the world to me when you did." He grasped her upper arms. "What it took me way too long to realize is that Valhalla Springs isn't just an address to you, either."

"No, but it's not the *permanent* kind, either. The cottage isn't mine, David. I don't own it and never will. I've never owned a home in my life."

She wrenched away. "All right, I should have told you about the wedding. About finally seeing myself living in the new house—our house—and about the agency idea, but none of that's anywhere *near* as drastic as selling out."

Moving to the table, she drank down her now luke-warm coffee. It didn't soothe the sickening, empty feeling in her stomach, the pounding at her temples. Carrying the empty mug to the coffeemaker, she said, "Celebrating. That's what I thought we'd be doing to-night. I wanted to take candles and sleeping bags and the wine up to the house and make love there for the first time."

She turned from the counter. "Instead, I'm unem-ployed, homeless, wedding-less, and I love you more than anything in the world, but I don't like you a damned bit."

"I should have told you."

"Too little, too late."

"I'm homeless and wedding-less, too, you know." He chuffed. "Gimme a coupla weeks. I may be job-less, right along with you."

"Ah, *there's* something to look forward to." She

hoisted her coffee mug. "Skoal, Sheriff. Between the two of us, we've hit the trifuckingfecta."

Delbert had no idea how long he'd been on Chlorine Moody's roof. Felt like a week, at least. An hour, for sure. Probably.

The shockproof, waterproof, fire-resistant watch he'd ordered from Private Spy Supply was on his dresser at home. It had gizmos galore and set him back a cool $29.99, plus shipping and handling, but its face glowed like a one-eyed alien in a bad sci-fi movie.

He supposed he could buzz IdaClare on the walkie-talkie and ask her the time. Chances were, the old bat would say the big hand's on this and the little hand's on that, knowing he couldn't yell at her.

However long he'd been at his post, the tar-and-bird stink had evaporated, or he'd ceased to smell them. Mosquitoes heckled his ears and the back of his neck, but the shoe-polish face paint repelled them. Delbert reckoned the basic ingredients minus the black dye ought to be worth millions.

The night air and fickle breeze had also cooled the roof considerably. Now it felt like he was stretched belly-down on a hard, slantwise water bed. Downright comfy, if he didn't need to keep his golf spikes pinioned in the shingles.

A sudden jaw-cracker of a yawn popped his ear-drums. Eyes watering, he obeyed the reflexive urge to stretch. It felt so good, he couldn't stanch the groan barreling up his throat. Smacking his lips, he blinked and googled his eyes several times to clear his vision.

Wonderfully refreshed and sleepy as hell at the same time, Delbert rose up on his forearms and peered through the binoculars. What the—

Holy camoglies. A lens adjustment blurred what he was seeing, rather than clarifying it. Changing the binoculars back to the previous setting, he commenced a corner-to-corner visual sweep of the perimeter.

When had Moody switched off the lights at the back of the house? The kitchen window still cast its pale patch on the grass along the driveway. Another larger area of the front yard gleamed yellowish from the porch light. With it on, Delbert couldn't tell whether the living room was as dark as the back of the house, or not.

Had she gone to bed? Delbert swore under his breath. Damned old fool. Yawning and stretching and derelicting in general's the same as abandoning your post. If you were Leo, there'd be hell and a piper to pay, yes-siree, Bob.

Binoculars leveled at the back door, Delbert pulled the red walkie-talkie from his right hip pocket.

"Team one, this is command central. Gimme a status report, *ASAP.*"

Silence. Garbled voices, then Leo said, "Now it is the team one, we are?"

Delbert held the walkie-talkie in front of the binoculars. Red as a dingdanged stop sign. "Goddamn it, Schnur. How'd you get IdaClare's walkie?"

"Huh? The one I got is the one you gave to me."

Again, Delbert checked the instrument in his gloved hand. Red. "Oh, yeah? What color is it?"

"The blue."

Trying to keep one eye on Moody's back door, Delbert tilted the binoculars and looked down at his transceiver. Blue. *Blue?* Thoroughly confused, he held it in front of the binoculars again. Red.

Because they're night-vision binoculars, you idiot. He thumbed the button. "Blue is correct, team two. Clear."

Temporarily holstering the blue walkie-talkie in his turtleneck collar, Delbert took the other one—the *red* one—from his left hip pocket. "Team one. Command central. Status report on the front of the house, ASAP."

"Delbert, is that you?" IdaClare drawled.

"Who the hell else—" He growled low in his throat. "Affirmative."

"Well, the status is the same."

"Lights still on the living room?"

"If they weren't, we'd have something different to look at," she snapped. "Do we have to stay here much longer? We're both bored to tears, and Marge needs to go to the bathroom."

"In a min—" A soft *whump* seemed to have come from every direction, save up. Delbert ducked behind the roofline. He flinched as his shoulder scraped against the shingles.

Moody's back door was still shut. He'd swear to it. So were all the rear windows. Was it the echo of a car door from down the street, he'd heard? Couldn't be. It was a wooden *whump,* not a metallic one.

Craning his neck, Delbert eased the binoculars above the ridge. A coppery pink halo wreathed the corner streetlight. He chastised himself for not ascertaining whether light at certain angles would glint off the glass lenses.

By God, the back door was definitely shut. Slowly sweeping right, he almost swallowed his upper plate when the other half of the cellar door *whumped* open. Pulse galloping faster than a man his age's should, he watched Chlorine Moody creep up the concrete steps and into the backyard.

With a dark scarf knotted under her chin, dressed in a black blouse and slacks, she was almost as invisible as Delbert hoped he was. In one hand, she carried a shovel; in the other was a trowel and a halogen penlight. Its slender, bluish beam didn't diffuse like a typical flashlight's. A silvery circle on the ground no larger than a quarter marked her progress across the yard.

Eureka, Delbert yelped to himself. He could scarcely breathe, and the roof felt fifty degrees hotter. For the love of Mike, he thought, let the Schnurs stay as still and quiet as Royal Moody.

The penlight beam jagged sharply to the left, away from what Delbert had pegged as the grave site. The shiny circle played over an upturned billed cap a few feet from the tunnel in the hedge—precisely where it had fallen when he'd pushed Leo's big fat butt through the gate. Delbert watched in horror as Chlorine bent to pick it up.

Yesterday, he'd tried talking Leo into distracting her at the front door while he slipped back into the yard for his cap. Leo's reply was in German. Delbert *sprechened* enough *Deutsch* to translate an obscene and physically impossible suggestion.

By penlight, Chlorine examined the sweat stains and the brand stamped on the cap's inner band. She peered at the hedge. The beam flicked across severed branches, their leaves wilting and brown at the edges.

Her head swiveled toward the garage. She looked up, straight at him.

His heart quivered behind his ribs. But Chlorine glanced back at the house, then tossed his cap aside.

She placed the penlight in the grass so that the beam pointed toward the alley and began to dig. Three shovelfuls of dirt had formed a small pyramid before Delbert could relax in the knowledge that she hadn't seen him. Slowly bending his knees, he inch-mealed downward below the peak of the roof. Nausea walloped him smack in the breadbasket. Elation lightened his head and set it spinning.

Chur-rekk…pause…*chur-rekk*…pause. Counting each shallow bite the shovel took had a strangely soothing effect. Delbert interpreted the sounds as a rescue of sorts. Twenty-three years late in some respects, but not all, by any means.

His ears pricked at the mewl of a worn-out fan belt and brakes squeaking to a halt. Judging by the sound, the car could have parked on either side of the street and up a house or two, or down.

A hand braced for leverage, Delbert leaned from the waist. He stretched just enough to see a taillight flash off.

The shoveling stopped. Chlorine heard the car pull up, too. And she damn well wasn't expecting company. Delbert huddled against the roof again. He couldn't see her, didn't hear footsteps—wasn't certain he would, if she'd returned to the house.

Then, came an ever-so-faint lilting refrain, like the lid of a music box being opened. Instead of a regular doorbell, Chlorine had one of those twist-key jobs that played "Edelweiss," or some such. Much closer, though muffled, a female voice whispered, "Delbert? *Delbert.* Oh, dear, how do you work this thing, Marge?"

Yanking the walkie-talkie out of his collar, he clapped it to his chest. Carefully, feeling the spikes on his right shoe losing their grip, he wriggled up the roof again.

The cellar doors were still open, but light shone through the curtains at the rear of the house. Chlorine must have gone inside. Whoever was at the door wouldn't have rung that rinky-dink chime if he'd had a key.

Into the red transceiver, he whispered, "Team one, come in."

"Delbert! Oh, Lord almighty, we thought you were a goner."

So had he, but that was beside the point. "Status report. Quick."

"Well, you'll never believe who just went into

Chlorine's house. Marge and I thought Chlorine had caught you for sure."

"Will you shut up and tell me who's here?"

"Detective Andrik, that's *who*. And that sweet young man that follows him around all the time. Phillips? Phipps? No, it's Phelps. Josh Phelps."

Delbert scowled. Hannah went to Marlin about that file on Royal. Hendrickson knew about it, too. But even if they suspected Chlorine of murder, they'd throw the investigation back to the Sanity PD. Most likely to Lieutenant Williams, that cold-case dick Hannah got a copy of the report from.

Whatever the county boys were here for, it had naught to do with Royal Moody. Except for putting the kibosh on Chlorine digging him up. The trench she'd started hadn't exposed anything, aside from a couple of gallons of dirt.

Be damned if the cops were never around when you needed 'em, but sure as God made green apples, they show up whenever you didn't.

Andrik was good for something, though. While he kept Chlorine occupied, Delbert would do the gentlemanly thing and give her a hand with the spadework.

"Team one, you still there?"

"Yes, but we're leaving and don't even try to talk

us out of it. We're both fit to bust and poor Itsy and Bitsy are, too."

"This is a code-red emergency. I repeat, code red. Find a pay phone and call 911. Report a prowler at this address. Use Chlorine's name. Got that?"

"A prowler?"

"Yes, a prowler. Then call Hannah. Hendrickson's likely at the cottage with her. Tell 'em to come on the double and hang up. Come back fast as you can, park around the corner and stay put. Do you read me?"

"Yes. 911, a prowler, Hannah, come back and wait. Oh, my stars and garters, this is so exciting, I'm about to— Never mind."

Out on the street, an engine roared to life. Delbert muttered, "Amateur," and threw the red transceiver in the backpack. Pulling out the blue one, he whispered, "Team two. Do you read me?"

Not a peep. He counted to five, tried again, then gave up. Delbert stowed the rest of his gear, then crab-walked to the rope ladder. Fresh as the Schnurs ought to be from their nap, *they'd* get the first turns with Chlorine's shovel and trowel.

17

Hannah frowned at her cell phone. The LED screen showed the incoming call originated from a pay phone with a Sanity prefix.

David looked over her shoulder. "Probably a wrong number."

Or not. Reluctant to ask if those in Sanity PD custody made their rightful phone calls from a pay phone, she pressed the connect button. "Valhalla Springs, Hannah—"

"Delbert says get to Chlorine Moody's house on the double. Oh, and if the sheriff's with you, bring him, too."

"IdaClare? What's wrong? IdaClare?" Hannah stared at the blank screen, then looked at David. "She hung up."

"What did she say?"

"Delbert told her to call me. He wants us at Chlorine's as fast as we can get there."

"Turn off the coffee, check the stove." David pushed past her and ran for the bedroom.

"She sounded more excited than scared," Hannah called after him. It also followed that if IdaClare was Delbert's mouthpiece, the entire gumshoe gang was in the vicinity.

She collected her shoulder bag from the couch and went into the kitchen. Dirty dishes were everywhere—on the table, the counter, piled in the sink. They'd been too caught up in an emotional mess to clean up the literal one.

Garvey vs. Hendrickson had been in its nine-hundred-and-sixty-seventh round when her cell phone rang. More accurately, rounds one through four had been in their nine-hundred-and-sixty-third replay.

No, she couldn't—wouldn't—unhire Willard. The job was as tailor-made for a writer as CEO of The Garvey Group was for Hannah.

No, David wouldn't tell Luke he'd changed his mind about selling his property. No, he wouldn't explain the situation to Luke, either, in the hope the offer would be retracted. A deal was a deal. And if David lost the election to Jessup Knox, he'd have to sell it, anyway.

He felt qualified to replace the retiring Cletus Orr, but that decision would be the new sheriff's. If Knox did hire him, David would have to answer to Elvis for the next four years. He wasn't confident he'd last four days.

Stalemate. Again. Except in this continuing episode of *Hannah and David Can't Win For Losing,* the original cast of two star-crossed lovers had rapidly expanded to include Luke Sauers, Willard Johnson and Jack Clancy.

David loomed in the doorway. He'd changed out of shorts and Birkenstocks into jeans and boots. A Kevlar vest covered all but the sleeves of his white T-shirt. A leather, sidearm-heavy utility belt creaked as he buckled it on.

"This could be none of my business," Hannah said, "but aren't you a little overdressed?"

"If Bisbee's involved, it's an automatic snafu." He motioned at the front door. "And if you don't know what that stands for, look it up."

She did, and it aptly described the entire evening. The aftermath of the dessert course, anyway. Proceeding David outside, she said, "Our first fight, and we can't even do *that* without somebody interrupting."

David unlocked the Crown Vic's passenger door and opened it for her. Waiting until she was seated, he snapped, "We aren't fighting," then slammed the door.

Hannah buckled the shoulder harness, watching

him stalk around the front bumper. The instant his butt hit the seat, she said, "We are, too."

"No, we aren't. We don't fight." He keyed the ignition. "I'm not putting anything out on the radio about this SOS call. Once it's official, whatever Delbert's gotten himself into will be harder to get him out of. If I need backup, Marlin and Phelps are probably still at the Outhouse."

"That's very kind of you, Sheriff. Thanks."

The cruiser seemed to hover, then took off, gliding over the rutted dirt lane. Hannah said, "So what's with this 'we don't fight' bit? What do you think we've been doing for the past almost two hours?"

"Having a difference of opinion."

"The *New York Times* and the *Washington Post* have a difference of opinion. We're fighting."

"No. We. Are. Not."

The car slowed, then jounced onto Turkey Creek Road. "Great," Hannah said. "Now we're fighting about whether we're fighting or not."

"We don't fight. Okay?"

Something in his voice beckoned a sidelong look. The expression illuminated by the dashboard light was one she'd seldom seen. Henry David Thoreau wrote of quiet desperation. David Hendrickson's face could illustrate it.

He seldom spoke of his first marriage. Rarer still were derogatory remarks about his ex-wife, which put him in the bottom one percent of divorced males. Particularly those whose wives were sleeping with their second husbands before filing for dissolution from the current ones.

What Hannah gathered from random snippets and allusions was that when David and Cynthia hadn't been arguing, they'd been either apart, asleep or not speaking at all.

"We are fighting," she said. "We haven't before, but this one isn't over and we'll have more fights. Lots more." Hannah laid her hand on his thigh. "I'm not your ex-wife. You aren't the same David you were then."

He glanced at her warily.

"Yes, I know you've seen a jillion arguments turn into domestics. Some with fatal, or near-fatal outcomes. None of those couples are us, either." She chuckled. "And you're the one with the gun, not me."

David rolled his eyes. "You almost had me, then you blew it."

"Oh, lighten up. This isn't the beginning of the end, you dork. It's the beginning of the beginning. You're stuck with me for life and I promise, you're going to love almost every minute of it."

Another glance, this one with a touch of the ol' killer grin. "Don't expect me to ever like getting mad and yelling at each other, because I don't. Never have, except with Marlin."

"Well, I'm not super keen on it, either, except with Marlin. But it beats the hell out of *not* fighting, and pretending everything's hunky freakin' dory, when you're shriveling up inside."

"Good point."

"I thought so."

Tension ebbing, he cocked his head and boasted, "I didn't bull up and go silent on you, like I used to."

"Another good point. See? We're making progress."

Hannah angled her shoulders toward him, which was as close to a face-to-face discussion as manageable in a speeding patrol unit. "While you're captive, I have a few compromises to get us out of the trifreakin'fecta we're in."

His face rumpled, as if stricken with acute appendicitis. "Like you said, I do have a gun."

"I'll bear that in mind."

"All right. Lay 'em on me."

"Luke's insane, but a wedding in the park will draw the right kind of attention to you for once. Plus, we get married. A two-fer, as IdaClare calls them. Okay?"

Heaven forbid the man just agree with her. "The married part, I'm all for. The Sunday before the election is mighty short notice for my folks and my brothers."

Hannah flapped a hand. "Pfft. It's your wedding. They'll be here. It'd be great if the whole clan could stay until election night and help us campaign, too."

"Uh-huh. What's an extra thirteen, fourteen people hanging around the house on our wedding night? And the night after that."

"I'll reserve town houses for everybody at Valhalla Springs. Your parents already know IdaClare. She and June can get reacquainted and Ed will get a kick out of Delbert."

"Yeah." David chuckled. "Nothin' like a visitor to lift an inmate's spirits."

"No matter what he's up to tonight, he'll make bail long before then."

No comment.

"Luke will be thrilled to have your entire family in the trenches for the final push before election day."

She hadn't met David's three younger brothers, but had seen photos. As Delbert would say, *hot ziggety,* in triplicate. While Kinderhook County's female constituency would swoon en masse, in Hannah's opinion, she had the pick of the litter.

"I can see the *Examiner*'s postelection headline now," she said. "David, Daniel, Darrin and Dillon. The Four Hendricksons of the Apocalypse Leave Elvis in the Dust."

"Wingate will never go for it," David said. "And damned if I can figure out how this is a compromise, but okay. You're on."

"*We're* on," she corrected. "Now, here's a real non-compromise. Win or lose, we aren't leaving Kinderhook County. Work with Marlin, the Sanity PD, the highway patrol—the CIA, for all I care. This is our home. We stay, no matter what."

David rubbed his jaw. Beat a drum riff on the steering wheel with his thumbs. Inhaled and blew out a massive sigh. "Deal."

From an arbitration standpoint, Hannah was confident the third leg of their conflict resolution was the easiest. She said, "As for selling out to Luke, here's a minor alteration. Sell him the A-frame and the land to more or less the middle of the valley. We keep the farmhouse and the rest of the acreage. He gets the new house, and keeps the view. We remodel and expand the old house, and keep the view. It's a win-win for everybody."

David's eyebrows met, then parted and rose. His mouth puckered and he shifted in the seat. With a snort, he said, "Not bad. Might even work. Luke mostly wants the land to look at, anyhow."

"And there are bonus amenities this way. He'll have an on-site sheriff, a rottweiler on patrol and a home-based advertising entrepreneur for a round-the-clock neighborhood watch committee."

"Yeah," David allowed, "but we'd also have to double the farmhouse's square footage. Maybe triple it. That'll take months, sugar. And we'd be back to sharing a bathroom."

"We'll manage. Our bathroom stuff will be in one place. So will the groceries. No to mention us. If the hammering gets too loud, I'll take the laptop I haven't bought yet and my cell phone out to the barn." She grinned. "You know, to conference with my partners, Malcolm and Rambo."

David's chuckle was downright lecherous. "Come to think of it, *we* haven't conferenced in the barn yet."

She laughed. "Does that mean yes, we'll split the place with Luke?"

"Affirmative, Miz Garvey." David took her hand and kissed the palm. "Does this mean we're through fighting?"

"For now, yeah." Her fingertips imitated a Dance of the Seven Veils on the back of his neck. "And if we didn't have to go save the Mod Squad from Chlorine Moody—or Chlorine Moody from the Mod Squad—we could be having our first make-up sex."

David's groan turned into a growl. "Compromise?"

Hannah glanced over her shoulder, then shook her head, albeit reluctantly. "Sorry. That'd be a first, too, but a quickie in the backseat isn't what I had in mind."

"Neither did I, darlin'. But after we save Delbert's butt, I'll do my damnedest to piss you off again, then we'll hit the daily double."

Heat licked up from Hannah's toes, concentrating in places he'd mapped so thoroughly and often. It was spreading to several lesser yet just as lovely principalities when the cruiser turned onto MacMillan Street.

Two Sanity patrol units with their lightbars flashing were parked nose-to-nose in the middle of the street. At the curb was an unmarked rustbucket of a Chevy sedan. Neighbors crowded the far sidewalk, gawking and pointing at Chlorine Moody's white bungalow. In the driveway, two uniformed PD officers were huddled with Marlin Andrik.

A shiver of fear eclipsed Hannah's reverie. "Oh, my God. I thought—" Junior Duckworth's hearse wheeled around the opposite corner, sending her heart lurching into her throat. "Somebody's dead. Oh, God, oh please, don't let it be Delbert. Don't let it be any of them."

"There's no ambulance," David said. "The EMTs would be here before Junior if anybody was...hurt."

"Maybe it already *left*."

He turned on the lightbar and parked behind the city car. "I monitored the radio all the way here. The only response from this address was about a prowler report."

Hannah hadn't heard any radio chatter. Then again, during previous ride-alongs, she'd rarely comprehended a word of it.

Marlin Andrik wasn't at all difficult to understand, even from a distance. The detective was smoking, but without benefit of a cigarette. "Cornelius, we've gone over this a hundred friggin' times. You're city. I'm county. The city's *in* the goddamned county, so it's my goddamned jurisdiction."

He pointed at David. "There's the sheriff. You want to bitch and moan, bitch and moan at him."

"Forget jurisdiction," David said. "I want to know what's going on. You first, Cornelius."

"Mrs. Moody called 911—"

"Ah-ah-ah," Marlin said. "A female who *identified* herself as Mrs. Moody called 911. Phelps and I were interviewing her when your dispatcher caught the call."

Cornelius began again. "Nine-one-one received a prowler complaint at this address." He nodded at the other officer. "Me and Sheib responded. Public Works had the alley barricaded, so we split up and walked around there on foot. A couple of old gents out looking for a lost puppy reported seeing a guy in a billed cap shinny down Moody's garage roof and into her yard."

Sheib, the younger of the two, chimed in, "There's rose bushes grown up over the fence clear to the power lines. We couldn't get through, but I shined the flashlight into the yard."

He rocked backward and blew out a breath. "Lemme tell ya, when I saw that big hole with a corpse in it, I tasted my dinner all over again."

Cornelius chuckled. "Whooee. I guarantee, that gomer ain't prowled nobody's house in a month of Sundays."

Twenty-three years' worth was a closer estimate. Hannah hugged herself as a gruesome montage of every zombie movie she'd ever seen scrolled through her mind.

The old fart was right. Chlorine had murdered her husband and buried him in the backyard. How he'd resurfaced was a mystery, and would hopefully stay that way. So would the absolute certainty that Ida-Clare had placed the 911 prowler call, and that the helpful puppy hunters were Sam Spade Bisbee and his faithful assistant, Leo Schnur.

Feeling David's eyes bore into her, Hannah surveyed the other available directions for a glimpse of a gumshoe, or two or five. The gang had to be around somewhere. Delbert couldn't be dragged away from his moment of glory with chains and a flatbed tow truck.

Marlin said to Cornelius, "I rest my case. No prowler, no city presence necessary. Except for maybe crowd and traffic control, which you aren't doing any of."

"Prowler, hell. We've got a dead body—a *very* dead body—to process back yonder."

"And we should all live long enough for your scene techs to roll in."

David looked hard at his chief of detectives, then asked Cornelius, "Are the backyard and the alley cordoned off?"

"Yes, sir."

"Your crime unit's en route?"

"Yes, sir. What's keepin' them, I can't hazard a guess."

"In the meantime, I'd appreciate you assigning somebody to disburse the rubberneckers—shoo 'em indoors, if he can. Whoever else is available, station them in back to keep that grave site secure. I'd also suggest contacting your dispatch about a city crew to take out that hedge and the fence."

Cornelius nodded. "Will do, Sheriff. Good thinkin'. Access from the alley is easier, and easier to control."

Marlin, now smoking for real, watched the two city officers stride away.

"We'll sort out the boundary disputes later," David said. "I've had almost enough arguing for one night." He winked at Hannah, then returned his attention to Marlin. "But I am a mite curious about what brought you and Phelps here. Before the prowler call ever went out, no less."

As casually as he'd answer a question about the weather, Marlin said, "To arrest Chlorine Moody for the murder of Bev Beauford. Phelps and a city uniform are still inside, taking her statement."

Hannah and David looked at each other, then at Marlin. All three of them turned toward an approaching clickety-clack sound on the sidewalk. Ignoring David and Marlin, the newcomer said, "Jiminy Christmas, ladybug. How'd you get here so fast? I didn't figure you and Hendrickson'd make it here for another half hour."

"Here's a better question, Bisbee," David said. "What are *you* doing here?"

Marlin gave Delbert a slow up-and-down. His hair was plastered down like a skullcap. From eyebrows to chin, his face had a greasy, grayish sheen to it. Mud spackled his golf spikes and black trousers, but his hands and wrinkled, black-and-white-striped shirt were clean.

"Interesting outfit," Marlin observed. "Since when do golf courses have referees?"

David glared at Hannah. Her widened eyes projected genuine innocence.

"So, where's IdaClare?" she asked Delbert.

"Parked around the corner. Leo, Rosemary, Marge and the poodles are whining to go home, but IdaClare promised she won't leave without me."

"The poodles?" Marlin repeated.

"I hear ya." Delbert rolled his eyes. "Itsy and Bitsy look like something a cat coughed up, but IdaClare won't go nary anywhere without 'em."

To Hannah, he said, "Did you hear they found Royal? As good as he looks— Well, he don't look *good,* mind you, being dead and all, but most of him's present and accounted for. Chlorine must have poked a whole bottle of arsenic down his gullet for his corpse to be that well-preserved."

Delbert clucked his tongue. "Cold-bloodedest female I ever heard tell of. She didn't just kill Royal and bury him, she set bricks around the grave and built a sandbox on top of it for Rudy."

Goose bumps raced up Hannah's arms. Cold-blooded? Add *heartless* and *cruel* and the description still fell short. Poisoning and burying her husband was a hideous act motivated by greed. Disguising his grave under a sandbox for his three-year-old son to play in was incomprehensible.

Delbert continued, his remarks pointedly directed at Hannah. "It'll be tough on Rudy to find out what really happened to his daddy. At least he'll know Royal wasn't a bum who didn't care two hoots about him."

The inference couldn't be clearer. Jack once told Hannah that her heart was as transparent as glass to anyone who loved her enough to see through her defenses.

She'd never find out who'd fathered her. What he looked like, what became of him, whether she had half siblings somewhere in the world—aunts, uncles, cousins. Delbert had sensed her need for Rudy to know the truth. To have answers to questions she couldn't resolve for herself.

David said, "How'd you get so knowledgeable about that grave site, Bisbee? Especially if the back-yard's as inaccessible as Sheib described."

The ever-sharp, book-learned Master of Criminal Investigation waved toward Officer Sheib, now dispersing the curbside spectators. "I heard him and that other cop talking. The tall cop was making sport of

Sheib for retching when he thought some grainy red-dish stuff around the grave was old, dried blood. Turns out, the bricks Chlorine laid were crumbling from moisture trapped in the sand and the dirt that gradually blew over it."

David shifted his weight, as though a seriously annoyed Incredible Hulk could intimidate Delbert. "Did you, uh, *hear* anything else you might want to share with us?"

"No," Delbert said, grinning. "I reckon that's about all I can say on the subject. You and Marlin'll want to take a gander at our Code Name: Epsilon file, though. It's a doozie."

"That's Detective Andrik to you, bub." Marlin's fingers waggled. "Now, why don't you tap-dance back to your chorus line, load up the poodles and scram."

"You mean, go home? But—"

"On your way there," David said, "I'd be much obliged if you'd drop off Hannah at my place to pick up her vehicle." He spread his hands. "I'm sorry, sugar, but as usual, I'm stuck for who knows how long."

Hannah nodded, exhaling a sigh of disappoint-ment. There went their daily double. Marlin wouldn't object to her hanging around the scene, but it wasn't exclusive to the sheriff's department.

Well, hell. She should have lured David into the Crown Vic's backseat when she had the chance.

David smiled wistfully as Hannah walked down the sidewalk, her arm slung around Delbert's shoulders. He knew she wanted to stay as much as he hated sending her home. Her home, not his, or theirs.

Only temporary, he thought. Two weeks from tomorrow, they'd be husband and wife and crammed cheek-to-jowl in a hundred-year-old farmhouse that'd fit inside her cottage with room to spare.

We'll manage, she'd said. That's all David needed to hear.

Marlin inquired, "You've argued enough for one night, huh? Smart money says toots won."

"Nope." David grinned. "We both did."

"Ya think?" Marlin blew out a raspberry. "Oh, yeah. I keep forgetting, you're not married yet."

Tempting as it was to issue a verbal wedding invitation, David demurred. Luke topped the needs-to-know list for several reasons. Once he did, the announcement in the *Sanity Examiner* would be old news before it hit the stands on Tuesday.

The always natty and usually stoic Junior Duckworth looked as though he'd just attended a snuff-film festival. He slumped against the fender of Marlin's

Chevy and wiped his face with his pocket square. "Growing up in a funeral home and after twelve years as county coroner, I thought I'd seen it all." Junior shook his head. "Never seen anything like that. Don't care to, ever again."

Marlin said, "The preliminary ID on the corpse is Royal Moody."

"Oh, it's Royal, all right. There's nothing preliminary about it."

David felt no compelling urge to witness what had knocked the whey out of a man who'd once handled with aplomb the discovery of a corpse dissected with a band saw and frozen like a side of beef. To Marlin, he said, "Hannah told me she left you a message about GMEI buying the company that Chlorine sold her card game to. Is that the link between her and Bev?"

"Yeah, but… What message? Me and Phelps put that one together."

David shrugged. "Maybe she misdialed your cell phone number. I don't catch the outgoing 'Yo, Andrik' on your voice mail most of the time."

"So, I'm a man of few words. Sue me. Now, do you want a briefing, or we can shoot the shit about Toots being incapable of dialing seven numbers in sequence."

Every poker player has a tell—a body language cue that signals a good hand, a poor one, a fence-straddler that could go either way or a bluff. For pros, the absence of a tell is a tell. For Marlin, a gruff tone and a smart-ass remark were as plain as the growing nose on Pinocchio's face.

He said, "The tip-offs were there from the start. Going after Kimmie Sue and her drone, the obvious suspects, made them easy to overlook. The phone company taking for friggin' ever to supply those records didn't help much."

Marlin explained his and Phelps's square-one brainstorming session at the Outhouse. Rather than focusing on a perpetrator who stood to gain from Bev's death, like Kimmie Sue or Jarek, they focused on the opposite effect—a threat posed by Bev's continued good health.

"It's a long story, children," Marlin said, "and some of it's speculation. Meaning it's logical, but won't ever be proved."

David said, "Larry Beaumont was involved, wasn't he?"

"That's what'll never be proved, boss. With the election a couple of weeks away, you'd better pray Mrs. Moody enters a guilty plea to go with that confession she's writing as we speak."

David knew that, in some people's minds, Larry's death had absolved many a sin. In others, he'd been elevated to near sainthood. Neither group would take kindly to his being dragged through the mud. Newcomers and those unaware of Beauford's shady reputation could assume his former chief deputy, now a candidate for sheriff, was as corrupt as his predecessor.

Marlin said, "Somehow *Deputy* Larry Beauford got wise to Chlorine killing Royal. At least, he wondered enough to request the missing person's file from the Sanity PD.

"Or, maybe he took pity on Chlorine and the kid, started out trying to help, *then* got wise. However it played out, Larry smelled dollar signs after Chlorine sold RUDY to Acer and Sons."

David nodded. "Larry might've thought if he worked the case freelance, it could pay off with a promotion. Except who needs a new stripe on his sleeve when he could do a little long-term extortion?"

"Excuse me for interrupting," Junior said. "You guys lost me way back there, but are you accusing Larry Beauford of blackmailing Chlorine Moody? For twenty-three years?"

"Off and on, yeah," Marlin said. "It's the only logical conclusion. He didn't tap her enough to draw attention. More like a rainy-day fund he dipped into when he needed extra cash."

"Or Kimmie Sue did," David said.

"And Bev knew about it and took over where Larry left off?" Junior shook his head. "That may seem logical to you, but Bev wouldn't do that. She just wouldn't."

"C'mon, Duckworth. She was Larry's wife. Mine would notice if my wallet stayed fat, and you *know* Larry was on the take. Nothing huge. Just regular bonuses he pissed away on girlfriends and no-tell motels across the county line."

Marlin paused to light a cigarette. "Considering the timing, it doesn't jibe that Bev knew all along that he was blackmailing Chlorine, specifically. If she had, she'd have hit the well sooner. Again, it's educated guesswork, but Bev must have found that missing file, photographs—whatever leverage Larry had on Chlorine—when she was cleaning out the house for a garage sale to pay her bills."

He pooched his lower lip to exhale upward. "Bev was desperate for money. By the call records on her phone, Kimmie Sue didn't blow into town to talk her mom into selling the house. She'd pressured Bev for months, but Bev didn't want to admit the house already had two mortgages on it. Kimmie Sue got tired of the shuck-and-jive and came here to get Bev's name on a listing contract."

"I'm assuming Chlorine found Larry's leverage and destroyed it," David said.

"Uh-huh. Along with a letter Bev received from GMEI. According to Chlorine, Bev hit her up for fifty grand, plus a thousand a month in perpetuity. In return, Bev would keep her mouth shut about Royal, and not use her influence to open an investigation into Larry's death."

"That's right," Junior said. "Rudy Moody was the one who found Larry in his patrol car after he had the stroke."

"Which sort of figured, at the time," David said, "since Rudy spent more hours on the road as an unpaid reservist, than a bona fide deputy working a double shift."

Marlin snorted. "I always had my doubts about Rudy's supposed rescue attempt. Especially after the trouble he got you into. The only reason I didn't look closer at Larry's death is because Rudy the Brown-Nosed Reindeer is dumber than a box of hair."

"Chlorine isn't," David said. "If Rudy found Beauford and called Mama in a panic, she might have told him to take his time getting Larry to the ER."

"Something else we'll never prove," Marlin said. "And Chlorine'll never confess to. Animals that eat their young are better mothers than she is, but she wouldn't implicate Rudy."

He went on to explain that Chlorine first stalled

Bev with a letter of agreement transferring ownership of the card game's royalties to Bev. A sweet deal, on the face of it. Chlorine had bragged for years about her cut of the game's profits. After GMEI bought Acer and Sons and released Classic RUDY, the *Examiner* quoted her as saying the first year's royalties alone would exceed the original game's purchase price.

And probably had. Except Chlorine had never received a dime in royalties and never would. She'd sold RUDY outright to Acer and Sons.

"Still," Marlin said, "a hundred grand ain't pocket change. Chlorine invested it and was set for life, but got greedy again. She told us she was a multimillionaire on paper till the dot-com bubble burst. That'd be my luck. Like Chlorine, I'd make a bundle, lose it, then have to pony up another bundle on the profits I don't have anymore to the IRS."

"For what it's worth," David said, "Hannah never believed Chlorine invented that game in the first place. It was Royal's idea and Chlorine killed him to capitalize on it."

"Motive, means, opportunity, zero proof and ancient history," Marlin said. "After the tax man cameth, Chlorine's nest egg shrunk from ostrich to hummingbird, but broke, she isn't. She just didn't have fifty large in her girdle to pay off Bev."

David slapped a mosquito whining past his ear. "Simple scenario, huh? Good God, Marlin. If it is, what the hell constitutes a complicated one?"

"Excellent question," Junior said. "So far, we've got Chlorine poisoning Royal to get rich off a card game, but not as rich as we thought. Larry had evidence she killed Royal, and blackmailed her for years. The night he died, Rudy Moody may or may not have heeded Chlorine's advice to drive as slow as possible to the hospital. Bev found Larry's evidence and tried to blackmail Chlorine, but was talked into settling for the game's royalties, which didn't exist."

"Like I said, man. Simple."

David and Junior exchanged glances. Truth be told, the coroner's summary had straightened the kinks out of the chain of events.

"That GMEI envelope was the key piece of evidence," Marlin said. "Not the envelope itself. The fact it was open and empty. We all assumed it was junk mail, and none of us wondered what happened to the contents."

It was found between the seat and console in Bev's car, along with a couple of other innocuous pieces of mail. David could now picture Bev pulling up in her car beside the curbside mailbox. It was raining; the box's contents were hastily retrieved, dropped in her lap, the lid pushed shut again. Spying the topmost envelope's return address, she ripped it open, expecting a check to fall out.

Whatever the letter said, it wasn't *Congratulations, Mrs. Beauford, Your Money Troubles Are Over.* In a rage, she drove into the garage, oblivious to the envelope and another few pieces of mail sliding off the clothing catalog's slick cover and landing beside the seat.

She stormed into the house, slapped her purse and the rest of the mail on the kitchen counter and called Chlorine Moody. Fifty thousand now, she'd surely demanded, or else.

"I'll grant that Chlorine killed Royal," David said, "and might have contributed to Larry's death. But even if Bev threatened Chlorine, I don't see that homicide as premeditated."

Marlin agreed. "At the scene, we all thought the scarf as a garrote leaned to opportunity more than means." He added, "That doesn't change the fact that once Bev called Chlorine, the proverbial powder keg was lit. Whether Chlorine consciously decided to kill Bev or not, the outcome was fated. If Bev hadn't been wearing a scarf, Chlorine would have bashed in her head, or stabbed her…or something."

Something alluded to a weapon she might have brought with her, then opted for one literally at hand. Chlorine wasn't an Amazon, but taller and considerably stouter than her blackmailer. Bev was angry and desperate. Chlorine was terrified, desperate and had already killed at least once.

Cops are trained not to pull their guns unless mentally prepared to use them. Chlorine might not have been armed, but Bev's fate had been sealed before Chlorine entered the house, the same way Bev did. That's why the doorknob was wiped clean.

Astonishment and a note of frustration laced Junior's voice. "I can't get over how nothing fit and now everything does. When Rudy wasn't playing cop, he was glued to TV crime shows. From them, or from tutoring him all those times he flunked out of the academy, Chlorine would have picked up some tricks like lowering the thermostat to delay decomposition."

Marlin added, "And how to fake an alibi. She got too cute, though. And not cute enough. She knew we'd get call records on Bev's phone. She didn't want her number to be the last dialed, so she called Glo-Brite Cleaners. Could be, she thought that'd help skew time of death, too.

"When Phelps contacted her about the call from Bev, Chlorine had a plausible explanation ready. As for Chlorine's alibi, my contact at the phone company confirmed that within minutes of Bev's call to Chlorine, an almost two-hour outbound call from Chlorine's number went to—get this—a national dial-a-prayer service."

"Called and left it off the hook," David said. "Can't prove she was listening. Can't prove she wasn't."

"It does infer premeditation. Why phone Jesus and leave him hanging? It might have worked, if Chlorine had put away Bev's groceries and taken that time-stamped receipt. Sure, Bev was so furious when she read that letter from GMEI, she forgot her frozen dinner, but if she was alive ninety-some minutes later to call Glo-Brite, she'd have unloaded her car by then."

"The jewelry," Junior said. "Chlorine didn't know Bev had already hocked it. That's how you knew the burglary was staged. A real thief wouldn't bother dumping her jewelry box."

Marlin clapped his shoulder. "Nice try, but me and Hendrickson knew it was staged from the get-go."

He went on, "Chlorine's getting rid of the evidence that Larry, then Bev, used to blackmail her was another dumb move. Natch, Chlorine thought she'd got away with Bev's homicide, too, but if she hadn't destroyed evidence of the Beaufords' extortion, a sharp defense attorney could've made an argument for mitigating circumstances."

Junior recoiled. "What difference would that make?" He pointed toward the backyard. "Her husband's mummified corpse is in a hole she dug twenty-three years ago. If Chlorine hadn't murdered the poor man, there wouldn't have been anything to blackmail her *with*."

Marlin flicked his smoldering cigarette into the gutter. "Spoken like an undertaker. If Moody goes to trial, her counsel will trot out everything from spousal abuse to diminished capacity to sway a jury."

His face reflected the numerous other contentions available to the defense. "Between Bev pressuring her and the new gas-line construction, Chlorine freaked. She shut up Bev permanently, but some dude from the public works department said they were widening the trench. Chlorine was digging up Royal to move him someplace safe when me and Phelps got here to ask about those phone records."

Marlin looked at David. "Amazing coincidence about that prowler complaint to the Sanity PD and the two geezers who pointed Constantine and Sheib at Royal's grave. Want to bet one of 'em was decked out like a referee and the other was fat and bald?"

"Nope."

"Want to bet the call to 911 came from the same pay phone as the one to Toots?"

"Nope."

"Want to bet a certain wacko wannabe Sherlock's fingerprints are on that shovel handle, along with Chlorine Moody's?"

"Yep. Twenty bucks?"

Marlin deliberated, then muttered a curse. "All right, all right. If the old bastard finished what Chlorine started, he'd have been smart enough to wear gloves."

"Black ones is my guess." David grinned. "You know. To match the paint job on his golf shoes."

18

From the outside, Claudina Burkholtz's house was a bleak, asphalt-shingled rental, but the home's drabness ended at the front door. Gallons of brightly hued paint had transformed the ugly birch paneling into pastel galleries for the kids' framed artwork.

Dressed in panties, nylons, ecru stiletto heels and a longline bra, Hannah stood on a sheet laid over the floor's crazy-quilt carpet squares, while the Great Slip Debate raged on behind her.

"Quit being so bossy, IdaClare. The slip goes on first, then the dress over it."

"I am not being bossy, *Margaret.* If you think Dixie Jo slaved for an hour on that mop of hair just to wreck it, you've gotta another think comin'."

Mop of hair? This from a woman who dyed hers pink? On purpose? Hannah gritted her teeth, determined not to morph into Bridezilla, regardless of provocation. The Constitution only guaranteed a fair trial, not the jury of twelve newlywedded women who'd acquit her in a nanosecond.

"Margaret?" Rosemary laughed. "Whenever I called one of my kids by his Christian name, it meant somebody was about to get a whipping."

IdaClare harrumphed. "The somebody that ought to be whipped is whoever thought one o'clock in the afternoon in August was the perfect time for an outdoor wedding."

Jeremy Burkholtz, sitting in the recliner in his underpants and black dress socks, aimed a sympathetic look at Hannah. He and his sisters had been privy to a couple of Claudina, Luke and Hannah's prenuptial meetings. Jeremy raised a small bowl of M&M's where she could reach them, as if it were a last treat before the flogging commenced.

"Thanks, sweetie, but I can't breathe as it is." Hannah smiled. "Okay, exhaling is doable. It's the inhaling that makes me see spots."

"How come?"

"Because wedding dresses are torture devices in disguise, and women are insane enough to buy them."

Jeremy's freckles shifted as he pondered, then asked the inevitable "Why?"

An attempted chuckle sounded like the Heimlich

maneuver performed on a duck. "For the same reason we buy blouses that button up the back and shoes that hurt to walk in. To look pretty for you guys."

"Sheriff David says you're pretty because you don't put too much gunk on your face, and you laugh a lot and you don't get mad when you get dirty."

Hannah's belly did a little flip-flop. Eat your heart out, Elizabeth Barrett Browning. "That's why I'm marrying him. Sheriff David likes me just the way I am."

Jeremy popped a few candies in his mouth and crunched them. "Then how come you've got a lotta gunk on your face and you haven't laughed once all day?" A rhetorical question, apparently, since he wriggled around in the recliner and returned his attention to the cartoon on TV.

Months ago, Polly had taken Hannah's breath away with a similar dead-on remark. Breathing being severely compromised at the moment didn't lessen the impact of Jeremy's observation. Whatever the older Burkholtz kids might have inherited from their father, their directness came from Claudina.

Rosemary gasped and said, "Hey, I know. We'll put a bag over her head while we pull the dress over it. Surely Claudina has a paper grocery sack, somewhere."

"If she doesn't," Marge said, "a plastic one will do. We'll just have to hurry so she won't suffocate."

IdaClare insisted, "Dress first. Slip pulled up from underneath. And that's final."

Hannah pictured herself in the strapless bra, hose and heels, with her head stuck in a Price-Slasher supermarket bag like a frozen Thanksgiving turkey. The giggles amped to whoops of laughter. It hurt like hell, but she couldn't stop.

At a teary-eyed glimpse of the three horrified god-mothers clutching her dress, the crinoline slip and, in Marge's case, a plastic shopping bag with the empty shoe box inside, Hannah lost it again. She clogged in place, as Dixie Jo's artful, sausage-curled creation yielded to hysterics and gravity.

Claudina rushed in from the back bedroom, where she'd been helping Polly and Lana into their flower girl ensembles. "What's going on? Hannah? Are you okay? Lord-a-mercy, girlfriend, are you laughing or crying?"

Both, actually. Hannah waved a hand, not trusting herself to answer without going loony tunes again.

IdaClare, who was seldom at a loss for words, di-agnosed prewedding jitters. She sniffed, huffed, then sniped, "I suppose we needn't worry about mussing her hair anymore. Dixie Jo is going to faint dead away when she sees what you've done."

"Let her," Hannah said, not unkindly. "Look, I

love you all and I appreciate everything you've done, but I'm just getting married, not ascending the freakin' throne."

She took the slip from IdaClare. Teetering on one leg, she inserted the other through the waistband. "I mean, c'mon. It's ninety-seven in the shade outside. Instead of birdseed bags, we're doling out tiny bottles of sunblock. The county coroner's officiating, so nobody'll get mad that we picked minister *A* over minister *B* through *Z*. A bluegrass band named for their overalls is playing the wedding march, and the ring bearer's still in his Batman Underoos."

Pulling the slip into position, Hannah fumbled for the zipper. "We—me, especially—caught a bad case of perfect wedding-itis." Chin down, more or less addressing her crotch, she added. "Heck with perfect. Legal, binding and fun, we can shoot for. If we're lucky, nobody'll pass out from heatstroke and need the ambulance standing by behind the gazebo."

She grinned and planted her hands on her hips. "So here's the drill. Claudina, pop a Travis Tritt CD into the stereo."

"Yeehaw." Claudina sashayed across the room, twirling her index fingers in the air. "Exactly what this party needs. A little boot-skootin' bootie shakin'."

Hannah regarded Lana, a frail blond angel in a

ruffled blue, dotted swiss dress. "Do you like your hair up in that french twist?"

The little girl touched a curly tendril with reverence. "Oh, yeth, Mith Hannah. It'th beeyootiful."

"It certainly is, honey. Now, would you please go find your brother's suit and his shoes?"

To Polly, the eldest, whose skinned knees matched her elbows, Hannah said, "I know you're mad about the dress, but I promise Sheriff David won't think you've gone over to the dark, girlie side."

"It's okay, I guess, on account of blue's his favorite color." The girl cut a scathing look at IdaClare, clad in pink from hairdo to pumps. "It's this doughnut thing stuck to my head that sucks."

Dixie Jo had wrapped and pinned Polly's waist-length braids into a coronet.

"You want your pigtails back?" Hannah asked. "Fine with me, but you've gotta make it quick."

IdaClare blanched and clapped a hand to her bosom. "No, please," she said, a tremor in her voice. "You can't… I won't let you spoil everything, I've…" Lips pressed tight, she struggled to fight back the tears rimming her eyes.

"Excuse us." Hannah led IdaClare into the kitchen for a private talk they should have had days ago. After seating her in a chair, Hannah looked for a tissue and settled for a paper napkin from a keeper on the counter.

IdaClare thanked her, and said, "I'm sorry, dear, for behaving like an old fool. And a cranky one at that. I swear, I don't know why weddings always do this to me."

Hannah knelt down, the voluminous slip billowing around her like a frothy cloud. "You were upset at Rosemary and Leo's wedding because it reminded you of yours and Patrick's and you miss him so much."

Nodding, IdaClare dabbed the inner corners of her eyes with the napkin. "I've missed him every minute he's been gone, but yes…it's hard to be happy for someone else—even when you *truly are*—and eaten up with envy at the same time."

"Except that's not why you're upset today, is it?" Hannah caressed a blue-veined, spotted hand. For decades, IdaClare worked as her rancher husband's number-one foreman, cattle-wrangler and calf-roper. "What's bothering you is that you wish I was marrying Jack instead of David."

Fresh tears rambled down IdaClare's face. "You'd be so perfect together. No insult to David, but I knew that from how Jack talked about you, before we ever met. If only that boy had come to his senses in time."

Hannah shook her head. "He did, IdaClare. Jack

tried for so long to be something he's not. And just because the love of his life is named Stephen, not Stephanie, or Hannah, doesn't mean you or Patrick did anything wrong."

Pain lanced those bright, Clancy-blue eyes. Hannah softened her tone but didn't blunt what needed to be said. "Jack is who he is, IdaClare. You'd love him with all your heart, even if he turned into an ax-murderer. I know you sometimes think that'd be easier to accept, but only when you put your happiness before his."

"I have *never*—"

"You can either stop crying about not being the mother of the groom and act like the mother of the bride—which you are, as far as I'm concerned—or keep making yourself miserable about a son who's done the Clancy name proud in every single respect that matters a damn."

IdaClare snatched away her hand. Pale, then flushed, she tensed as though ready to storm out of the house. "You have no right to speak to me like that."

Staring into the distance, she wicked the moisture from her face and her wattled neck. "But it's high time somebody did."

That somebody should have been her son, Hannah thought. But Jack feared his Irish temper as much as

IdaClare's and likely didn't want to risk saying something he didn't mean, and couldn't ever take back.

IdaClare picked apart the soggy napkin. "People are going to ask who Stephen is. What do I say? How do I introduce him to people?"

"Well," Hannah said, "I think, 'This is Dr. Stephen Riverton, the best OB/GYN in St. Louis' will do just fine."

"But what if someone asks if he and Jack are…a couple?"

"'A couple of what?' is the best comeback I know of."

"A couple of what?" IdaClare repeated. Straightening in the chair, a defiant smirk crimped her lips. "Hah. That'll nip it in the bud, won't it."

"Works for me." Hannah grinned. IdaClare was a long way from accepting Jack's lifestyle, but at the moment, she looked almost eager to try out her new zinger.

The honorary mother of the bride pushed upright so fast, Hannah nearly tumbled backward on her butt. "Heavens to Betsy, young lady. That's a slip, not a dust mop. Just 'cause that dress is beige doesn't mean the dirt won't show underneath."

Hannah took the hand she offered, saying, "It isn't beige, it's cream-white."

"I don't care if it's fire-engine-red with tassels on the bust." IdaClare pointed at the clock on the opposite wall. "We've got eighteen minutes to get to the park, lest that poor boy thinks you've left him at the altar."

Fifteen minutes elapsed before IdaClare, Marge and Rosemary stepped back, their eyes brimming with tears at the creation they'd buttoned, poked, prodded and bickered into shape.

The resourceful, practical Claudina had taken a closet door with a built-in mirror off its hinges and leaned it against the living room wall. The glass was cloudy and the silvering worn away in places, but all Hannah saw was a reflection she hardly recognized.

She'd never thought of herself as an ugly duckling—well, not since her knees were constantly scabbed and her eyes too big for her face. A swan she'd never been, either. Not even close…until now.

The strapless satin gown was banded at the top and hem in a pale, bronzy taupe. The gentle belled skirt nipped her waist and narrowed her hips, the fabric folding into soft pleats at the back below a crisscross-laced panel.

Its simple, elegant design effected a grace and sophistication no child raised in a trailer park known as Tin Can Alley bothered dreaming of, because silk purses can't be made of sow's ears no matter how many stars you wish on, or prayers you whisper.

Vaguely aware of the Battle of the Veil erupting around her, Hannah twirled this way and that, entranced by the skirt's fluid dips and sways. She couldn't wait to see the look on David's face when he saw her. A childish second self wished everyone in Effindale, Illinois, who'd ever taunted her for being a no-account Garvey could, too. It wouldn't change any minds, though, and plenty of family members had lived down to that reputation.

I'm not a silk purse, she thought, smiling at the lovely lady in the mirror, *and I'm not a sow's ear. I'm just Hannah Marie Garvey, soon to be Hannah Marie Garvey Hendrickson, who doesn't wear too much gunk on my face and laughs a lot and doesn't get mad if I get dirty.*

"Hannah wants the veil down," Marge said.

"She certainly does," Rosemary concurred. "Like brides used to wear them."

IdaClare said, "Well, that's the silliest thing I've ever heard. What's the sense in nobody being able to see her face?"

"David will," Rosemary said, with a dreamy sigh. "When he lifts it to kiss his bride."

"Oh, pshaw." IdaClare fussed with the headpiece,

gouging craters in Hannah's skull. Fluffing the veil forward, she retreated a few steps, then crossed her arms, her head angled like a curator examining a Rembrandt.

"Beautiful," Marge said.

"It's so sheer, you can hardly tell it's there," Rosemary agreed. "And I love those tiny little spangly thingies. They'll sparkle like diamond dust when the sun hits them."

IdaClare clucked her tongue in disgust. "Well, I still don't like it—"

"You wouldn't admit it, if you did," Marge snapped.

"—but if that's what she wants, at least it'll keep the skeeters off of her."

"The limo's here," Claudina yelled from the front bedroom. "Ready or not, it's time to rock 'n' roll."

David stood in a copse of walnut trees where Luke had dropped him off. The wedding planners had won more arguments than they'd lost in the past couple of weeks, but David refused to wade into the crowd gathering in the park. The groom wasn't expected to mingle before a church wedding, and he damn well wouldn't here.

Besides, a little peace, quiet and solitude gave him

a chance to admire the miracle Luke and Claudina had pulled off. They'd drafted a small army of helpers, but the results were nothing short of amazing.

A white canvas runner divided row upon row of chairs obtained from every rental outfit in a hundred-mile radius. At the far end was a flower-twined arbor backdropped with a hurricane candelabra where David and Hannah would repeat their vows.

Off to one side, a gazebo was hung with gauzy curtains, where Hannah would wait, unseen, until her walk down the aisle. Between it and the bandstand, tables clothed in starched white linens were shaded by green canopies, courtesy of Duckworth's Funeral Home.

From a refrigerated delivery truck, Willard Johnson and his mother, Benita, the special-event baker at Petits Fours & More, were unloading boxes of individually decorated squares of cake for the reception. Ruby Amyx, a vision in sequined, scarlet lace, was arranging and rearranging silver paper cake plates, forks and imprinted napkins.

The squad of official greeters were all surnamed Hendrickson. David's mother and sisters-in-law were each armed with a guest book, and his father and brothers ushered the multitudes to their seats. His nieces and nephews scurried from one row to another doling out sunblock and old-fashioned paddle fans.

Plain ones, not the imprinted "Hendrickson for Sher-iff" kind Luke had wanted him to get.

David ran a finger under his shirt collar, telling himself he'd be roasting from the inside out if he'd worn a black tuxedo instead of his dress uniform. Any discomfort he felt now from feeling less like a groom, and more like a politician masquerading as one.

Hannah had insisted on the uniform. Like she'd said, the last time he'd worn it was to Bev Beauford's funeral. From now on, when he took it from the clo-set, wouldn't he rather be reminded of their wedding?

The fact that Hannah considered his profession a point of pride, not something he should apologize for, made David smile. The most amazing woman in the world was marrying him because she loved the man he was, not the one she hoped he'd change into.

"If I was you, I'd be hiding back here, too, old buddy."

Startled, David turned, the voice not registering, until he found himself practically nose-to-nose with Jessup Knox. His opponent's presence wasn't a sur-prise. His triumphant expression wasn't, either.

"Mighty fine party you and Sauers done cooked up here, Dave. Real festive. Romantic, even." Knox sur-veyed the hundreds of people laughing and talking in their seats, waving their fans at friends and neighbors spied in adjacent rows.

"Leastwise, it is, if you got no more respect for the sanctity of holy matrimony than you do a cattle auction at the feedlot."

"Sorry to disappoint you," David said, clenching his teeth, "but if you're spoiling for a fight, it won't be with me."

"Spoiling, huh?" Knox chuckled. "Funny choice of words, Dave, since that's exactly what I aim to do to this dog-and-pony show of yours."

"What's going on?" Luke demanded, rushing up beside David. Behind him were Chase Wingate, Jimmy Wayne McBride and Junior Duckworth.

For the benefit of the newspaperman in particular, David replied, "I was telling Mr. Knox that his opinion of the wedding was another of about ten thousand things we don't agree on."

"Wedding," Knox spat. "It's electioneering and you know it." He gestured at David's uniform. "You getting all duded up and calling this a wedding is about as ridiculous as your bride'll look wearing a white dress."

Jimmy Wayne took a step forward. "That's enough."

David motioned him back. He hadn't anticipated

the slur against Hannah, either, but it wasn't every day that a man bent on hanging himself brought along his own rope.

"Not that being born on the wrong side of the blanket is the sin it used to be," Knox went on. "I've talked to some folks from Ms. Garvey's hometown in the past coupla weeks. They give her all kinds of credit for being a big-shot ad executive. What she must've done to get there, they ain't real proud of, but you know what they say, like mama, like daughter."

Pity leavened David's chuckle—or what the other men would interpret as such. "Spew all you want, Knox. I won't take a swing at you, and I can't throw you out of a public park. Wouldn't if I could."

He shook his head. "There's any number of people who'd think poorly of me for it, because they believe you're a fine Christian man, not a gutless wonder that wants to be sheriff for all the wrong reasons."

Knox's complexion flushed a deep red, but his voice was oddly composed. "You're right, Dave, ol' buddy. This here is a public park, only it's me that's throwing *you* out."

He yanked a folded sheet of paper from his shirt pocket. "The mayor made me this copy of the city-use permits issued for the month of August. You bein' hazy about the law and all, I s'pose you didn't know that without one, you're violatin' city statutes and subject to arrest for unlawful assembly."

David nodded at Chase Wingate. "Did you get all that down?"

The editor, scribbling furiously in his notebook, muttered, "Almost."

Luke peered over Wingate's shoulder. "Why they don't teach shorthand in school anymore is a mystery to me." He tapped his suit-coat pocket. "But, anything you might have missed, I've got on tape."

Knox looked from him to Jimmy Wayne to David, who said, "The problem with dirty politics, *ol' buddy,* is that sooner or later, that mud splashes back all over you."

"And the mayor," Jimmy Wayne said, "who ought to know better than to copy city documents for his or anyone else's personal use."

With a dramatic flourish, Luke presented a notarized document he'd obtained in the event Knox acted precisely as he'd anticipated. "You're the one who's hazy about the law. As an officer of the court, it's my duty to inform you of codicil to that statute you and Mayor Wilkes are so fond of.

"To wit, Mr. Knox, when this land was deeded to the city, the donor retained a proprietary right to its usage, until his death, plus fifty years. The clause was designed to keep the city from selling the land to a developer, or for uses other than a public park."

Luke tapped the spidery signature at the bottom of page. "The donor couldn't have been happier to oblige Sheriff Hendrickson's and Ms. Garvey's request to hold their wedding here."

He pointed at the white mansion atop the adjacent hill. "Go ahead, Knox. Give him a wave, why don't you. It's a shame the heat and rheumatism discouraged his attendance, but he has a telescope set up on the second-floor veranda."

"Gotcha, asshole," Duckworth sneered, who had never, to anyone's knowledge, uttered a crude remark in his life. Much less with so much undisguised glee.

Jimmy Wayne laughed and nudged Chase Wingate. "If you aren't gonna take a picture, give me the camera. Big as Elvis's mouth is hanging open, the sheriff could stick his boot in there without scraping the sides."

Polly and Lana, then Jeremy walked down the runner to the accompaniment of the bluegrass band's rendition of the wedding march. What might have been hokey, even irreverent to some ears, was a respectful, beautiful homage to Mendelssohn's famed composition.

A brief pause cued Luke and Claudina to pull open

the gazebo's filmy drapes. Hannah grinned at Delbert, took a breath, then stepped out.

The cream-colored rose pinned to the lapel of his blue swallow-tailed tux had been lifted from her bouquet when Claudina realized she'd forgotten to order his boutonniere.

Delbert sawed a finger under his nose. "I couldn't be prouder if you were my own, ladybug."

"Don't you dare make me cry, you old fart," Hannah said, sniffling. "Because I am yours, and you're mine, in every way that counts."

She tucked her hand under his arm as a single violin recommenced playing. For a moment, she couldn't move, couldn't imagine a lone instrument sounding sweeter, purer, than a symphony orchestra's entire string section.

Gliding along the aisle felt more like a movie dream sequence than reality. Hannah was only vaguely aware of the smiling faces, whispered compliments and best wishes directed her way. But once her eyes, filmy with tears, found David's, she never looked away.

Not as Delbert helped her up the steps to the platform. Not when he rose on tiptoes to kiss her cheek through her veil. Grinning at David, she was so overwhelmed with joy, she couldn't hear, couldn't think, couldn't respond at all, when he said, "I love you, darlin'. More than I'll ever be able to tell you, or show you in just one lifetime."

Then Junior recited, "We are gathered together today to celebrate the joining of this man and this woman…"

To David, Hannah mouthed the one word she thought she'd ceased to believe in. That had until now been little else than a hopeful empty promise and an easy rhyme for songwriters and poets.

Forever.

HENDRICKSON WINS PRIMARY ELECTION BY A LANDSLIDE

by Chase Wingate

Few in Kinderhook County seemed surprised at David M. Hendrickson's defeat of Republican opponent, Jessup Knox, than the sheriff-elect himself.

Hendrickson's three-to-one margin of victory is the largest since Homer John McMillan prevailed over Webster Ploutt in 1895. Ploutt was subsequently hanged for gunning down his political nemesis in broad daylight, as McMillan was being sworn into office on the east portico of the newly completed Kinderhook County courthouse.

Hannah Garvey Hendrickson, the sheriff's bride of

nine days and owner of The Garvey Group, the county's newest and only advertising agency, said she had "no doubt whatsoever" that voters would overwhelmingly approve of "the job my husband and the entire sheriff's department has done to protect and serve them to the absolute best of their ability."

Sheriff Hendrickson expressed gratitude to his tireless election campaign staff, led by manager Lucas Sauers. "I'm honored and humbled by the trust the citizens of this county have placed in me," Hendrickson said. "It's a privilege I don't take lightly and will never take for granted."

Repeated requests for a response from Mr. Knox, of Fort Knox Security, were declined. Sources close to that campaign have confirmed his intention to run against Hendrickson in the next election, as well as Knox's expectation that the outcome will be reversed by an even wider margin.

The perennial Democratic candidate for sheriff, Jefferson Davis Oglethorpe, received a total of two primary votes. Mr. Oglethorpe noted that figure is twice the number received in several previous elections, then extended his heartiest congratulations to Sheriff-elect and Mrs. Hendrickson.

New York Times bestselling author

DEBBIE MACOMBER

It was the year that changed everything...

At fifty, Susannah finds herself regretting the paths not
taken. Long married, a mother and a teacher, she should
be happy. But she feels there's something missing in her
life. Not only that, she's balancing the demands of an aging
mother and a temperamental twenty-year-old daughter.

In returning to her parents' house, her girlhood friends and
the garden she's always loved, she discovers that things are
not always as they once seemed. Some paths are dead ends.
But some gardens remain beautiful....

Susannah's Garden

"[A] touching and recognizable."
—*Booklist*

Available the first week of May 2007
wherever books are sold.

A compelling new book in the
VIRGIN RIVER series by

ROBYN CARR

John "Preacher" Middleton is about to close the bar when a young
woman and her three-year-old son come in out of a wet October
night. A marine who has seen his share of pain, Preacher knows
a crisis when he sees one—the woman is covered in bruises. He
wants to protect them, and he wants to punish whoever did this
to her. Paige Lassiter is stirring up emotions in this gentle giant of
a man—emotions that he has never allowed himself to feel.

SHELTER
MOUNTAIN

"A beautiful romance entangled with passion and intrigue."
—*New York Times* bestselling author Clive Cussler

Available the first week of May 2007
wherever paperbacks are sold!

www.MIRABooks.com   MRC2429

REQUEST YOUR FREE BOOKS!

2 FREE NOVELS
FROM THE ROMANCE/SUSPENSE
COLLECTION PLUS 2 FREE GIFTS!

YES! Please send me 2 FREE novels from the Romance/Suspense Collection and my 2 FREE gifts. After receiving them, if I don't wish to receive any more books, I can return the shipping statement marked "cancel." If I don't cancel, I will receive 4 brand-new novels every month and be billed just $5.49 per book in the U.S., or $5.99 per book in Canada, plus 25¢ shipping and handling per book plus applicable taxes, if any*. That's a savings of at least 20% off the cover price! I understand that accepting the 2 free books and gifts places me under no obligation to buy anything. I can always return a shipment and cancel at any time. Even if I never buy another book from the Reader Service, the two free books and gifts are mine to keep forever.

185 MDN EF5Y   385 MDN EF6C

Name	(PLEASE PRINT)	
Address		Apt. #
City	State/Prov.	Zip/Postal Code

Signature (if under 18, a parent or guardian must sign)

Mail to The Reader Service:
IN U.S.A.: P.O. Box 1867, Buffalo, NY 14240-1867
IN CANADA: P.O. Box 609, Fort Erie, Ontario L2A 5X3

Not valid to current subscribers to the Romance Collection,
the Suspense Collection or the Romance/Suspense Collection.

Want to try two free books from another line?
Call 1-800-873-8635 or visit www.morefreebooks.com.

* Terms and prices subject to change without notice. NY residents add applicable sales tax. Canadian residents will be charged applicable provincial taxes and GST. This offer is limited to one order per household. All orders subject to approval. Credit or debit balances in a customer's account(s) may be offset by any other outstanding balance owed by or to the customer. Please allow 4 to 6 weeks for delivery.

Your Privacy: Harlequin is committed to protecting your privacy. Our Privacy Policy is available online at www.eHarlequin.com or upon request from the Reader Service. From time to time we make our lists of customers available to reputable firms who may have a product or service of interest to you. If you would prefer we not share your name and address, please check here. ☐

BOB07

LEDBETTER

323005 ONCE A THIEF   ___ $6.99 U.S. ___ $8.50 CAN.
(limited quantities available)

TOTAL AMOUNT $ _____
POSTAGE & HANDLING $ _____
($1.00 FOR 1 BOOK, 50¢ for each additional)
APPLICABLE TAXES* $ _____
TOTAL PAYABLE $ _____
(check or money order—please do not send cash)

To order, complete this form and send it, along with a check or money order for the total above, payable to MIRA Books, to: **In the U.S.:** 3010 Walden Avenue, P.O. Box 9077, Buffalo, NY 14269-9077; **In Canada:** P.O. Box 636, Fort Erie, Ontario, L2A 5X3.

Name: _____
Address: _____ City: _____
State/Prov.: _____ Zip/Postal Code: _____
Account Number (if applicable): _____

075 CSAS

*New York residents remit applicable sales taxes.
*Canadian residents remit applicable GST and provincial taxes.

MIRA®

www.MIRABooks.com   MSLE0507BL